LIBRARY OF SELECTED SOVIET LITERATURE

НИКОЛАЙ ОСТРОВСКИЙ

Как закалялась сталь

РОМАН
В ДВУХ ЧАСТЯХ

ЧАСТЬ ПЕРВАЯ

ИЗДАТЕЛЬСТВО ЛИТЕРАТУРЫ
НА ИНОСТРАННЫХ ЯЗЫКАХ
Москва · 1952

NIKOLAI OSTROVSKY

How the Steel Was Tempered

A NOVEL
IN TWO PARTS

PART ONE

FOREIGN LANGUAGES
PUBLISHING HOUSE
Moscow · 1952

TRANSLATED FROM THE RUSSIAN
BY R. PROKOFIEVA

ILLUSTRATIONS
BY A. REZNICHENKO
DESIGNED
BY I. TSAREVICH

NIKOLAI OSTROVSKY
AND HIS NOVEL

Nikolai Ostrovsky's novel, *How the Steel Was Tempered*, occupies a place of prominence in the history of Soviet literature. The making of the book, as well as the whole of Ostrovsky's literary work, was a deed of valour crowning the life of a heroic Bolshevik.

Ostrovsky was born in 1904, in the village of Viliya, Ostrozhsky District, Rovno Region. His father was a seasonal worker, but earnings were so meagre that his mother and young sisters had to work as agricultural labourers on landed estates. His elder brother was apprenticed to a locksmith who maltreated his workers. The dire poverty and ruthless exploitation which overshadowed the childhood of the future writer sowed the seeds of bitter hatred for his class enemies and wrathful protest against social injustice and human degradation. He was a shepherd boy at nine, and at eleven a kitchen boy in a railway station buffet in the Ukrainian town of Shepetovka, where the family had moved after the outbreak of the world war.

To escape the atmosphere of corruption and servility prevailing in the buffet, the young Nikolai spent much of his time with his brother, mechanic in the railway depot.

It was there that he learned of the workers' struggle for human rights, and heard the Bolsheviks speak of Lenin and Lenin's ideas.

5

In the village school young Nikolai Ostrovsky had shown himself a pupil of extraordinary promise. When they moved to Shepetovka Nikolai's parents sent him to a two-year school. In a few months, however, he was expelled on the insistence of the priest who taught the Scripture and whom the inquisitive lad had harassed with discomfiting questions.

It took the Revolution of 1917 to open the doors of learning to Nikolai Ostrovsky. He managed to combine his arduous stoker's job at the power station with his studies and participation in the school literary journal and a literary circle he himself organized. In his adolescent years Nikolai Ostrovsky's heroes were men like Garibaldi and the Gadfly. He was a voracious reader, and the works of the great Ukrainian revolutionary poet Taras Shevchenko, Gogol's romantic tale *Taras Bulba* and other classic writers captured the lad's imagination.

The civil war, which raged with especial ferocity in the Ukraine, then, according to J. V. Stalin, "the very centre of the day's international life, the meeting point of the workers' revolution begun in Russia and imperialist counterrevolution coming from the West," drew the younger generation into the vortex of the class struggle. Young Ostrovsky and his friends helped the underground Revolutionary Committee to fight the invaders and the Ukrainian bourgeoisie who had treacherously opened the front to the German troops. On the liberation of Shepetovka young Ostrovsky was active in aiding the Revolutionary Committee to bring life back to normal, and combat black-marketeering and counterrevolution.

Nikolai Ostrovsky was among the first five Komsomol members of Shepetovka. In August 1919 he ran away from home and joined the Red Army, proving himself to be a valiant fighter. In the summer of 1920 he returned to his home town with a unit of the First Mounted Army, which had covered itself with glory in the war against the White Poles. But the war was not yet over, and 15-year-old Ostrovsky soon volunteered for active service again. In the fighting at Lvov he was severely wounded and lost the sight of his right eye. Being demobilized after two months in hospital, he returned to Shepetovka.

In the summer of 1921 Ostrovsky moved to Kiev, where he headed a local Komsomol organization, working as electrician in the railway workshops and going through a technical course at the same time. These were difficult times. Bread and fuel were scarce. Nikolai Ostrovsky led a brigade of young workers on the construction of a spur line to bring much-needed firewood to the city. The job, accomplished under extremely rigorous conditions, was successfully completed but it cost Nikolai Ostrovsky his health. The following autumn Nikolai Ostrovsky barely recovered from his illness, joined his Komsomol comrades in salvaging rafted timber from the autumn floods, working knee-deep in the icy water of the Dnieper.

His battle wound, typhus and acute rheumatism undermined Ostrovsky's health to such an extent that he was forced to give up his job in Kiev. But the very idea of being officially invalided and divorced from the political and creative life of the country went against his grain. He insisted on being given work, and in compliance with his wishes was sent to Berezdov, a small Ukrainian town on the old Western border, where he threw himself into important Party and Komsomol work.

In 1924 Ostrovsky became a member of the Communist Party. By this time his health had deteriorated to a point that made work impossible. Despite the efforts of the best specialists and prolonged sanatorium treatment provided by the Party and Soviet Government, the disease (*ankylotic polyarthritis*) progressed rapidly. At the close of 1926 it became clear that the heroic youth was fated to be bedridden for life. Three years later he became totally blind and in 1930 complete fixation of the joints, excepting the hands and elbows, set in.

7

With all hope of recovery gone, Nikolai Ostrovsky devised "a plan that would give meaning to life, something that would justify existence." Tragic as his position was, the young Bolshevik could not conceive of life apart from the people's work and struggle. He resolved to return to the fighting ranks, armed with a new weapon—the written word. His heart was set on writing a book about the heroic past which would help the Party to bring up the rising generation in the spirit of Communism. This would be his contribution to the cause.

It must have been in the year 1925 or 1926, during the first period of his terrible illness, that this idea first occurred to Ostrovsky. He was fond of reminiscing about the days and deeds of the first Komsomol members, and his stories showed him a gifted narrator. In those days, however, Ostrovsky did not think of himself as a writer. It was not until later, when he took a correspondence course at the Communist University which gave him a thorough grounding in Marxism and Leninism, that he began to see his experiences in a new light, to understand the role played by the Party of Lenin and Stalin in the liberation of his Motherland, the power of the ideas of Communism which had transfigured his land, his people and himself.

Ostrovsky delved avidly into the works of the classic Russian writers—Pushkin, Gogol, Turgenev, Tolstoy, Chekhov and, above all, Gorky. A volume of selected works by Gorky, his *Mother* and a few others were Ostrovsky's favourite reading. In later years he asked his friends and relatives to read Gorky to him and to copy out passages from Gorky on literature and on the tasks of the proletarian writer. He made a thorough study of political literature and books about the Civil War, primarily *Chapayev* and *Mutiny* by Dmitri Furmanov, *The Iron Flood* by A. Serafimovich, and Fadeyev's *Debacle*, books dealing with the Russian people's heroic struggle for freedom, and the birth of the new Soviet man.

Then came the years of the First Stalin Five-Year Plan. "History had never known," says the *History of the C.P.S.U.(B.), Short Course,* "industrial construction on such a gigantic scale, such enthusiasm for new development, such labour heroism on the part of the working-class millions."

Hundreds of thousands of Komsomol members in common with the whole of the Soviet people took part in building the Magnitogorsk Iron and Steel Works, the Lenin Hydroelectric Station on the Dnieper, the Stalingrad Tractor Plant, and other great construction undertakings of the First Stalin Five-Year Plan. At the same time millions of peasants joined the mass collectivization movement.

It was under the influence of these great events that Nikolai Ostrovsky's hero, "the hero of our time," as his creator called him, took final shape in his mind.

In November 1930, blind and prostrate, he began work on the novel *How the Steel Was Tempered.* Part of the book was written by the author's own hand, despite the cruel pain and difficulties he must have experienced; the rest was dictated to his wife, his sister and his closest friends. In June 1933 the book was finished.

* * *

How the Steel Was Tempered is a book about the birth of the New Man, the man of the socialist epoch who dares all and achieves all in the struggle for the happiness of humanity.

The very conditions in which the book was written—the gallant fight put up by the author against pain and disease, the help rendered him by Party and Soviet authorities and, as often as not, by people who were neither his friends nor relatives—are in themselves indicative of the great changes that had been wrought in human relations, and of the birth of the New Man.

The potent, life-asserting force of the idea which had gripped the mind of the young writer who had dedicated himself heart and soul to "the finest thing in the world—the struggle for the liberation of mankind," captivated all who came in contact with Nikolai Ostrovsky.

How the Steel Was Tempered is the story of the author's life, yet it is more than that—"it is a novel, and not simply the biography of Komsomol member Ostrovsky," as the author himself has put it. The fact that in Pavel Korchagin we can easily detect a likeness to his creator is a characteristic feature of Ostrovsky, the writer—his affinity with his hero; the private, social and creative lives of both hero and author form one organic whole subordinated to service of the people. This is a feature common to all Soviet writers and one that lends convincing power and veracity to the characters they depict.

Recasting his own biography, which was also to a large extent the biography of his generation, Nikolai Ostrovsky begins the novel with a picture of the hero's childhood, showing the reader how the mind and character of Pavel Korchagin are moulded by his resistance to a hostile environment; how he matures and awakens to the necessity of remaking this environment and the entire social system; how the people's struggle for Socialism, by changing the economic conditions of social life, calls into being a new socialist consciousness and establishes a new code of social and individual behaviour, the basis of a genuinely humane morality.

Labour, its character, form and content came in for great changes under the socialist system, welding millions of men in a single creative collective engaged in building, under a master plan, a new life for the Motherland. These changes, in their turn, reshape the ideas, sentiments and relations of Ostrovsky's heroes.

In the case of Pavel Korchagin the new attitude toward labour and socialist property appears immediately after his return from the frontlines. The feeling is born within him that he is the master of his workshops and of his country. This novel feeling, an outgrowth of the new relations of production, is the motive force behind Korchagin's fight against slackers and self-seekers, against workers who are criminally careless of their tools, forgetting that these now belong to the people. The same feeling makes Korchagin an ardent Komsomol worker, an implacable fighter against wreckers and smugglers and a fiery organizer of collectivization in the countryside. The period of socialist upbuilding raised the sense of proprietorship to a new, higher plane. Millions of people became conscious builders of the socialist industry, the state and collective farms. The irresistible urge to be part of the creative labours of the people brought Pavel to his final creative exploit.

Pavel Korchagin's is the heroism inherent in the Russian working class. The nature of this heroism changes with each new period in Pavel Korchagin's life. It is not a full-fledged revolutionary that rescues Zhukhrai from the Petlyura patrol; Pavel Korchagin's spontaneous protest against the conditions of life draws him into the class struggle and gives way to a growing socialist consciousness. From self-denial in the name of lofty ideals in the Civil War, there springs a conscious communist self-discipline, serving as an example to the masses, which, in its turn, develops, towards the end of the novel, into a mature socialist consciousness determining Korchagin's character and conduct. For, indeed, the disabled hero was under no obligation to launch his amazing struggle for a return to the ranks, none, that is, excepting the vital urge to take part in the life of the millions working for Socialism.

Pavel Korchagin's initial interpretation of his duty to the Revolution involved wholesale rejection of private life, of even so natural an attribute of youth as love. Pavel breaks off his friendship with Tonya, who came of a middle-class family, and suppresses a budding love for the Communist girl Rita Ustinovich.

In a few years, however, Pavel Korchagin, like his creator in real life, renounces his asceticism—the senseless tragedy of agonizing will-tests, so popular among the first Komsomol members.

Pavel's mother and Taya, his well-loved wife, are his comrades-in-arms in the revolutionary struggle. He himself brought them into the Communist Party. Through them he continues selflessly to serve the people.

* * *

In portraying his hero, Nikolai Ostrovsky shows how Korchagin's best qualities ripen in the process of his participation in the people's struggle for Socialism. The spiritual beauty of Ostrovsky's hero, the triumph of what he stands for are predetermined by the course of events depicted in the novel, by their historical truth. It is precisely this that makes Pavel Korchagin so typical of his generation.

We cannot imagine Pavel Korchagin apart from the collective, from such comrades as Seryozha Bruzzhak, who goes to war so that there might be no more wars; as Seryozha's sister Valya, the heroic young patriot executed by the White Poles; Ivan Zharky, the orphan who was adopted by a Red Army company; Nikolai Okunev, secretary of the District Komsomol Committee; Ivan Pankratov, the young stevedore.

Like his comrades, Pavel Korchagin has inherited the finest qualities of the old Bolshevik guard, the leaders and teachers of youth in the revolutionary struggle. The elder generation is represented in the novel by the indefatigable Dolinnik, chairman of the underground Volost Revolutionary Committee; by the courageous revolutionary ex-sailor Fyodor Zhukhrai, a member of the Bolshevik Party since 1915; by Tokarev, a worker of the revolutionary underground; by the Military Commissar Kramer, and many others. The two generations are bound by invisible but unbreakable ties.

Korchagin's deeds of heroism are matched by those of his comrades. Pavel Korchagin is no exception among the many thousands that tread the same path. Throwing caution to the winds, Pavel attacks the Petlyura man guarding the arrested Zhukhrai; Seryozha Bruzzhak, moved by a powerful feeling of protest against brutality and love of mankind, shields with his body an old Jew from a vicious sabre cut aimed by a drunken Petlyura trooper. Pavel Korchagin takes part in the famous operations of the First Mounted Army; Ivan Zharky distinguishes himself in the liberation of the Crimea from the White Guards.

In building the railway spur Korchagin's friends are as self-sacrificing as Pavel himself. It is a notable fact that Sergei Bruzzhak, another of his favourite characters, was also drawn from Ostrovsky's own biography. The fact that so many of the novel's characters share the same qualities makes them all the more typical and lifelike.

Pavel and his friends aspire to an exacting moral purity in love and friendship. The theme of love and friendship runs through the whole novel and is given special prominence in such scenes as Pavel's meeting with Tonya and Seryozha's with Rita, in which the birth of a young love is described, and in the relations of Pavel and Taya, his wife and comrade. Rita Ustinovich, Anna Borhardt, Lydia Polevykh and the other feminine characters of the novel are pure and noble and reflect the great changes which have taken place in human relationships.

The novel condemns all that is sordid and degrading to human dignity, as may be seen from Pavel's attitude towards the depraved Trotskyite Dubava, his encounter with the lewd Failo, and from the author's treatment of what passed between Razvalikhin and Lida. Nikolai Ostrovsky shows how political double-dealing goes hand in hand with moral dissipation in private life, revealing the coarse construction placed upon sex relationships by enemies of the people and chance followers of the Party and Komsomol. Bolshevik ideals are inseparably linked with the highest moral standards—this is one of the underlying ideas of the novel.

The novel's individual characters blend into a single image of the people, who may be said to be its main hero. The people are well portrayed in the numerous mass scenes: battle episodes, the building of the railway branch line, Party and Komsomol meetings which repulse the Trotskyites, the holiday demonstration on the Soviet-Polish border, etc. These scenes are bound up with the private lives of the characters. In them the major problems facing the nation as a whole find their solution. Love of Country, implacable hatred of its foes, heroism in all things, big and small, in the name of lofty aims, a strong sense of proletarian internationalism and socialist humanism thus become more than individual traits, peculiar to Ostrovsky's heroes, they are the traits of a whole people. Significantly enough, it is at the site of the back-breaking railway job that the words were uttered: Thus is the steel tempered!

Ostrovsky, the artist, does not endeavour to by-pass life's sharp contradictions or underestimate the hardships of the struggle for the new world, a world of creative labour, against the dying world of oppression and exploitation. He does not conceal the influence the accursed past exerted on the working class, an influence but gradually eradicated in the process of the formation of the new socialist society. Nor does he gloss over the shortcomings of his hero, Pavel Korchagin. Ostrovsky's novel owes much of its popularity to the fact that in describing the making of a hero it *shows how* the survival of capitalism in men's consciousness can be overcome.

Ostrovsky carries on the traditions of the Russian novel famed for its depth of content and insight into social contradictions and the social struggle. Pavel Korchagin is one of the best heroic characters created by Russian literature.

But Ostrovsky has invested his hero with a new quality,

to the Bolshevik education of the young generation of our Socialist Motherland."

The young author kept his word. Popular recognition, a brilliant comeback, thousands of letters from enthusiastic readers, and hundreds of visitors anxious to make his acquaintance, the care and solicitude shown him by his Country, the Soviet Government, the Communist Party and the Komsomol, made the last years of Ostrovsky's life radiant with happiness and sharpened his talent.

While still working on his first novel for a re-edition, Nikolai Ostrovsky started his second book *Born of the Storm.* A second world war was then darkening the horizon. Encouraged by Anglo-American imperialism, the German and Japanese fascists were preparing war against the Land of Socialism.

"We are all engaged in peaceful labour," wrote Nikolai Ostrovsky, "our banner is Peace. The Party and Government have raised high this banner. . . . We want peace, for we are building the crystal edifice of Communism. But it would be treachery to forget about the evil and vicious enemies surrounding us."

The task Ostrovsky set himself in his new book was to show the young generation, reared in the conditions of a socialist society, who their enemies were.

"I am doing this," Nikolai Ostrovsky explained his task, "so that in the battles to come—if they are thrust upon us—no young hand will falter."

The author's attention in his new novel is focussed on the upper bourgeois and landlord strata of Poland, then embarked on the road to fascism. He was able to finish only the first part of this book which introduces an historically true, lifelike cast of characters, Bolshevik workers and revolutionary youth who lead the working masses in the struggle with the White Poles backed, once again, by American-British and French imperialism.

18

a quality unshared by any of Pavel Korchagin's predecessors, one that was engendered by the process of building Socialism and by the socialist society—the individual's freedom of expression in the course of the struggle for an advanced social ideal. Life itself in the late 'twenties and early 'thirties showed the author the Soviet man not only as a leader, a commander, or an organizer, but as a rank-and-file Bolshevik, an ordinary Komsomol member, with his rich spiritual world and his new attitude towards his social obligations and his personal life. An integral character, Pavel Korchagin typifies a whole period in the development of Soviet society, during which the new human being, a newcomer in history, took shape.

The depiction of the people's struggle for Socialism, which furnishes the background of the novel's plot, and of the experiences, actions and destinies of its heroes; the depiction of labour, which transforms life and those who labour, and lastly, the depiction of new relations between men—all this makes Ostrovsky's novel a genuine work of socialist realism. Like other Soviet authors, Nikolai Ostrovsky wrote in the Gorky tradition, which, however, did not prevent him from being a bold innovator, the creator of a new literary hero.

Pavel Korchagin will always be the hero of the youth for many generations to come. Each generation produces more young people of the Korchagin mettle than the one before. With a perspicacity worthy of his great teacher Maxim Gorky, Ostrovsky discerned the truth of the future in the realities of his own time: the heroic traits and qualities of Pavel Korchagin are becoming more and more typical of the Soviet youth. The Great Patriotic War showed that these traits were shared by millions of Soviet people. Today, many of the best brigades of young Stakhanov workers at the great Stalin construction works are named after Nikolai Ostrovsky and his hero.

* * *

15

Nikolai Ostrovsky was a purposeful artist fully aware of the task he set himself—the task of creating the portrait of a young fighter whose example the youth should follow. To achieve this, the book would have to be an *ordinary biography,* one which showed that a similar path was possible for any young man. At the same time it had to be a *heroic biography,* for Ostrovsky saw a deeply romantic quality and much that was worthy of emulation in the everyday heroism which he believed to be typical of the working people, and with this spirit he imbued his main hero and his other characters. The concrete details he took from his own experiences and the life of his coevals.

Characteristically enough, Ostrovsky refused to write about many heroic incidents of his past on the grounds that he was "afraid of overdoing it," as he explained to his editor. He refrained from mentioning the fact that, as a boy, he once pasted up a number of leaflets printed by the underground Revolutionary Committee under the very nose of a German sentry; or the fact that as a fifteen-year-old youngster he blew up a bridge near Novograd-Volynsky; or the story of his scouting in a town seized by a kulak band. With the tact of the true artist Ostrovsky rejected all that would have made the life story of his hero extraordinary or unique.

While incorporating some dangerous episode from his own biography in his book, Ostrovsky often tends to strip the incident of the perils and gallantry actually involved. For example, in describing the convoying of valuables from Berezdov to the regional centre over a dangerous road he merely states that the valuables were delivered safe and sound, although actually the trip was successful only thanks to the courage of Ostrovsky and the two militiamen accompanying him, who repelled a bandit attack en route.

The radio looms large in Korchagin's later life. In the novel the set which brought such comfort to the bedridden Pavel is assembled by his friend Bersenev. In reality Ostrovsky assembled it himself, spending one and a half or two months on the job. Here is what Ostrovsky himself told a friend about this remarkable exploit:

"Just think! Blind as I was, I began assembling a radio set, using such wretched material that even anyone with perfect eyesight would have sweated over it. What a job that was, working with only the sense of touch to guide me! To hell with it! When it was all over and the one-tube radio set was ready, I vowed never to undertake anything of the kind again."

The writing of the novel under the most arduous of conditions was, without doubt, Ostrovsky's supreme act of heroism. It is this exploit that we recall when we think of Ostrovsky. Yet, in the novel the stress is laid not on the exploit as such but on all that is typical in the hero's life, all that went into the preparation of the crowning exploit of a splendid life. What in Ostrovsky's life took years of heroic struggle is over in the story of Korchagin in a few months. With the modesty of the true hero, Ostrovsky devotes only two or three pages to the creation of the book.

In his portrayal of a young worker in the early years of the Revolution, Nikolai Ostrovsky revealed the typical features of not only the first Komsomol generation, but of the young man of the Lenin and Stalin epoch. This constitutes the chief contribution of Ostrovsky, the artist, and a victory for the method of socialist realism. And it is this that makes Pavel Korchagin immortal.

* * *

In 1935, on hearing that he had been awarded the Order of Lenin, Nikolai Ostrovsky addressed these fervent words of thanks to Joseph Stalin:

"I have been reared by the Komsomol, the Party's faithful assistant, and as long as my heart beats my life will be devot

Patriotism and proletarian internationalism, loyalty to the banner of Lenin and heroic courage distinguish the behaviour of the elder generation of revolutionaries as represented by Sigismund Raewski and the Bolshevik workers who lead the rising.

It is safe to presume that the life story of Andrei Ptakha, the most memorable of the book's characters, would have served to illustrate the formation of a Bolshevik, the birth of a New Man.

Death interfered with the plans of the Bolshevik writer. Nikolai Ostrovsky died on December 22, 1936, the day the first part of his second and last novel, *Born of the Storm*, appeared.

"What can be finer than for a man to continue to serve mankind even when he is no more," Nikolai Ostrovsky said.

The writings of this Bolshevik novelist, his ardent articles and the speeches he made to the youth are to this day a valuable contribution to the struggle of the peoples of the world for peace, for creative labour, for popular democracy—for human happiness.

N. Vengrov

HOW THE STEEL
WAS TEMPERED

Part One

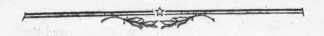

CHAPTER ONE

"THOSE of you who came to my house to be examined before the Easter holidays, stand up!"

The speaker, a corpulent man in the garb of a priest, with a heavy cross dangling from his neck, fixed the class with a baleful glare.

His small hard eyes seemed to bore through the six children—four boys and two girls—who rose from their seats and looked at the man in the cassock with apprehension.

"You sit down," the priest said, motioning to the girls.

The girls hastily complied, with sighs of relief.

Father Vasili's slits of eyes focussed on the other four.

"Now then, my fine lads, come over here!"

Father Vasili rose, pushed back his chair and walked up to the group of boys who stood huddled close together.

"Which of you young ruffians smokes?"

"We don't smoke, father," the four answered timidly.

The blood rushed to the priest's face.

"You don't smoke, eh, you scoundrels? Then who put the tobacco in the dough? Tell me that! We'll see whether you smoke or not. Now then, turn out your pockets! Come on, turn them out, I say!"

Three of the boys proceeded to empty the contents of their pockets onto the table.

The priest inspected the seams carefully for grains of tobacco, but found nothing, whereupon he turned to the fourth lad, a dark-eyed youngster in a grey shirt and blue trousers patched at the knees.

"What are you standing there for like a dummy?"

The lad threw a look of silent hatred at his questioner.

"I haven't any pockets," he replied sullenly.

"No pockets, eh? You think I don't know who could have played such a scoundrelly trick as to spoil my dough? You think I'm going to let you off again? Oh no, my boy, you shall suffer for this. Last time I allowed you to stay in this school because your mother begged me to keep you, but now I've finished with you. Out with you!" He seized the boy painfully by the ear and threw him out into the corridor, slamming the door after him.

The class sat silent, cowed. None of the children could understand why Pavel Korchagin had been expelled, none but Sergei Bruzzhak, who was Pavel's closest friend. He had seen him sprinkle a fistful of homegrown tobacco into the Easter cake dough in the priest's kitchen where six backward pupils had waited for the priest to come and hear them repeat their lesson.

Now the ejected Pavel sat down on the bottom step of the schoolhouse and wondered dismally what his mother would say when he told her what had happened, his poor hard-working mother who toiled from morning till night as cook at the excise inspector's.

Tears choked him.

"What shall I do? It's all because of that damned priest. What on earth made me go and put that tobacco in his dough. It was Seryozhka's idea. 'Let's play a trick on the old beast,' he says. So we did. And now Seryozhka's got off and I'll likely be kicked out."

His feud with Father Vasili was of long standing. It dated back to the day he had a scrap with Mishka Levchukov and in punishment was kept in after lessons. To keep the lad out of mischief in the empty classroom, the teacher took him to the second grade to sit in at a lesson.

Pavel took a seat at the back. The teacher, a wizened little man in a black jacket, was telling the class about the earth and the heavenly bodies, and Pavel gaped with amazement when he learned that the earth had been in existence for millions of years and that the stars too were worlds. So startled was he by what he had heard that he barely refrained from getting up and blurting out: "But that isn't what the Bible says!" But he was afraid of getting into more hot water.

The priest had always given Pavel full marks for Scripture. He knew almost the whole prayer book practically by heart, and the Old and New Testament as well. He knew exactly what God had created on each day of the week. Now he resolved to take the matter up with Father Vasili. At the very next lesson, before the priest had time to settle himself properly in his chair, Pavel raised his hand and, having obtained permission to speak, he got up.

"Father, why does the teacher in the second grade say the earth is millions of years old, instead of what the Bible says, five thou...." A hoarse cry from Father Vasili cut him short.

"What did you say, you scoundrel? So that's how you learn your Scripture!"

And before Pavel knew what had happened the priest had seized him by the ears and was banging his head against the wall. A few minutes later, shaken with fright and pain, he found himself outside in the corridor.

His mother too had given him a good scolding that time. And the following day she had gone to the

26

school and begged Father Vasili to take him back. From that day Pavel hated the priest with all his soul. Hated and feared him. His childish heart rebelled against any injustice, however slight. He could not forgive the priest for the undeserved beating, and he grew sullen and bitter.

Pavel suffered many a slight at the hands of Father Vasili after that. The priest was forever sending him out of the classroom; day after day for weeks on end he made him stand in the corner for trifling misdemeanours and never called on him to answer questions, with the result that on the eve of the Easter holidays Pavel had to go with the backward boys to the priest's house to be re-examined. It was there in the kitchen that he had dropped the tobacco into the dough.

No one had seen him do it, yet the priest had guessed at once who was to blame.

The lesson ended at last and the children poured out into the yard and crowded round Pavel, who maintained a gloomy silence. Sergei Bruzzhak lingered behind in the classroom. He felt that he too was guilty, but he could do nothing to help his friend.

Yefrem Vasilievich, the head master, poked his head out of the open window of the teachers' room and shouted:

"Send Korchagin to me at once!" Pavel jumped at the sound of the Head's deep bass voice, and with pounding heart obeyed his summons.

The proprietor of the railway station restaurant, a pale middle-aged man with faded, colourless eyes, glanced briefly at Pavel.

"How old is he?"

"Twelve."

"All right, he can stay. He'll get eight rubles a month and his food on the days he works. He'll work twenty-four hours at a stretch every other day. But mind, no pilfering."

"Oh no, sir. He won't steal, I'll answer for that," the mother hastened fearfully to assure him.

"Let him start in today," ordered the proprietor and, turning to the woman behind the counter, said: "Zina, take the boy to the kitchen and tell Frosya to put him to work instead of Grishka."

The barmaid laid down the knife with which she had been slicing ham, nodded to Pavel and led the way across the hall to a side door opening into the scullery. Pavel followed her. His mother hurried after him and whispered quickly into his ear: "Now Pavlushka, dear, do your best, and don't disgrace yourself."

With sad eyes she watched him go, and left.

Work in the scullery was in full swing; plates, forks and knives were piled high on the table and several women were drying them with towels flung over their shoulders.

A boy with a shaggy mop of red hair, slightly older than Pavel, was tending two huge samovars.

The scullery was full of steam that rose from the large vat of boiling water in which the dishes were washed, and Pavel could not see the faces of the women at first. He stood waiting uncertainly for someone to tell him what to do.

Zina, the barmaid, went over to one of the dishwashers and touched her shoulder.

"Here, Frosya, I've brought you a new boy to take Grishka's place. You tell him what he's to do."

"She's in charge here," Zina said to Pavel, nodding toward the woman she had called Frosya. "She'll tell you what you have to do." And with that she turned and went back to the buffet.

"All right," Pavel replied softly and looked questioningly at Frosya. Wiping her perspiring brow she examined him critically from head to foot as if sizing him up, then, rolling up her sleeve which had slipped over her elbow, she said in a deep and remarkably pleasant voice:

"It's not much of a job, dearie, but it will keep you busy enough. That copper over there has to be heated in the morning and kept hot so there's boiling water all the time; then there's the wood to chop and the samovars to take care of besides. You'll have to clean the knives and forks sometimes and carry out the slops. There'll be plenty to do, lad," she said, speaking with a marked Kostroma accent laying the stress on the "a's." Her manner of speaking and her flushed face with the small turned-up nose made Pavel feel better.

"She seems quite decent," he concluded, and overcoming his shyness he said: "What am I to do now, Auntie?"

A burst of loud laughter from the dishwashers met his words.

"Ha! Ha! Frosya's gone and got herself a nephew...."

Frosya herself laughed even more heartily than the others.

Through the cloud of steam Pavel had not noticed that Frosya was a young girl; she was no more than eighteen.

Covered with confusion, he turned to the boy and asked:

"What am I supposed to do now?"

But the boy merely chuckled. "You ask Auntie, she'll tell you all about it. I'm off." Whereupon he darted through the door leading to the kitchen.

"Come over here and help dry the forks," one of the dishwashers, a middle-aged woman, called.

"Stop your cackling," she admonished the others. "The lad didn't say anything to laugh at. Here, take this," she handed Pavel a dish towel. "Hold one end between your teeth and pull it tight by the other. Here's a fork, run the towel back and forth between the prongs, and see you don't leave any dirt. They're very strict about that here. The customers always inspect the forks and if they find a speck of dirt, they make a terrible fuss, and the mistress will send you flying out in a jiffy."

"The mistress?" Pavel echoed. "I thought the master who hired me was in charge."

The dishwasher laughed.

"The master, my lad, is just a stick of furniture around here. The mistress is the boss. She isn't here today. But if you work here a while you'll see for yourself."

The scullery door opened and three waiters entered carrying trays piled high with dirty dishes.

One of them, a broad-shouldered cross-eyed man with a heavy, square jaw, said: "You'd better put on a little speed. The 12 o'clock is due any minute, and here you are dawdling about."

He looked at Pavel. "Who's this?" he asked.

"That's the new boy," said Frosya.

"Ah, the new boy," he said. "Well, listen, my lad," he laid his heavy hand on Pavel's shoulders and pushed him over to the samovars. "You're supposed to keep them boiling all the time, and look, one of them's out, and the other is barely going. We'll let it pass today, but if it happens again tomorrow, you'll get your face pushed in, see?"

Pavel busied himself with the samovars without a word.

Thus began his life of toil. Never had Pavka exerted himself as much as on that first day at work. He realized that this was not home where he could afford to disobey his mother. The cross-eyed waiter had made it quite plain that if he did not do as he was told, he would suffer for it.

Placing one of his topboots over the chimney and using it as a bellows, Pavel soon had the sparks flying from the large pot-bellied samovars. He picked up the slop pail and rushed out to the garbage dump, added firewood to the water boiler, dried the wet dish towels on the hot samovars—in a word, did everything he was told to do. Late that night when the weary Pavel went down to the kitchen, Anisia, the middle-aged dishwasher, with a glance at the door that had closed behind him, remarked: "Something queer about that boy, look at the way he dashes about like mad. Must have been a good reason for putting him to work."

"He's a good worker," said Frosya. "Needs no speeding up."

"He'll soon cool off," was Lusha's opinion. "They all try hard in the beginning. . . ."

At seven o'clock the next morning, Pavel, utterly exhausted after a whole night spent on his feet, turned the boiling samovars over to the boy who was to relieve him. The latter, a puffy-faced youngster with an ugly glint in his eyes, examined the boiling samovars, and having assured himself that all was in order, thrust his hands into his pockets and spat through his teeth with an air of scornful superiority.

"Now listen, snotnose!" he said in an aggressive tone, fixing Pavel with his colourless eyes. "See you're on the job here tomorrow at six sharp."

"Why at six?" Pavka wanted to know. "The shift changes at seven, doesn't it?"

"Never mind when the shift changes. You get here at six. And you'd better not blab too much or I'll smash your silly mug for you. Some cheek, only started in today and already putting on airs."

The dishwashers who had just finished their shift listened with interest to the exchange between the two boys. The blustering tone and bullying manner of the other enraged Pavel. He took a step toward his tormentor and was about to lash out at him with his fists when the fear of losing his newly-acquired job stopped him.

"Stop your noise," he said, his face dark with rage, "and keep off or you'll get more than you bargained for. I'll be here at seven tomorrow, and I can use my fists as good as you can. Maybe you'd like to try? I'm game."

His adversary cowered back against the boiler, gaping with surprise at the bristling Pavel. He had not expected such a determined rebuff.

"All right, all right, we'll see," he muttered.

Pavel, his first day at work having passed without mishap, hurried home with a sense of having honestly earned his rest. Now he too was a worker and no one could accuse him of being a parasite.

The morning sun was already climbing above the sprawling buildings of the sawmill. Before long the tiny house where Pavel lived would come into view, just behind the Leszczinski garden.

"Mother must have just got up, and here I am coming home from work," Pavel thought, and he quickened his pace, whistling as he went. "It turned out not so bad being kicked out of school. That damned priest wouldn't have given me any peace anyway, and now he can go to hell for all I care," Pavel reflected as he approached the house and opened the gate. "As for that gingerhead I'll punch his face for certain."

His mother, who was busy firing the samovar in the yard, looked up at her son's approach and asked anxiously:

"Well, how was it?"

"Fine," Pavel replied.

His mother was about to say something when through the open window Pavel caught a glimpse of his brother Artem's broad back.

"So Artem's here?" he asked anxiously.

"Yes, he came last night. He's going to stay here and work at the railway yards."

With some hesitation he opened the front door.

The man seated at the table with his back to the door turned his huge frame as Pavel entered and the eyes under the thick black brows wore a stern look.

"Ah, here comes the tobacco lad. Well, how goes it?"

Pavel dreaded the forthcoming interview.

"Artem knows all about it already," he thought. "I'm in for a good row and a hiding to boot." Pavel stood somewhat in awe of his elder brother.

But Artem evidently had no intention of chastising the lad. He sat on a stool, leaning his elbows on the table and studied Pavel's face with a mingled expression of amusement and scorn.

"So you've graduated from university, eh? Learned all there is to learn and now you're busying yourself with slops, eh?"

Pavel stared down at a crack in the floor, scrutinizing the head of a nail. Artem got up from the table and went out into the kitchen.

"Looks as if I won't get a thrashing after all," Pavel thought with a sigh of relief.

Later on at tea Artem questioned Pavel about the incident at school. Pavel told him all that had happened.

"What will become of you if you grow up to be such a scamp," the mother said sadly. "What shall we do with him? Who does he take after, I wonder? Dear God, to think of all I've had to suffer from that boy," she complained.

Artem pushed his empty cup away and turned to Pavel.

"Now listen to me, mate," he said. "What's done can't be undone. Only now take care and do your work properly and no monkey business, because if you get yourself kicked out of this place I'll give you a proper thrashing. Remember that. You've given mother enough trouble as it is. You're always getting into some sort of mess. But that's got to stop. When you've worked for a year or thereabouts I'll try and get you taken on at the depot as an apprentice, because you'll never amount to anything if you mess about with slops all your life. You've got to learn a trade. You're a bit too young just now, but in a year's time I'll see what I can do, maybe they'll take you. I'll be working here now. Ma won't need to go out to work any more. She's slaved enough for all sorts of swine. Only see here, Pavka, you've got to be a man."

He stood up, his huge frame dwarfing all about him, and putting on the jacket that hung over the chair, said to his mother: "I've got to go out for an hour or so," and went out, stooping a little in the doorway.

Passing by the window on his way to the gate he

looked in and called out to Pavel: "I've brought you a pair of boots and a knife. Mother will give them to you."

The station restaurant was open day and night.

Six different railway lines met at this junction, and the station was always packed with people; only for two or three hours at night during a gap between trains was the place comparatively quiet. Hundreds of trains passed through this station in all directions. Trains on their way from one section of the front to another, trains bringing back thousands of maimed and crippled men, and taking away a constant stream of new men in monotonous grey overcoats.

Pavel worked there for two years—two years in which he saw nothing more than the scullery and kitchen. The twenty odd people employed in the huge basement kitchen worked at a feverish pace. Ten waiters scurried constantly back and forth between the restaurant and the kitchen.

By now Pavel was receiving ten rubles instead of eight. He had grown taller and broader in these two years, and many were the trials that fell to his lot. For half a year he had worked as a kitchen boy but had been sent back to the scullery again; the all-powerful chef had taken a dislike to him—you never knew but what the unruly cub might stick a knife into you if you boxed his ears too often. Indeed Pavel's fiery temper would have lost him the job long since had it not been for his tremendous capacity for hard work. For he could work harder than anyone else and he never seemed to get tired.

During rush hours he would dash with loaded trays up and down the kitchen stairs like a whirlwind, taking four or five steps at a time.

At night, when the hubbub in both halls of the restaurant subsided, the waiters would gather downstairs in the kitchen storerooms and wild, reckless card games would begin. On more than one occasion Pavel saw banknotes of large denominations change hands. He was not surprised to see so much money lying about for he knew that each waiter received between thirty and forty rubles a shift in ruble and half ruble tips, which they spent later in drinking and gambling. Pavel hated them.

"The damned swine!" he thought. "There's Artem, a first-class mechanic, and all he gets is forty-eight rubles a month, and I get ten. And they rake in all that money in one day. And just for carrying trays back and forth. And then they spend it all on drink and cards."

To Pavel the waiters were as alien and hostile as his employers. "They crawl on their bellies here, the pigs, but their wives and sons strut about town like rich folk."

Sometimes they brought their sons wearing smart Gymnasium uniforms, and sometimes their wives, plump and soft with good living. "I bet they have more money than the gentry they serve," Pavel thought. Nor was the lad shocked any longer by what went on at night in the dark corners of the kitchen or in the storerooms. He knew very well that no dishwasher or barmaid would hold her job long if she did not sell herself for a few rubles to those who held the whip hand here.

Pavel had a glimpse of the bottommost depths of life, the very sump of its ugly pit, and from it a musty, mouldy stench, the smell of swamp rot, was wafted up to him who so eagerly reached out for everything new and unexplored.

Artem failed to get his brother taken on as an apprentice at the railway yards; they would not have anyone under fifteen. But Pavel was drawn to the huge soot-blackened brick building, and he looked forward to the day when he could get away from the restaurant.

He went to see Artem at the yards frequently, and would go with him to look over the cars, helping him whenever he could.

He felt particularly lonely after Frosya left. With the gay, laughing girl gone, Pavel felt more keenly than ever how strong his friendship with her had grown. Now as he came in the morning to the scullery and listened to the shrill quarrelling of the refugee women he felt a gnawing sense of emptiness and solitude.

One night as he fired the boiler he squatted in front of the open firebox and stared squinting at the flames, revelling in the heat of the stove. He was alone in the scullery.

Involuntarily he fell to thinking of Frosya, and a scene he had recently witnessed rose before his mind's eye.

During the night interval on Saturday Pavel was on his way downstairs to the kitchen, when curiosity prompted him to climb onto a pile of firewood to look into the storeroom on the lower landing where the gamblers usually assembled.

The game was in full swing. Zalivanov, flushed with excitement, was keeping the bank.

Just then footsteps sounded on the stairs. Looking around, Pavel saw Prokhoshka coming down, and he slipped under the staircase to let the man pass into the kitchen. It was dark there under the stairs and Prokhoshka could not see him.

As Prokhoshka passed the turning in the stairs, Pavel caught a glimpse of his broad back and huge head. Just then someone else came hurrying lightly down the steps after the waiter and Pavel heard a familiar voice call out:

"Prokhoshka, wait!"

Prokhoshka stopped and turned around to look up the stairway.

"What d'you want?" he growled.

The footsteps pattered down and soon Frosya came into sight.

She seized the waiter by the arm and spoke in a broken, choking voice.

"Where's the money the Lieutenant gave you, Prokhoshka?"

The man wrenched his arm away from the girl.

"What money? I gave it to you, didn't I?" his tone was sharp and vicious.

"But he gave you three hundred rubles," Frosya's voice broke into muffled sobs.

"Did he now? Three hundred!" Prokhoshka sneered. "Want to get it all, eh? Flying high for a dishwasher, aren't you, my fine young lady? The fifty I gave you is plenty. Girls a damn sight better than you, educated too, don't take that much. You ought to be thankful for what you got—fifty rubles clear for a night is damn good. Alright, I'll give you another ten, maybe twenty, that's all—and if you're not a fool you can earn some more. I can help you." With this Prokhoshka spun around and disappeared into the kitchen.

"Scoundrel! Swine!" Frosya screamed after him and, leaning against the woodpile, sobbed bitterly.

Words cannot convey the emotion that seized Pavel as he stood in the darkness under the staircase watching Frosya convulsively beat her head against the logs of wood. But he did not show himself; only his fingers spasmodically gripped the cast-iron supports of the staircase.

"So they've sold her too, damn them! Oh Frosya, Frosya. . . ."

His hatred for Prokhoshka seared deeper than ever and everything around him was revolting and hateful to him. "If I had the strength I'd beat the scoundrel to death! Why am I not big and strong like Artem?"

The flames under the boiler flared up and died down, their trembling red tongues intertwining into a long bluish spiral; it seemed to Pavel that some jeering, mocking imp was showing its tongue at him.

It was quiet in the room; only the fire crackled and the tap dripped at measured intervals.

Klimka put the last pot, scrubbed until it shone, on the shelf and wiped his hands. There was no one else in the kitchen. The cook on duty and the kitchen help were asleep in the cloakroom. Quiet settled over the kitchen for the three night hours, and these hours Klimka always spent upstairs with Pavel, for a firm friendship had sprung up between the young kitchen boy and the dark-eyed boiler attendant. Upstairs, Klimka found Pavel squatting in front of the open firebox. Pavel saw the shadow of the familiar shaggy figure cast against the wall and said without turning around:

"Sit down, Klimka."

The boy climbed onto the wood pile, stretched out on it and looked at the silent Pavel.

"Trying to tell your fortune in the fire?" he asked, smiling.

Pavel tore his gaze away from the licking tongues of flame and turned on Klimka two large shining eyes brimming with unspoken sadness. Klimka had never seen his friend look so sad.

"What's wrong with you today, Pavel?" After a pause he asked: "Anything happened?"

Pavel got up and sat next to Klimka.

"Nothing's happened," he replied in a low voice. "Only it's hard for me here, Klimka." And his hands resting on his knees clenched into fists.

"What's come over you today?" Klimka insisted, propping himself up on his elbows.

"Today? It's been like this ever since I got this job. Just look at this place! We work like horses and instead of thanks we get blows—anyone can beat you and there's nobody to stick up for you. The masters hire us to serve them, but anyone who's strong enough has the right to beat us. After all, you can run yourself ragged but you'll never please everybody and those you can't please always have it in for you. No matter how you try to do everything right so that nobody could find fault, there's always bound to be somebody you haven't served fast enough, and then you get it in the neck just the same. . . ."

"Don't shout like that," Klimka interrupted him, frightened. "Somebody might walk in and hear you."

Pavel leapt to his feet.

"Let them hear, I'm going to quit anyway. I'd rather shovel snow than hang around this . . . this hole full of crooks. Look at all the money they've got! They treat us like dirt, and do what they like with the girls. The decent girls who won't do what they want are kicked out, and starving refugees who have no place to go are taken on instead. And that sort hang on because here at least they get something to eat, and they're so down and out they'll do anything for a piece of bread."

He spoke with such passion that Klimka, fearing that someone might overhear, sprang up to close the door leading to the kitchen, while Pavel continued to pour out the bitterness that was overflowing in his soul.

"And you, Klimka, take the beatings lying down. Why don't you ever speak up?"

Pavel dropped onto a stool at the table and rested his head wearily on the palm of his hand. Klimka threw some wood into the fire and also sat down at the table.

"Aren't we going to read today?" he asked Pavel.

"There's nothing to read," Pavel replied. "The bookstall's closed."

"Why should it be closed today?" Klimka wondered.

"The gendarmes picked up the bookseller. Found something on him," Pavel replied.

"Picked him up? What for?"

"For politics, they say."

Klimka stared at Pavel, unable to grasp his meaning.

"Politics. What's that?"

Pavel shrugged his shoulders.

"The devil knows! They say it's politics when you go against the tsar."

Klimka looked startled.

"Do people do that sort of thing?"

"I dunno," replied Pavel.

The door opened and Glasha, her eyes puffed from sleepiness, walked into the scullery.

"Why aren't you two sleeping? There's time for an hour's nap before the train pulls in. You'd better take a rest, Pavka, I'll see to the boiler for you."

Pavel quit his job sooner than he expected and in a manner he had not foreseen.

One frosty January day when Pavel had finished his shift and was ready to go home he found that the young man who was to relieve him had not shown up. Pavel went to the proprietor's wife and announced that he was going nevertheless, but she would not hear of it. There was nothing for him to do but to carry on, exhausted though he was after a day and night of work. By evening he was ready to drop with weariness. During the night interval he had to fill the boilers and bring them to the boil in time for the three-o'clock train.

Pavel turned the tap but there was no water; the

pump evidently was not working. Leaving the tap open, he lay down on the woodpile; but fatigue got the better of him, and he was soon fast asleep.

A few minutes later the tap began gurgling and hissing and the water poured into the boiler, filling it to overflowing and spilling over the tiled floor of the scullery which was deserted as usual at this hour. The water flowed on until it covered the floor and seeped under the door into the restaurant.

Puddles of water gathered under the bags and portmanteaus of the dozing passengers, but nobody noticed it until the water reached a passenger lying on the floor and he jumped to his feet with a shout. There was a rush for luggage and a terrific uproar broke out.

And the water continued to pour in.

Prokhoshka, who had been clearing the tables in the second hall, ran in when he heard the commotion. Leaping over the puddles he made a dash for the door and pushed it open violently. The water dammed behind it burst into the hall.

There was more shouting. The waiters on duty rushed into the scullery. Prokhoshka threw himself on the sleeping Pavel.

Blows rained down on the boy's head, stunning him.

Still half asleep, he had no idea of what was happening. He was only conscious of blinding flashes of lightning before his eyes and agonizing pain shooting through his body.

Pavel was so badly beaten that he barely managed to drag himself home.

In the morning Artem, grim-faced and scowling, questioned his brother as to what had happened.

Pavel told him everything.

"Who beat you?" Artem asked hoarsely.

"Prokhoshka."

"All right, now lie still."

Without another word Artem pulled on his jacket and walked out.

"Where can I find Prokhor, the waiter," he asked one of the dishwashers. Glasha looked at the stranger in workingman's clothes who stood before her.

"He'll be here in a moment," she replied.

The man leaned his enormous bulk against the door jamb.

"All right, I can wait."

Prokhor, carrying a mountain of dishes on a tray, kicked the door open and entered the scullery.

"That's him," Glasha nodded at the waiter.

Artem took a step forward and laying a heavy hand on Prokhor's shoulder looked him straight in the eye.

"What did you beat up my brother Pavka for?"

Prokhor tried to shake his shoulder loose, but a smashing blow laid him out on the floor; he tried to rise, but a second blow more terrible than the first pinned him down.

47

The terror-stricken dishwashers scattered on all sides.

Artem spun around and headed for the exit.

Prokhoshka sprawled on the floor, his battered face bleeding.

That evening Artem did not come home from the railway yards.

His mother learned that he was being held by the gendarmes.

Six days later Artem returned late at night when his mother was already asleep. He went up to Pavel, who was sitting up in bed, and said gently:

"Feeling better, boy?" Artem sat down next to Pavel. "Might have been worse." After a moment's silence he added: "Never mind, you'll go to work at the electric station; I've spoken to them about you. You'll learn a real trade there."

Pavel seized Artem's powerful hand with both of his.

CHAPTER TWO

Like a whirlwind the stupendous news broke into the small town: "The tsar's been overthrown!"

The townsfolk refused to believe it.

From a train that crawled into the station in a blizzard two students in army greatcoats and with rifles slung over their shoulders and a detachment of revolutionary soldiers wearing red armbands tumbled out onto the platform and arrested the station gendarmes, an old colonel and the chief of the garrison. Now the townsfolk believed the news. Thousands streamed down the snowbound streets to the town square.

Eagerly they drank in words they had not known before: liberty, equality and fraternity.

Turbulent days followed, days full of excitement and jubilation. Then a lull set in, and the red flag flying over the town hall where the Mensheviks and adherents of the Bund had ensconced themselves was the sole reminder of the change that had taken place. Everything else remained as before.

Towards the end of the winter a regiment of the cavalry guards was billeted in the town. In the mornings they sallied out in squadrons to hunt for deserters from the Southwestern Front at the railway station.

The troopers were great, beefy fellows with well-fed faces. Most of their officers were counts and princes; they wore golden shoulder straps and silver piping on their breeches, just as they had in the tsar's time—for all the world as if there had been no revolution.

For Pavel, Klimka and Sergei Bruzzhak nothing had changed. The bosses were still there. It was not until November that something out of the ordinary began to happen. People of a new kind had appeared at the station and were beginning to stir things up; a steadily increasing number of them were soldiers from the firing lines and they bore the strange name of "Bolsheviks."

Where that firm and weighty word came from no one knew.

The guardsmen found it increasingly hard to detain the deserters. The crackle of rifles and the splintering of glass was heard more and more often down at the station. The men came from the front in groups and when stopped they fought back with bayonets. In the beginning of December they began pouring in by trainloads.

The guardsmen came down in force to the station with the intention of holding the soldiers, but they found themselves raked by machine-gun fire. The men who poured out of the railway cars were inured to death.

The grey-coated frontliners drove the guards back into the town and then returned to the station to continue on their way, trainload after trainload.

One day in the spring of nineteen eighteen, three chums on their way from Sergei Bruzzhak's where they had been playing cards dropped into the Korchagin garden and threw themselves on the grass. They were bored. All the customary occupations had begun to pall, and they were beginning to rack their brains for some more exciting way to spend the day when they heard the clatter of horses' hoofs behind them and saw a horseman come galloping down the road. With one bound the horse cleared the ditch between the road and the low garden fence and the rider waved his whip at Pavel and Klim.

"Hi there, my lads, come over here!"

Pavel and Klim sprang to their feet and ran to the fence. The rider was covered with dust; it had settled in a heavy grey layer on the cap which he wore pushed to the back of his head, and on his khaki blouse and breeches. A revolver and two German grenades dangled from his heavy soldier's belt.

"Can you get me a drink of water, boys?" the horseman asked them. While Pavel dashed off into the house for the water, he turned to Sergei who was staring at him. "Tell me, boy, who's in authority in your town?"

Sergei breathlessly related all the local news to the newcomer.

"There's been nobody in authority for two weeks. The homeguard's the government now. All the inhabitants take turns patrolling the town at night. And who might you be?" Sergei asked in his turn.

"Now, now—if you know too much you'll get old too soon," the horseman smiled.

Pavel ran out of the house carrying a mug of water.

The rider thirstily emptied the mug at one gulp and handed it back to Pavel. Then jerking the reins he started off at a gallop, heading for the pinewoods.

"Who was that?" Pavel asked Klim.

"How do I know?" the latter replied, shrugging his shoulders.

"Looks like the authorities are going to be changed again. That's why the Leszczinskis left yesterday. And if the rich are on the run that means the partisans are coming," declared Sergei, settling the political question firmly and with an air of finality.

The logic of this was so convincing that both Pavel and Klim agreed with him at once.

Before the boys had finished discussing the question a clatter of hoofs from the highway sent all three rushing back to the fence.

Over by the forest warden's cottage, which was barely visible among the trees, they saw men and carts emerging from the woods, and nearer still on the highway a party of fifteen or so mounted men with rifles across their pommels. At the head of the horsemen rode an elderly man in khaki jacket and officer's belt with field glasses slung on his chest, and beside him the man the boys had just spoken to. The elderly man wore a red ribbon on the front of his chest.

"What did I tell you?" Sergei nudged Pavel in the ribs. "See the red ribbon? Partisans. I'll be damned

if they aren't partisans. . . ." And whooping with joy he leapt over the fence into the street.

The others followed suit and all three stood by the roadside gazing at the approaching horsemen.

When the riders were quite close the man whom the boys had met before nodded to them, and pointing to the Leszczinski house with his whip asked:

"Who lives over there?"

Pavel paced alongside trying to keep abreast the rider.

"Leszczinski the lawyer. He ran away yesterday. Must have been scared of you. . . ."

"How do you know who we are?" the elderly man asked, smiling.

"What about that?" Pavel pointed to the ribbon. "Anybody can tell. . . ."

People poured into the street to stare with curiosity at the detachment entering the town. Our three young friends too stood watching the dusty, exhausted Red Guards go by. And when the detachment's lone cannon and the carts with machine guns clattered over the cobblestones the boys trailed after the partisans, and did not go home until after the unit had halted in the centre of the town and the billeting began.

That evening four men sat around the massive carved-legged table in the spacious Leszczinski parlour: detachment commander Comrade Bulgakov, an elderly man whose hair was touched with grey, and three members of the unit's commanding personnel.

Bulgakov had spread out a map of the gubernia on the table and was now running his finger over it.

"You say that we ought to put up a stand here, Comrade Yermachenko," he said, addressing the man with prominent cheekbones and strong teeth facing him, "but I think we must move out in the morning. Better still if we could get going during the night, but the men are in need of a rest. Our task is to withdraw to Kazatin before the Germans get there. To resist with the strength we have would be ridiculous. One gun with thirty rounds of ammunition, two hundred infantry and sixty cavalry. A formidable force, isn't it, when the Germans are advancing in an avalanche of steel. We cannot put up a fight until we join up with other withdrawing Red units. Besides, Comrade, we must remember that apart from the Germans there'll be numerous counterrevolutionary bands of all kinds to deal with en route. I propose that we should withdraw in the morning after first blowing up the railway bridge beyond the station. It'll take the Germans two or three days to repair it and in the meantime their advance along the railway will be held up. What do you think, Comrades? It's up to us to decide..." he turned to the others around the table.

Struzhkov, who sat diagonally across from Bulgakov, sucked in his lips and looked first at the map and
then at Bulgakov.

"I agree with Bulgakov," he said finally.

The youngest of the men, who was dressed in a
worker's blouse, also concurred.

"Bulgakov's right," he said.

But Yermachenko, the man who had spoken with
the boys earlier in the day, shook his head.

"What the devil did we get the detachment together
for? To retreat from the Germans without putting up
a fight? As I see it, we've got to have it out with them
here. I'm sick and tired of running. If it was up to me,
I'd fight them here without fail...." Pushing his
chair back sharply, he rose and began pacing the room.

Bulgakov looked at him with disapproval.

"We must use our heads, Yermachenko. We can't
throw our men into a battle that is bound to end in
defeat and destruction. That would be ridiculous.
There's a whole division with heavy artillery and armoured cars just behind us.... This is no time for
schoolboy heroics, Comrade Yermachenko...." Turning to the others, he continued: "So it's decided, we
evacuate tomorrow morning.... Now for the next question, liaison," Bulgakov proceeded. "Since we are the
last to leave, it's our job to organize work in the
German rear. This is a big railway junction and there
are two stations in the town. We must see to it that there

is a reliable comrade to carry on the work on the railway. We'll have to decide here whom to leave behind to get the work going. Have you anyone in mind?"

"I think Fyodor Zhukhrai the sailor ought to remain," Yermachenko said, moving up to the table. "In the first place he's a local man. Secondly, he's a fitter and mechanic and can get himself a job at the station. Nobody's seen Fyodor with our detachment—he won't get here until tonight. He's got a good head on his shoulders and he'll get things going properly. I think he's the most suitable man for the job."

Bulgakov nodded.

"Right. I agree with you, Yermachenko. No objections, Comrades?" he turned to the others. "None. Then the matter is settled. We'll leave Zhukhrai some money and the credentials he'll need for his work. . . . Now for the third and last question, Comrades. About the arms stored here in the town. There's quite a stock of rifles, twenty thousand of them, left over from the tsarist war and forgotten by everybody. They are piled up in a peasant's shed. I have this from the owner of the shed who happens to be anxious to get rid of them. We are not going to leave them to the Germans; in my opinion we ought to burn them, and at once, so as to have it over and done with by morning. The only trouble is that the fire might spread to the surrounding cottages. It's on the fringes of the town where the peasant poor live."

Struzhkov stirred in his chair. He was a solidly built man with a heavy stubble that had not seen a razor for some time.

"Why burn the rifles? I would distribute them among the population."

Bulgakov turned quickly to face him.

"Distribute them, you say?"

"A splendid idea!" Yermachenko responded enthusiastically. "Give them to the workers and anyone else who wants them. At least there will be something to hit back with when the Germans make life impossible. They're bound to do their worst. And when things come to a head, the men will be able to take to arms. Struzhkov's right: the rifles must be distributed. Wouldn't be a bad thing to take some to the villages too; the peasants will hide them away, and when the Germans begin to requisition everything the rifles are sure to come in handy."

Bulgakov chuckled.

"That's all right, but the Germans are sure to order all arms turned in and everybody will obey."

"Not everybody," Yermachenko objected. "Some will but others won't."

Bulgakov looked questioningly at the men around the table.

"I'm for distributing the rifles," the young worker supported Yermachenko and Struzhkov.

"All right then, it's decided," Bulgakov agreed. "That's all for now," he said, rising from his chair. "We can take a rest till morning. When Zhukhrai comes, send him in to me, I want to have a talk with him. Yermachenko, you'd better inspect the sentry posts."

When the others left, Bulgakov went into the bedroom next to the parlour, spread his greatcoat on the mattress and lay down.

The following morning Pavel was coming home from the electric power station where he had been working as a stoker's helper for a year now.

He saw at once that the town was in the grip of unusual excitement. As he went along he met more and more people carrying one or two and sometimes even three rifles each. He could not understand what was happening and he hurried home as fast as he could. Outside the Leszczinski garden he saw his acquaintances of yesterday mounting their horses.

Pavel ran into the house, washed quickly and, learning from his mother that Artem had not come home yet, dashed out again and hurried over to see Sergei Bruzzhak, who lived on the other side of the town.

Sergei's father was an engine driver's helper and had his own tiny house and a small piece of land.

Sergei was out, and his mother, a stout, pale-faced woman, eyed Pavel sourly.

"The devil knows where he is! He rushed out first thing in the morning like one possessed. Said they were giving out rifles somewhere, so I suppose that's where he is. What you snot-nosed warriors need is a good hiding—you've gotten out of hand completely. Hardly out of pinafores and already dashing off after firearms. You tell the scamp that if he brings a single cartridge into this house I'll skin him alive. Who knows what he'll be dragging in and then I'll have to answer for it. You're not going there too, are you?"

But before Sergei's garrulous mother had finished speaking, Pavel was already racing down the street.

On the highway he met a man carrying a rifle on each shoulder. Pavel dashed up to him.

"Please, uncle, where did you get them?"

"They're giving them away over there in Verkhovina."

Pavel set out as fast as his legs could carry him. Two streets down he collided with a boy who was lugging a heavy infantry rifle with bayonet attached. Pavel stopped him.

"Where'd you get the gun?"

"Fellows from the detachment were giving them away out there opposite the school, but there aren't any more. All gone. Handed them out all night and now only the empty cases are left. This is my second one," the boy declared proudly.

Pavel was utterly dismayed by the news.

"Damn it, I should've gone straight there," he thought bitterly. "How could I have been caught napping like this?"

Suddenly an idea struck him. Spinning around he overtook the receding boy in two or three bounds and wrenched the rifle from his hands.

"One's enough for you. This is going to be mine," he said in a tone that brooked no opposition.

Infuriated by this robbery in broad daylight, the boy flung himself at Pavel, but the latter leapt back and pointed the bayonet at his antagonist.

"Look out or you'll get hurt!" Pavel shouted.

The boy burst into tears of sheer vexation and ran away, cursing with impotent rage. Pavel, vastly pleased with himself, trotted home. Leaping over the fence he ran into the shed, laid his acquisition on the crossbeams under the roof, and, whistling gaily, walked into the house.

Lovely are the summer evenings in the Ukraine. In small Ukrainian towns like Shepetovka, which are more like villages on the outskirts, these calm summer nights lure all the young folk out of doors. You will see them in groups and in pairs—on the porches, in the little front gardens, or perched on piles of timber lying by the side of the road. Their gay laughter and singing echo in the evening stillness.

The air is heavy and tremulous with the fragrance of flowers. There is a faint pinpoint glimmer of stars in the depths of the sky, and voices carry far, far away....

Pavel dearly loved his accordion. He would lay the melodious instrument tenderly on his knees and let his nimble fingers run lightly up and down the double row of keys. A sighing from the bass, and a cascade of rollicking melody would pour forth....

How can you keep still when the sinuous bellows weave in and out and the accordion breathes its warm compelling harmonies. Before you know it your feet are answering its urgent summons. Ah how good it is to be alive!

This is a particularly jolly evening. A merry crowd of young folk have gathered on the pile of logs outside Pavel's house. And gayest of them all is Galochka, the daughter of the stonemason who lives next door to Pavel. Galochka loves to dance and sing with the lads. She has a deep velvety contralto.

Pavel is a wee bit afraid of her. For Galochka has a sharp tongue. She sits down beside Pavel and throws her arms around him, laughing gaily.

"What a wonder you are with that accordion!" she says. "It's a pity you're a bit too young or you'd make me a fine hubby. I adore men who play the accordion, my poor heart just melts."

Pavel blushes to the roots of his hair—luckily it is too dark for anyone to see. He edges away from the vixen but she clings fast to him.

"Now then, dearie, you wouldn't run away from me, would you? A fine sweetheart you are," she laughs.

Her firm breast brushes Pavel's shoulder, and he is strangely stirred in spite of himself, and the loud laughter of the others breaks the accustomed stillness of the lane.

"Move up, I haven't any room to play," says Pavel giving her shoulder a slight push.

This evokes another roar of laughter, jokes and banter.

Marusya comes to Pavel's rescue. "Play something sad, Pavel, something that tugs at your heartstrings."

Slowly the bellows spread out, gently Pavel's fingers caress the keys and a familiar well-loved tune fills the air. Galina is the first to join in, then Marusya, and the others.

> *All the boatmen to their cottage*
> *Gathered on the morrow,*
> *O, 'tis good*
> *And O, 'tis sweet*
> *Here to sing our sorrow . . .*

The vibrant young voices of the singers were carried far away into the wooded distances.

"Pavka!" It was Artem's voice.

Pavel compressed the bellows of his accordion and fastened the straps.

"They're calling me. I've got to go."

"Oh, play just a little more. What's your hurry?" Marusya tried to wheedle him into staying.

But Pavel was adamant.

"Can't. We'll have some music tomorrow again, but now I've got to go. Artem's calling." And with that he ran across the street to the little house opposite.

He opened the door and saw two men in the room besides Artem: Roman, a friend of Artem's, and a stranger. They were sitting at the table.

"You wanted me?" Pavel asked.

Artem nodded to him and turned to the stranger:

"This is that brother of mine we've been talking about."

The stranger extended a gnarled hand to Pavel.

"See here, Pavka," Artem said to his brother. "You told me the electrician at the power plant is ill. Now what I want you to do is to find out tomorrow whether they want a good man to take his place. If they do you'll let us know."

The stranger interrupted him.

"No need to do that. I'd rather go with him and speak with the boss myself."

"Of course they need someone. Today the power plant didn't work simply because Stankovich was sick.

63

The boss came around twice—he'd been looking high and low for somebody to take his place but couldn't find anyone. He was afraid to start the plant with only a stoker around. The electrician's got the typhus."

"That settles it," the stranger said. "I'll call for you tomorrow and we'll go over there together," he added addressing Pavel.

"Good."

Pavel's glance met the calm grey eyes of the stranger who was studying him carefully. The firm, steady scrutiny somewhat disconcerted him. The newcomer was wearing a grey jacket buttoned from top to bottom—it was obviously a tight fit for the seams strained on his broad, powerful back. His head and shoulders were joined by a muscular, oxlike neck, and his whole frame suggested the sturdy strength of an old oak.

"Goodbye and good luck, Zhukhrai," Artem said accompanying him to the door. "Tomorrow you'll go along with my brother and get fixed up in the job."

The Germans entered the town three days after the detachment left. Their coming was announced by a locomotive whistle at the station which had latterly been quite deserted.

"The Germans are coming," the news flashed through the town.

The town stirred like a disturbed anthill, for although the townsfolk had known for some time that the Germans were due, they had somehow not quite believed it. And now these terrible Germans were not only somewhere on their way, but actually here, in town.

The townsfolk clung to the protection of their front-garden fences and wicket gates. They were afraid to venture out into the streets.

The Germans came, marching single file on both sides of the highway; they wore olive-drab uniforms and carried their rifles at the ready. Their rifles were tipped with broad knife-like bayonets; they wore heavy steel helmets, and carried enormous packs on their backs. They came from the station into the town in an endless stream, came cautiously, prepared to repel an attack at any moment, although no one dreamed of attacking them.

In front strode two officers, Mausers in hand, and in the centre of the road walked the interpreter, a sergeant-major in the Hetman's service wearing a blue Ukrainian coat and a tall fur cap.

The Germans lined up on the square in the centre of the town. The drums rolled. A small crowd of the more venturesome townsfolk gathered. The Hetman's man in the Ukrainian coat climbed onto the porch of the chemist's shop and read aloud an order issued by the commandant, Major Korf.

§ 1

I hereby order:

All citizens of the town are to turn in within
24 hours any firearms or other lethal weapons
in their possession. The penalty for violation
of this order is death by shooting.

§ 2

Martial law is declared in the town and
citizens are forbidden to appear in the streets
after 8 p. m.

Major Korf, Town Commandant.

The German *Kommandantur* took up quarters in
the building formerly used by the town administration
and, after the revolution, by the Soviet of Workers'
Deputies. At the entrance a sentry was posted wearing
a parade helmet with an imperial eagle of enormous
proportions. In the backyard of the same building
were storage premises for the arms to be turned in by
the population.

All day long weapons were brought in by townsfolk
scared by the threat of shooting. The adults did not
show themselves; the arms were delivered by youths
and small boys. The Germans detained nobody.

Those who did not want to come in person dumped
their weapons out on the road during the night, and

in the morning a German patrol picked them up, loaded them into an army cart and hauled them to the *Kommandantur*.

At one o'clock in the afternoon, when the time limit expired, German soldiers began to take stock of their booty: fourteen thousand rifles. That meant that six thousand had not been turned in. The dragnet searches they conducted yielded very insignificant results.

At dawn the next morning two railwaymen in whose homes concealed rifles had been found were shot at the old Jewish cemetery outside the town.

As soon as he heard of the commandant's order, Artem hurried home. Meeting Pavel in the yard, he took him by the shoulder and asked him quietly but firmly:

"Did you bring any weapons home?"

Pavel had not intended to say anything about the rifle, but he could not lie to his brother and so he made a clean breast of it.

They went into the shed together. Artem took the rifle down from its hiding place on the beams, removed the bolt and bayonet, and seizing the weapon by the barrel swung it with all his might against a fence post. The butt splintered. What remained of the rifle was thrown far away into the waste lot beyond the garden. The bayonet and bolt Artem threw into the privy pit.

When he was finished, Artem turned to his brother.

"You're not a baby any more, Pavka, and you ought to know you can't play with guns. You must not bring anything into the house. This is dead serious. You might have to pay with your life for that sort of thing nowadays. And don't try any tricks, because if you do bring something like that home and they find it I'd be the first to be shot—they wouldn't touch a youngster like you. These are brutal times, understand that!"

Pavel promised.

As the brothers were crossing the yard to the house, a carriage stopped at the Leszczinskis' gate and the lawyer and his wife and two children, Nelly and Victor, got out.

"So the fine birds have flown back to their nest," Artem muttered angrily. "Now the fun begins, blast them!" He went inside.

All day long Pavel thought regretfully of the rifle. In the meantime his friend Sergei was hard at work in an old, abandoned shed, digging a hole in the ground next to the wall. At last the pit was ready. In it Sergei deposited three brand-new rifles well wrapped up in rags. He had obtained them when the Red Guard detachment distributed arms to the people and he did not have the slightest intention of giving them up to the Germans. He had laboured hard all night to make sure that they were safely hidden.

He filled up the hole, tramped the earth down level, and then piled a heap of refuse on top. Critically reviewing the results of his efforts and finding them satisfactory, he took off his cap and wiped the sweat off his forehead.

"Now let them search, and even if they find it, they'll never know who put it there, because the shed is nobody's anyway."

Imperceptibly a friendship sprang up between Pavel and the grim-faced electrician who had been working a full month now at the electric station.

Zhukhrai showed the stoker's helper how the dynamo was built and how it was run.

The sailor took a liking to the bright youngster. He frequently visited Artem on free days and listened patiently to the mother's tale of domestic woes and worries, especially when she complained about her younger boy's escapades. Thoughtful and serious-minded, Zhukhrai had a calming, reassuring effect on Maria Yakovlevna, who would forget her troubles and grow more cheerful in his company.

One day Zhukhrai stopped Pavel as he was passing between the high piles of firewood in the power station yard.

"Your mother tells me you're fond of a scrap," he said, smiling. " 'He's as bad as a game-cock,' she says." Zhukhrai chuckled approvingly. "As a matter of fact, it doesn't hurt to be a fighter, as long as you know whom to fight and why."

Pavel was not sure whether Zhukhrai was joking or serious.

"I don't fight for nothing," he retorted, "I always fight for what's right and fair."

"Want me to teach you to fight properly?" Zhukhrai asked unexpectedly.

"What d'you mean, properly?" Pavel looked at the other in surprise.

"You'll see."

And Pavel was given a brief introductory lecture on boxing.

Proficiency in this art did not come easy to Pavel. Time and again he found himself rolling on the ground, knocked off his feet by a blow from Zhukhrai's fist, but for all that he proved a diligent and patient pupil.

One warm day after he had returned from Klimka's place and fidgeted about in his room for a while wondering what to do with himself, Pavel decided to climb up to his favourite spot—the roof of a shed that stood in the corner of the garden behind the house. He crossed the backyard into the garden, went over to the clapboard shack, and climbed up onto its roof. Pushing through the dense branches of the cherry trees that hung over the shed, he made his way to the centre of the roof and lay down to bask in the sunshine.

One side of the shed jutted out into the Leszczinski garden, and from the end of the roof the whole garden and one side of the house were visible. Poking his head over the edge Pavel could see part of the yard and a carriage standing there. The batman of the German Lieutenant quartered at the Leszczinskis' was brushing his master's clothes.

Pavel had often seen the Lieutenant at the gate leading to the grounds. He was a squat, ruddy-faced man who wore a tiny clipped moustache, pince-nez and a cap with a shiny lacquered peak. Pavel also knew that he lived in the side room, the window of which opened onto the garden and was visible from the shed roof.

At this moment the Lieutenant was sitting at the table writing. Presently he picked up what he had written and went out of the room. He handed the paper to the batman and walked off down the garden path leading to the gate. At the summer house he paused to talk to someone inside. A moment later Nelly Leszczinska came out. The Lieutenant took her arm and together they went out of the gate into the street.

Pavel watched the proceedings from his vantage point. Presently a drowsiness stole over him and he was about to close his eyes when he noticed the batman entering the Lieutenant's room; he hung up a uniform, opened the window into the garden and tidied up the room. Then he went out, closing the door behind him.

The next moment Pavel saw him over by the stable where the horses were.

Through the open window Pavel had a good view of the whole room. On the table lay a belt and some shining object.

Driven by an irresistible curiosity, Pavel quietly climbed noiselessly off the roof onto the cherry tree and slipped down into the Leszczinski garden. Bent double, he bounded across the garden and peered through the window into the room. Before him on the table were a belt with a shoulder strap and holster containing a splendid twelve-shot Mannlicher.

Pavel caught his breath. For a few seconds he was prey to an inward struggle, but reckless daring gained the upper hand and reaching into the room, he seized the holster, pulled out the new blue-steel weapon and sprang down to the ground. With a swift glance around he cautiously slipped the pistol into his pocket and dashed across the garden to the cherry tree. With the agility of a monkey he climbed to the roof and paused to look behind him. The batman was still chatting pleasantly with the groom. The garden was silent and deserted. Pavel slid down the other side and ran home.

His mother was busy in the kitchen cooking dinner and paid no attention to him.

He seized a rag from behind a trunk and shoved it into his pocket, then slipped out unnoticed, ran across the yard, scaled the fence and emerged on the road leading to the woods. Holding the heavy revolver to prevent it from pounding against his thigh, he ran as fast as he could to the abandoned ruins of a brick kiln nearby.

His feet seemed barely to touch the ground and the wind whistled in his ears.

Everything was quiet at the old brick kiln. It was a depressing sight, with the wooden roof fallen in here and there, the mountains of brick rubble and the collapsed ovens. The place was overgrown with weeds; no one ever visited it except Pavel and his two friends who sometimes came here to play. Pavel knew a great many hiding places where the stolen treasure could be concealed.

He climbed through a gap in one of the ovens and looked around him cautiously, but there was no one in sight. Only the pines soughed softly and a slight wind stirred the dust on the road. There was a strong smell of resin in the air.

Pavel placed the revolver wrapped in the rag in a corner of the oven floor and covered it with a small pyramid of old bricks. On the way out he filled in the entrance into the old kiln with loose bricks, noted the exact location, and slowly set out for home, feeling his knees trembling under him.

"How is it all going to end?" he thought and his heart was heavy with foreboding.

To avoid going home he went to the power station earlier than usual. He took the key from the watchman and opened the wide doors leading into the powerhouse. And while he cleaned out the ashpit, pumped water into the boiler and started the fire going, he wondered what was happening at the Leszczinskis'.

It was about eleven o'clock when Zhukhrai came and called Pavel outside.

"Why was there a search at your place today?" he asked in a low voice.

Pavel started.

"A search?"

"I don't like the look of it," Zhukhrai continued after a brief pause. "Sure you haven't any idea what they were looking for?"

Pavel knew very well what they had been looking for, but he could not risk telling Zhukhrai about the theft of the revolver. Trembling all over with anxiety, he asked:

"Have they arrested Artem?"

"Nobody was arrested, but they turned everything upside down in the house."

This reassured Pavel slightly, although his anxiety did not pass. For a few minutes both he and Zhukhrai stood there each wrapped in his own thoughts. One of the two knew why the search had been made and was worried about the consequences, the other did not and hence was on the alert.

74

"Damn them, maybe they've got wind of me some-how," Zhukhrai thought. "Artem knows nothing about me, but why did they search his place? Got to be more careful."

The two parted without a word and returned to their work.

The Leszczinski house was in a turmoil.

The Lieutenant, noticing that the revolver was missing, called in his batman, who declared that the weapon must have been stolen; whereupon the officer's usual restraint deserted him and he struck the batman on the ear with all his might. The batman, swaying from the impact of the blow, stood stiffly at attention, blinking and submissively awaiting further developments.

The lawyer, called in for an explanation, was indignant at the theft and apologized to the Lieutenant for having allowed such a thing to occur in his house.

Victor Leszczinski suggested to his father that the revolver might have been stolen by the neighbours, and in particular by that young ruffian Pavel Korchagin. The father lost no time in passing on his son's conjecture to the Lieutenant, who at once ordered a search made.

The search was fruitless, and the episode of the missing revolver reassured Pavel that even enterprises as risky as this can sometimes succeed.

CHAPTER THREE

Tonya stood at the open window and pensively surveyed the familiar garden bordered by the stalwart poplars now stirring faintly in the gentle breeze. She could hardly believe that a whole year had passed since she had been here where her childhood years had been spent. It seemed that she had left home only yesterday and returned by this morning's train.

Nothing had changed: the rows of raspberry bushes were as neatly trimmed as ever, and the garden paths were laid out with the same geometric precision and lined with pansies, mother's favourite flowers. Everything in the garden was neat and tidy. Everywhere was the imprint of the pedantic hand of the dendrologist. The sight of these clean-swept, neatly drawn paths bored Tonya.

She picked up the novel she had been reading, opened the door leading to the veranda and walked down the stairs into the garden; she pushed open the little painted wicket gate and slowly headed for the pond next to the station pump house.

She passed the bridge and came out on the tree-lined road. On her right was the pond fringed with willows and alders; on the left the forest began.

She was on her way to the ponds at the old stone-quarry when the sight of a fishing rod bobbing over the water made her pause.

Leaning over the trunk of a twisted willow, she parted the branches and saw before her a sun-tanned, barefoot boy with trouser legs rolled up above the knee. Next to him was a rusty tin can with worms. The lad was too engrossed in his occupation to notice her.

"Do you think you can catch fish here?"

Pavel glanced angrily over his shoulder.

Holding on to the willow and bending low over the water was a girl Pavel had never seen before. She was wearing a white sailor blouse with a striped blue collar and a short light-grey skirt. Short socks with a coloured edging clung to her shapely sun-tanned legs. Her chestnut hair was gathered in a heavy braid.

A slight tremor shook the hand holding the fishing rod and the goose-feather float bobbed, sending circles spreading over the smoothness of the water.

"Look, look, a bite!" the excited voice piped behind Pavel.

He now lost his composure completely and jerked at the line so hard that the hook with the squirming worm on the end of it fairly leapt out of the water.

"Not much chance to fish now, damn it! What the devil brought her here," Pavel thought irritably and in order to cover up his clumsiness cast the hook farther out, landing, however, exactly where he should not have—between two burdocks where the line could easily get caught.

He realized what had happened and without turning around hissed at the girl sitting above him on the bank:

"Can't you keep quiet? You'll scare off all the fish that way."

From above came the mocking voice:

"Your black looks have scared the fish away long ago. No self-respecting angler goes fishing in the afternoon anyway!"

Pavel had done his best to behave politely but this was too much for him. He got up, and pushed his cap over his eyes as he usually did when roused.

"You'd do better, miss, if you took yourself off," he muttered through his teeth, drawing on the most inoffensive part of his vocabulary.

Tonya's eyes narrowed slightly and laughter danced in them.

"Am I really interfering?"

The teasing note had gone from her voice and given way to a friendly, conciliatory tone, and Pavel, who had primed himself to be really rude to this "missy" who had sprung from nowhere, found himself disarmed.

"You can stay and watch, if you want to. It's all the same to me," he said grudgingly and sat down to attend to the float again. It had got stuck in the burdock and there was no doubt that the hook had caught in the roots. Pavel was afraid to pull at it. If it caught he would not be able to get it loose. And the girl would be sure to laugh. He wished she would go away.

Tonya, however, had settled more comfortably on the slightly swaying willow trunk and with her book on her knees was watching the sun-tanned dark-eyed rough-mannered young man who had given her such an ungracious reception and was now deliberately ignoring her.

Pavel saw the girl clearly reflected in the mirror-like surface of the pond, and when she seemed to be absorbed in her book he cautiously pulled at the entangled line. The float ducked under the water and the line grew taut.

"Caught, damn it!" flashed in his mind and at the same moment he saw out of the corner of his eye the laughing face of the girl looking up at him from the water.

Just then two young men, both seventh-grade Gymnasium students, were coming across the bridge at the pump house. One of them was the seventeen-year-old son of engineer Sukharko, the chief of the railway yards, a loutish, fair-haired, freckle-faced scapegrace whom his schoolmates had dubbed Pockmarked Shurka. He was carrying a fancy fishing rod and line and had a cigarette stuck in the corner of his mouth. With him was Victor Leszczinski, a tall, effeminate youth.

"Now this girl is a peach, there's nobody like her

about here," Sukharko was saying, winking significantly as he bent toward his companion. "You can take my word for it that she's chock-full of r-r-romance. She's in the sixth grade and goes to school in Kiev. Now she's come to spend the summer with her father —he's the chief forest warden here. My sister Liza knows her. I wrote her a letter once in a sentimental sort of vein. 'I love you madly'—you know the sort of thing—'and await your answer in trepidation.' Even dug up some suitable verses from Nadson."

"Well, what came of it?" Victor asked curiously.

"Oh, she was frightfully stuck up about it," Sukharko muttered rather sheepishly. "Told me not to waste paper writing letters and all that. But that's how it always is in the beginning. I'm an old hand at this sort of thing. As a matter of fact I can't be bothered with all that romantic nonsense—mooning about for ages, sighing. It's much simpler to take a stroll of an evening down to the repairmen's barracks where for three rubles you can pick up a beauty that'd make your mouth water. And no nonsense either. I used to go out there with Valka Tikhonov—do you know him? The foreman on the railway."

Victor scowled in disgust.

"Do you mean to tell me you go in for foul stuff like that, Shura?"

Shura chewed at his cigarette, spat and replied with a sneer:

"Don't pretend to be so virtuous. We know what you go in for."

Victor interrupted him.

"Will you introduce me to this peach of yours?"

"Of course. Let's hurry or she'll give us the slip. Yesterday morning she went fishing by herself."

As the two friends came up to Tonya, Sukharko took the cigarette out of his mouth and greeted her with a gallant bow.

"How do you do, Mademoiselle Tumanova. Have you come to fish too?"

"No. I'm just watching," replied Tonya.

"You two haven't met, have you?" Sukharko hastened to put in, taking Victor by the arm. "This is my friend Victor Leszczinski."

Victor extended his hand to Tonya in some confusion.

"And why aren't you fishing today?" Sukharko inquired in an effort to keep up the conversation.

"I forgot to bring my line," Tonya replied.

"I'll get another one right away," Sukharko said. "In the meantime you can have mine. I'll be back in a minute."

He had kept his promise to Victor to introduce him to the girl and was now anxious to leave them alone.

"I'd rather not, we should only be in the way. There's somebody fishing here already," said Tonya.

"In whose way?" Sukharko asked. "Oh, you mean him?" For the first time he noticed Pavel who was sitting under a bush. "Well, I'll get rid of him in two shakes."

Before Tonya could stop him he had slipped down to where Pavel was busy with his rod and line.

"Pull in that line of yours and clear out," Sukharko told Pavel. "Hurry up now. . . ." he added as Pavel continued fishing calmly.

Pavel looked up and gave Sukharko a glance that boded no good.

"Shut up, you! Hold your noise!"

"Wha-a-t!" Sukharko exploded. "You've got the cheek to answer back, you wretched tramp! Clear out of here!" He kicked violently at the tin of worms which spun around in the air and fell into the pond, splashing water in Tonya's face.

"You ought to be ashamed of yourself, Sukharko!" she cried.

Pavel leapt to his feet. He knew that Sukharko was the son of the chief of the railway yards where Artem worked, and that if he hit that flabby, mousy mug of his he would complain to his father and Artem would get into trouble. This alone prevented him from settling the matter then and there.

Sensing that Pavel would hit out at him in another moment, Sukharko rushed forward and pushed him in the chest with both hands. Pavel, standing at the

82

water's edge, teetered dangerously, but by frantically waving his arms regained his balance and saved himself from falling in.

Sukharko was two years older than Pavel and notorious as a troublemaker and bully.

The blow in the chest made Pavel see red.

"So that's what you want! Take this!" And with a short swing of his arm he drove a cutting blow into Sukharko's face. Before the latter had time to recover, Pavel seized him firmly by his uniform blouse, clinched him and dragged him into the water.

Knee-deep in the pond, his polished shoes and trousers soaking wet, Sukharko struggled with all his might to wrench himself loose from Pavel's powerful grip. Having achieved his purpose, Pavel jumped ashore. The enraged Sukharko charged after him, ready to tear him to pieces.

As he spun around to face his opponent, Pavel remembered:

"Rest your weight on your left foot, with your right leg tense and right knee bent. Put the weight of your whole body behind the blow, striking upward, at the point of the chin."

Crack!

There was a harsh click of teeth. Then, squealing from the excruciating pain that shot through his chin and his tongue which was caught between the teeth,

Sukharko flailed wildly with his arms and fell back into the water with a loud splash.

Up on the bank Tonya was doubled up with laughter.

"Bravo, bravo!" she cried, clapping her hands. "Well done!"

Seizing his entangled fishing line, Pavel jerked at it so hard that it snapped, and scrambled up the bank to the road.

"That's Pavel Korchagin, a hooligan if there ever was one," he heard Victor say to Tonya as he went.

There was trouble brewing at the station. Rumour had it that the railwaymen on the line were downing tools. The workers of the yards at the next large station had started something big. The Germans arrested two engine drivers suspected of carrying proclamations with them. And among the workers who had ties with the countryside there was serious ferment because of the requisitioning and the return of landlords to their estates.

The lashes of the Hetman's guards seared the backs of the peasants. The partisan movement was developing in the gubernia; the Bolsheviks had already organized nearly a dozen partisan detachments.

There was no rest for Zhukhrai these days. During his stay in the town he had accomplished a great deal. He had made the acquaintance of many railway work-

ers, attended gatherings of young folk, and built up a
strong group among the mechanics at the railway
yards and the sawmill workers. He tried to find
out where Artem stood, and he asked him once
what he thought about the Bolshevik Party and its
cause.

"I don't know much about these parties, Fyodor,"
the burly mechanic replied. "But if there's help needed,
you can count on me."

Fyodor was satisfied, for he knew that Artem was
made of the right stuff and would stand by his word.
As for the Party, he wasn't ready for that yet. "Never
mind," he thought, "in times like these he'll soon
learn for himself."

Fyodor left the power station for a job at the railway yards, where it was easier for him to carry on his
work. At the electric station he had been cut off from
the railway.

Traffic on the railway was exceedingly heavy. The
Germans were shipping carloads of loot by the thousand from the Ukraine to Germany: rye, wheat,
cattle. . . .

One day the Hetman's guards arrested Ponomarenko, the station telegrapher. The blow fell quite
unexpectedly. He was taken to the guardhouse and
brutally beaten. It was he, evidently, who gave away
Roman Sidorenko, a workmate of Artem's.

Two Germans and a Hetman's guard, the Station Commandant's Assistant, came for Roman during working hours. Without saying a word the Assistant Commandant walked over to the bench where Roman was working and cut him across the face with his riding whip.

"You come along, you sonofabitch!" he said. "We've got something to talk to you about." With an ugly leer he seized hold of the mechanic's arm and wrenched it violently. "We'll teach you to go around agitating!"

Artem, who had been working at the vise next to Roman, dropped his file and came at the Assistant Commandant, his massive frame menacingly poised.

"Keep your fists off him, you bastard!" Artem spoke hoarsely, doing his best to restrain his rising fury.

The Assistant Commandant fell back, unfastening his holster as he did so. One of the Germans, a squat, stocky man, unslung his heavy rifle with the broadbladed bayonet from his shoulder and sharply clicked the bolt.

"Halt!" he barked, ready to shoot at another move.

The tall, brawny mechanic stood helpless before the puny soldier; he could do nothing.

Both Roman and Artem were placed under arrest. Artem was released an hour later, but Roman was locked up in a luggage room in the basement.

Ten minutes after the arrest not a single man was working. The depot workers assembled in the station park where they were joined by the switchmen and the men employed at the supply warehouses. Feeling ran high and someone drafted a written demand for the release of Roman and Ponomarenko.

Indignation rose higher still when the Assistant Commandant rushed into the park at the head of a group of guards brandishing a revolver and shouting:

"Back to work, or we'll arrest every last man of you on the spot! And put some of you up against the wall!"

The enfuriated workers replied with a bellow that sent him running for cover to the station. In the meantime, however, the Station Commandant had summoned German troops from the town and truckloads of them were already careering down the road leading to the station.

The workers dispersed and hurried home. No one, not even the stationmaster, remained on the job. Zhukhrai's work was beginning to make itself felt; this was the first time the workers at the station had taken mass action.

The Germans mounted a heavy machine gun on the platform; it stood there like a pointer that has spotted a quarry. Next to it squatted a German corporal, his hand resting on the trigger grip.

The station grew deserted.

At night the arrests began. Artem was among those taken. Zhukhrai escaped by not going home that night.

All the arrested men were herded together in a huge freight shed and given the alternative of either returning to work or being court-martialled.

Practically all the railwaymen were on strike all along the line. For a day and a night not a single train went through, and one hundred and twenty kilometres away a battle was being fought with a large partisan detachment which had cut the railway line and blown up the bridges.

During the night a German troop train pulled in but was held up because the engine driver, his helper and the fireman had deserted the locomotive. There were two more trains on the station sidings waiting to leave.

The heavy doors of the freight shed swung open and in walked the Station Commandant, a German lieutenant, his assistant, and a group of other Germans.

"Korchagin, Polentovsky, Bruzzhak," the Commandant's Assistant called out. "You will make up an engine crew and take a train out at once. If you refuse, you will be shot on the spot. What do you say?"

The three workers nodded sullen consent. They were escorted under guard to the locomotive while the Commandant's Assistant went on to call out the names of the driver, helper and fireman for the next train.

The locomotive snorted angrily, sending up geysers of sparks. Breathing heavily it breasted the gloom ahead as it pounded along the track into the depths of night. Artem, who had just shovelled coal into the firebox, kicked the door shut, took a gulp of water from the snubnosed teapot standing on the toolbox, and turned to Polentovsky, the old engine driver.

"Well, pa, are we taking it through?"

Polentovsky's eyes blinked irritably under their overhanging eyebrows.

"You will when there's a bayonet at your back."

"We could chuck everything and make a dash for it," suggested Bruzzhak, watching the German soldier sitting on the tender from the corner of his eye.

"I think so too," muttered Artem, "if it wasn't for that bird behind our backs."

"That's right," Bruzzhak was noncommittal as he stuck his head out of the window.

Polentovsky moved closer to Artem.

"We can't take the train through, understand?" he whispered. "There's fighting going on ahead. Our fellows have blown up the track. And here we are bringing these swine there so they can shoot them down. You know, son, even in the tsar's time I never drove an engine when there was a strike on, and I'm not going to do it now. We'd disgrace ourselves for life if we brought destruction down on our own kind. The other engine-crew ran away, didn't they? They risked their lives, but they did it. We just can't take the train through. What do you think?"

"You're right, pa, but what are you going to do about him?" and he indicated the soldier with a glance.

The engine driver scowled. He wiped his sweating forehead with a handful of waste and stared with bloodshot eyes at the pressure gauge as if seeking an answer there to the question tormenting him. Then he swore in fury and desperation.

Artem drank again from the teapot. The two men were thinking of one thing, but neither could bring himself to break the tense silence. Artem recalled Zhukhrai's: "Well, brother, what do you think about the Bolshevik Party and the Communist idea?" and his own reply: "I am always ready to help, you can count on me. . . ."

"A fine way to help," he thought, "driving a punitive expedition. . . ."

Polentovsky was now bending over the toolbox next to Artem. Hoarsely he said:

"That fellow, we've got to do him in. Understand?"

Artem started. Polentovsky added through clenched teeth:

"There's no other way out. Got to knock him over the head and chuck the throttle and the levers into the firebox, cut off the steam and then run for it."

Feeling as if a heavy weight had dropped off his shoulders Artem said:

"Right!"

Leaning toward Bruzzhak, Artem told him of their decision.

Bruzzhak did not answer at once. They all were taking a very great risk. Each had a family at home to think of. Polentovsky's was the largest: he had nine mouths to feed. But all three knew that they could not take the train to its destination.

"Good, I'm with you," Bruzzhak said. "But what about him? Who's going to...." He did not finish the sentence but his meaning was clear enough to Artem.

Artem turned to Polentovsky, who was now busy with the throttle, and nodded as if to say that Bruzzhak agreed with them, but then, tormented by a question still unsettled, he stepped closer to the old man.

"But how?"

Polentovsky looked at Artem.

"You begin, you're the strongest. We'll conk him with the crowbar and it'll be all over." The old man was violently agitated.

Artem frowned.

"I can't do it. I can't. After all, when you come to think of it, the man isn't to blame. He's also been forced into this at the point of the bayonet."

Polentovsky's eyes flashed.

"Not to blame, you say? Neither are we for being made to do this job. But don't forget it's a punitive expedition we're hauling. These innocents are going out to shoot down partisans. Are the partisans to blame then? No, my lad, you've mighty little sense for all that you're strong as an ox...."

"All right, all right," Artem's voice cracked. He picked up the crowbar, but Polentovsky whispered to him:

"I'll do it, be more certain that way. You take the shovel and climb up to pass down the coal from the tender. If necessary you give him one with the shovel. I'll pretend to be loosening up the coal."

Bruzzhak heard what was said, and nodded. "The old man's right," he said, and took his place at the throttle.

The German soldier in his forage cap with a red band around it was sitting at the edge of the tender holding his rifle between his feet and smoking a cigar. From time to time he threw a glance at the engine crew going about their work in the cab.

When Artem climbed up on top of the tender the sentry paid little attention to him. And when Polentovsky, who pretended he wanted to get at the larger chunks of coal next to the side of the tender, signed to him to move out of way, the German readily slipped down in the direction of the door leading to the cab.

The sudden crunch of the German's skull as it

caved in under the crowbar made Artem and Bruzzhak jump as if touched by red-hot iron. The body of the soldier rolled limply into the passage leading to the cab.

The blood seeped rapidly through the grey wool forage cap and the rifle clattered against the iron side of the tender.

"Finished," Polentovsky whispered as he dropped the crowbar. "No turning back for us now," he added, his face twitching convulsively.

His voice broke, then rose to a shout to repel the silence that descended heavily on the three men.

"Unscrew the throttle, quick!" he shouted.

In ten minutes the job was done. The locomotive, now out of control, was slowly losing speed.

The dark ponderous shapes of trees on the wayside lunged into the radius of light around the locomotive only to recede into the impenetrable gloom behind. In vain the engine's headlights sought to pierce the thick shroud of night for more than a dozen metres ahead, and gradually its stertorous breathing slowed down as if it had spent the last of its strength.

"Jump, son!" Artem heard Polentovsky's voice behind him and he let go of the handrail. The momentum of the train sent his powerful body hurtling forward until with a jolt his feet met the earth surging up from below. He ran for a pace or two and tumbled heavily head over heels.

Two other shadows left the locomotive simultaneously, one from each side of the cab.

Gloom had settled over the Bruzzhak house. Antonina Vasilievna, Sergei's mother, had eaten her heart out during the past four days. There had been no news from her husband; all she knew was that the Germans had forced him to man an engine together with Korchagin and Polentovsky. And yesterday three of the Hetman's guards had come around and questioned her in a rough, abusive manner.

From what they said she vaguely gathered that something had gone wrong and, gravely perturbed, she threw her kerchief over her head as soon as the men left and set out to see Maria Yakovlevna in hope of learning some news of her husband.

Valya, her eldest daughter, who was tidying up the kitchen, noticed her slipping out of the house.

"Where you off to, Mother?" the girl asked.

"To the Korchagins," Antonina Vasilievna replied, glancing at her daughter with eyes brimming with tears. "Perhaps they know something about father. If Sergei comes home tell him to go over to the station to see the Polentovskys."

Valya threw her arms around her mother's shoulders.

"Don't worry, dear," she said as she saw her to the door.

As usual, Maria Yakovlevna gave Antonina Vasilievna a hearty welcome. Each of the two women hoped that the other would have some news to tell, but the hope vanished as soon as they got talking.

The Korchagins' place had also been searched during the night. The soldiers had been looking for Artem, and had told Maria Yakovlevna on leaving to report to the *Kommandantur* as soon as her son returned.

The coming of the patrol had frightened Korchagina almost out of her wits. She had been home alone, for Pavel as usual was on the night shift at the power plant.

When Pavel returned from work early in the morning and heard from his mother about the search, he felt a gnawing anxiety for his brother's safety. Despite differences in character and Artem's seeming coldness, the two brothers were deeply attached to one another. It was a stern, undemonstrative affection, but Pavel knew that there was no sacrifice he would hesitate to make for his brother's sake.

Without stopping to rest, Pavel ran over to the station to look for Zhukhrai. He could not find him, and the other workers he knew could tell him nothing about the missing men. Engine driver Polentovsky's family too was completely in the dark; all he could learn from Polentovsky's youngest son, Boris, whom he met in the yard, was that their house too had been searched that night. The soldiers had been looking for Polentovsky.

Pavel came back to his mother with no news to report. Exhausted, he threw himself on the bed and dropped instantly into fitful slumber.

Valya looked up as the knock came at the door.

"Who's there?" she asked, unhooking the catch.

The dishevelled carroty head of Klimka Marchenko appeared in the open door. He had evidently been running, for he was out of breath and his face was red from exertion.

"Is your mother home?" he asked Valya.

"No, she's gone out."

"Where to?"

"To the Korchagins, I think," Valya seized hold of Klimka's sleeve as the boy was about to dash off.

Klimka looked up at the girl in hesitation.

"I've got to see her about something," he ventured.

"What is it?" Valya would not let him go. "Out with it, you redheaded bear you, and stop keeping me in suspense," the girl said in an imperative tone.

Klimka forgot Zhukhrai's warnings and his strict instructions to deliver the note into Antonina Vasilievna's hands, and he pulled a soiled scrap of paper out of his pocket and handed it to the girl. He could not refuse anything to Sergei's pretty fair-haired sister, for truth to tell he had a soft spot in his heart for her.

He was far too timid, however, to admit even to himself that he liked Valya. The girl quickly read the slip of paper he had handed to her.

> "Dear Tonya! Don't worry. All's well. They're safe and sound. Soon you will have more news. Let the others know that everything is all right so they needn't worry. Destroy this note. *Zakhar*."

Valya rushed over to Klimka.

"My dear little brown bear, where did you get it? Who gave it to you?" And she shook Klimka so violently that he quite lost his presence of mind and made his second blunder before he knew it.

"Zhukhrai gave it to me down at the station." Then, remembering that he should not have said it, he added: "But he told me not to give it to anybody but your mother."

"That's all right," Valya laughed. "I won't tell anybody. Now you run along like a good little bear to Pavel's place and you'll find mother there." And she gave the lad a light push in the back.

A second later Klimka's red head had disappeared through the garden gate.

None of the three railwaymen returned home. In the evening Zhukhrai came to the Korchagins and told Maria Yakovlevna what had happened on the train. He did his best to calm the fear-stricken mother, and assured her that all three were safe with Bruzzhak's uncle who lived in an out-of-the-way village ; they could not come back now, of course, but the Germans were in a tight fix and the situation was likely to change any day.

The disappearance of the three men brought their families closer together than ever. The rare notes that were received from them were read with rejoicing, but home seemed an empty and dreary place without them.

One day Zhukhrai dropped in to see Polentovsky's wife as if in passing, and gave her some money.

"Here's something from your husband to keep you going," he said. "Only see you don't mention it to anyone."

The old woman gratefully clasped his hand.

"Thanks. We need it badly. There's nothing to give the children to eat."

The money actually came from the fund left by Bulgakov.

"Well, now we'll see what comes next," said Zhukhrai to himself as he walked back to the station. "Even if the strike's broken under the threat of shooting, even if the workers are back at the job, the fire has been kindled and it can't be put out any more. As for those three, they're stout fellows, true proletarians." A wave of elation swept him.

In a little old smithy whose soot-blackened front faced the road in the outskirts of the village of Vorobyova Balka, Polentovsky stood before the glowing forge, his eyes narrowed from the glare, and turned over a red-hot piece of iron with a pair of long-handled tongs.

Artem pumped the bellows suspended from a cross-beam overhead.

"A skilled worker won't go under in the villages these days—there's as much work to be had as you might want," chuckling good-naturedly in his beard the engine driver said. "A week or two like this and we'll be able to send some fat back and flour home to the folks. The peasant always respects a smith, son. You'll see, we'll feed ourselves up like capitalists, ha-ha! Zakhar's a bit different from us—he hangs on to the peasantry, has his roots in the land through that uncle of his. Well, I can't say as I blame him. You and me, Artem, we've got neither harrow nor barrow, so to say, nought but a strong back and a pair of hands—what they call eternal proletarians, that's us—ha-ha—but old Zakhar's kind of split in two, one foot in the locomotive and the other in the village." He shifted the red-hot metal with the tongs and continued in a more serious vein: "As for us, son, things look bad. If the Germans aren't smashed pretty soon we'll have to get through to Yekaterinoslav or Rostov; otherwise we might find ourselves nabbed and strung up between heaven and earth before we know it."

"You're right there," Artem mumbled.

"I wish I knew how our people are getting on out there. Are the Haydamaks leaving them alone, I wonder."

"Yes, pa, we're in a mess. We'll just have to give up thinking of going home."

The engine driver pulled the hot piece of glowing blue metal from the forge and with a dexterous movement laid it on the anvil.

"Lay on to it, son!"

Artem seized a heavy hammer, swung it high above his head and then brought it down on the anvil. A fountain of bright sparks spurted with a hiss in all directions, lighting up for a moment the darkest corners of the smithy.

Polentovsky turned over the red-hot slab under the powerful blows and the iron obediently flattened out like so much soft wax.

Through the open doors of the smithy came the warm breath of the dark night.

Down below lay the lake, dark and vast. The pines surrounding it on all sides nodded their lofty heads.

"Like living things," thought Tonya looking up at them. She was lying in a grass-carpeted depression on the granite shore. High above her beyond the hollow was the forest's edge, and below, at the very foot of the bluff, the lake. The shadows of the cliffs pressing in on the lake gave the dark sheet of water a still darker fringe.

This old stone quarry not far from the station was Tonya's favourite haunt. Springs had burst forth in the deep abandoned workings and now three lakes had formed there. The sound of splashing from where the shore dropped into the water caused Tonya to raise her head. Parting the branches in front of her, she looked in the direction of the sound. A supple, sun-tanned body was swimming away from the shore with strong strokes. Tonya caught sight of the swimmer's brown back and dark head; he was blowing like a walrus, paddling briskly in the water, rolling over, somersaulting and diving, then he turned over on his back and floated, squinting in the bright sun, his arms stretched out and his body slightly bent.

Tonya let the branch fall back into place. "It's not nice to look," she smiled to herself and returned to her reading.

She was so engrossed in the book which Leszczinski had given her that she did not notice someone climb over the granite rocks that separated the hollow from the pine woods; only when a pebble, inadvertently set into motion by the intruder, rolled onto the book did she look up with a start to see Pavel Korchagin standing before her. He too was taken aback by the encounter and in his confusion turned to go.

"It must have been him I saw in the water," Tonya thought as she noticed his wet hair.

"Did I frighten you? I didn't know you were here." Pavel laid his hand on the rocky ledge. He had recognized Tonya.

"You aren't interfering at all. If you care to, you can stay and talk with me for a while."

Pavel looked at Tonya in surprise.

"What could we talk about?"

Tonya smiled.

"Why don't you sit down—here, for instance?" She pointed to a stone. "What is your name?"

"Pavka Korchagin."

"My name's Tonya. So now we've introduced ourselves."

Pavel twisted his cap in embarrassment.

"So you're called Pavka?" Tonya broke the silence. "Why Pavka? It doesn't sound nice, Pavel would be ever so much better. That's what I shall call you—Pavel. Do you come here often...." She wanted to say "to swim," but not wishing to admit having seen him in the water, she said instead: "for a walk?"

"No, not often. Only when I've got time off," Pavel replied.

"So you work somewhere?" Tonya questioned him further.

"At the power plant. As a stoker."

"Tell me, where did you learn to fight so skil-fully?" Tonya asked unexpectedly.

"What's my fighting to you?" Pavel blurted out in spite of himself.

"Now don't be angry, Korchagin," said Tonya hastily, seeing that her question had annoyed him. "I'm just interested, that's all. What a punch that was! You shouldn't be so merciless." She burst out laugh-ing.

"Sorry for him, eh?" Pavel asked.

"Not at all. On the contrary, Sukharko only got what he deserved. I enjoyed it immensely. I hear you get into scraps quite often."

"Who says so?" Pavel pricked up his ears.

"Well, Victor Leszczinski claims you are a profes-sional scrapper."

Pavel's features darkened.

"Victor's a swine and a softy. He ought to be thank-ful he didn't get it then. I heard what he said about me, but I didn't want to muck up my hands."

"Don't use such language, Pavel. It's not nice," Tonya interrupted him.

Pavel bristled.

"Why did I have to start talking to this ninny?" he thought to himself. "Ordering me about like this: first it's 'Pavka' doesn't suit her and now she's finding fault with my language."

"What have you against Leszczinski?" Tonya asked.

"He's a sissy, a mama's boy without any guts! My fingers itch at the sight of his kind: always trying to walk all over you, thinks he can do anything he wants because he's rich. But I don't give a damn for his wealth. Just let him try to touch me and he'll get it good and proper. Fellows like that are only asking for a punch in the jaw," Pavel went on, roused.

Tonya regretted having mentioned Leszczinski. She could see that this young man had old scores to settle with the dandified schoolboy. To steer the conversation into more placid channels she began questioning Pavel about his family and work.

Before he knew it, Pavel was answering the girl's questions in great detail, forgetting that he had wanted to go.

"Why didn't you continue studying?" Tonya asked.

"Got thrown out of school."

"Why?"

Pavel blushed.

"I put some shag in the priest's dough, and so they chucked me out. He was mean, that priest was; he'd worry the life out of you." And Pavel told her the whole story.

Tonya listened with interest. Pavel got over his initial shyness and was soon talking to her as if she were an old acquaintance. Among other things he told her about his brother's disappearance. Neither of the two noticed the hours pass as they sat there in the hollow engrossed in friendly conversation. At last Pavel sprang to his feet.

"It's time I was at work. I ought to be firing the boilers instead of sitting here gassing. Danilo is sure to raise a fuss now." Ill at ease once more he added: "Well, goodbye, miss. I've got to dash off to town now."

Tonya jumped up, pulling on her jacket.

"I must go too. Let's go together."

"Oh no, couldn't do that. I'll have to run."

"All right. I'll race you. Let's see who gets there first."

Pavel gave her a disdainful look.

"Race me? You haven't the ghost of a chance!"

"We'll see. Let's get out of here first."

Pavel jumped over the ledge of stone, then extended a hand to Tonya, and the two trotted through the woods to the broad, level clearing leading to the station.

Tonya stopped in the middle of the road.

"Now let's go: one, two, three, go! Try and catch me!" She was off like a whirlwind down the track, the soles of her shoes flashing and the tail of her blue jacket flying in the wind.

Pavel raced after her.

"I'll be up with her in two shakes," thought Pavel as he sped after the flying jacket, but it was only at the end of the lane quite close to the station that he overtook her. Making a final spurt, he caught up with her and seized her shoulders with his strong hands.

"Tag! You're it!" he cried gaily, panting from the exertion.

"Don't! You're hurting me!" Tonya resisted.

As they stood there panting, their pulses racing, Tonya, exhausted by the wild chase, leaned ever so lightly against Pavel in a fleeting moment of sweet intimacy that he was not soon to forget.

"Nobody has ever overtaken me before," she said as she drew away from him.

At this they parted and with a farewell wave of his cap Pavel ran toward town.

When Pavel pushed open the boiler-room door, Danilo, the other stoker, was already busy firing the boiler.

"Couldn't you make it any later?" he growled. "Expect me to do your work for you, or what?"

Pavel patted his mate on the shoulder placatingly.

"We'll have the fire going full blast in a jiffy, old man," he said cheerfully and applied himself to the firewood.

Toward midnight, when Danilo was snoring lustily on the woodpile, Pavel finished oiling the engine, wiped his hands on waste, pulled out the sixty-second instalment of *Giuseppe Garibaldi* from a toolbox, and was soon engrossed in the fascinating account of the interminable adventures of the Neapolitan "Redshirts'" legendary leader.

"She gazed at the duke with her beautiful blue eyes. . . ."

"She's also got blue eyes," thought Pavel. "And she's different, not at all like rich folk. And she can run like the devil."

Engrossed in the memory of his encounter with Tonya during the day, Pavel was oblivious of the rising whine of the engine which was now straining under the pressure of excess steam; the huge flywheel whirled madly and a nervous tremor ran through the concrete mounting.

A glance at the pressure gauge showed Pavel that the needle was several points above the red warning line.

"Damn it!" Pavel leapt to the safety valve, gave it two quick turns, and the steam ejected through the exhaust pipe into the river hissed hoarsely outside the boiler room. Pulling a lever, Pavel threw the drive belt onto the pump pulley.

He glanced at Danilo, but the latter was fast asleep, his mouth wide open and his nose emitting fearful sounds.

Half a minute later the pressure gauge needle had returned to normal.

After parting with Pavel, Tonya headed for home, her thoughts occupied by her encounter with the dark-eyed young man; although she was unaware of it herself, she was happy because she had met him.

"What spirit he has, what grit! And he isn't at all the ruffian I imagined him to be. At any rate he's nothing like all those silly schoolboys. . . ."

Pavel was of another mould, he came from an environment to which Tonya was a stranger.

"But he can be tamed," she thought. "He'll be an interesting friend to have."

As she approached home, she saw Liza Sukharko and Nelly and Victor Leszczinski in the garden. Victor was reading. They were obviously waiting for her.

They exchanged greetings and she sat down on a bench. In the midst of the empty small talk, Victor sat down beside her and asked:

"Have you read the novel I gave you?"

"Novel?" Tonya looked up. "Oh, I . . ." She almost told him she had forgotten the book on the lakeshore.

"Did you like the love story?" Victor looked at her questioningly.

Tonya was lost in thought for a moment, then, slowly tracing an intricate pattern on the sand of the walk with the toe of her shoe, she raised her head and looked at Victor.

"No. I have begun a far more interesting love story."

"Indeed?" Victor drawled, annoyed. "Who's the author?"

Tonya looked at him with shining, smiling eyes. "There is no author...."

"Tonya, ask your visitors in. Tea's served," Tonya's mother called from the balcony.

Taking the two girls by the arm, Tonya led the way to the house. As he followed them, Victor puzzled over her words, unable to fathom their meaning.

This strange new feeling that had imperceptibly taken possession of him vaguely disturbed Pavel; he did not understand it and his rebellious spirit was troubled.

Tonya's father was the chief forest warden, which, as far as Pavel was concerned, put him in the same class as the lawyer Leszczinski.

Pavel had grown up in poverty and want, and he was hostile to anyone whom he considered to be wealthy. And so his feeling for Tonya was tinged with apprehension and misgiving; Tonya was not one of his own crowd, she was not simple and easy to understand like Galina, the stonemason's daughter, for instance. With Tonya he was always on his guard, ready to rebuff any hint of the mockery or condescension he would expect a beautiful and cultivated girl like her to show towards a common stoker like himself.

He had not seen her for a whole week and today he decided to go down to the lake. He deliberately chose the road that took him past her house in the hope of meeting her. As he sauntered along by the fence, he caught sight of the familiar sailor blouse at the far end of the garden. He picked up a pine cone lying on the road, aimed it at the white blouse and let fly.

Tonya swung round and ran over to him, stretching out her hand over the fence with a warm smile.

"You've come at last," she said and there was gladness in her voice. "Where have you been all this time? I went down to the lake to get the book I had left there. I thought you might be there. Won't you come in?"

Pavel shook his head.

"No."

"Why not?" Her eyebrows rose in surprise.

"Your father wouldn't like it, I bet. He'd likely give you hell for letting a ragamuffin like me into the garden."

"What nonsense, Pavel," Tonya said in anger. "Come inside at once. My father would never say anything of the kind. You'll see for yourself. Now come in."

She ran to open the gate for him and Pavel followed her uncertainly.

"Do you like books?" she asked him when they were seated at a round garden table.

"Very much," Pavel replied eagerly.

"What book do you like best of all?"

Pavel pondered the question for a few moments before replying: "Jeezeppy Garibaldi."

"Giuseppe Garibaldi," Tonya corrected him. "So you like that book particularly?"

"Yes. I've read all the sixty-eight instalments. I buy five of them every pay day. Garibaldi, that's a man for you!" Pavel exclaimed. "A real hero! That's what I call the real stuff. All those battles he had to fight and he always came out on top. And he travelled all over the world! If he was alive today I would join him, I swear I would. He used to take young workers into his band and they all fought together for the poor folk."

"Would you like me to show you our library?" Tonya said and took his arm.

"Oh no, I'm not going into the house," Pavel objected.

"Why are you so stubborn? What is there to be afraid of?"

Pavel glanced down at his bare feet which were none too clean, and scratched the back of his head.

"Are you sure your mother or your father won't throw me out?"

"If you don't stop saying such things I'll get really annoyed with you," Tonya flared up.

"Well, Leszczinski would never let the likes of

111

us into his house, he always talks to us in the kitchen. I had to go there for something once and Nelly wouldn't even let me into the room—must have been afraid I'd spoil her carpets or something," Pavel said with a grin.

"Come on, come on," she urged him, taking him by the shoulder and giving him a friendly little push toward the porch.

She led him through the dining room into a room with a huge oak bookcase. And when she opened the doors Pavel beheld hundreds of books standing in neat rows. He had never seen such wealth in his life.

"Now we'll find an interesting book for you, and you must promise to come regularly for more. Will you?"

Pavel nodded happily.

"I love books," he said.

They spent several pleasant hours together that day. She introduced him to her mother. It was not such a terrible ordeal after all. In fact he liked Tonya's mother.

Tonya took Pavel to her own room and showed him her own books.

On the dressing table stood a small mirror. Tonya led Pavel up to it and said with a little laugh:

"Why do you let your hair grow wild like that? Don't you ever cut it or comb it?"

"I just shave it clean off when it grows too long. What else should I do with it?" Pavel said, embarrassed.

Tonya laughed, and picking up a comb from the dressing table she ran it quickly a few times through his unruly locks.

"There, that's better," she said as she surveyed her handiwork. "Hair ought to be neatly cut, you shouldn't go around looking like an oaf."

She glanced critically at his faded brown shirt and his shabby trousers but made no further comment.

Pavel noticed the glance and felt ashamed of his clothes.

When they said goodbye, Tonya invited him to come again. She made him promise to come in two days' time and go fishing with her.

Pavel left the house by the simple expedient of jumping out of the window; he did not care to go through the other rooms and meet Tonya's mother again.

With Artem gone, things grew hard for the Korchagins. Pavel's wages did not suffice.

Maria Yakovlevna suggested to Pavel that she go out to work again, especially since the Leszczinskis happened to be in need of a cook. But Pavel was against it.

"No, mother, I'll find some extra work to do. They need men at the sawmill to stack the timber. I'll put in a half a day there and that'll give us enough to live on. You mustn't go to work, or Artem will be angry with me for not being able to get along without that."

His mother tried to insist, but Pavel was adamant.

The next day Pavel was already working at the sawmill stacking up the freshly sawn boards to dry. There he met several lads he knew, Misha Levchukov, an old schoolmate of his, and Vanya Kuleshov. Misha and he teamed together and working at piece rates they earned rather well. Pavel spent his days at the sawmill and in the evenings went to his job at the power plant.

On the evening of the tenth day Pavel brought his earnings to his mother.

As he handed her the money, he fidgeted uneasily, blushed and said finally:

"You know what, mother, buy me a sateen shirt, a blue one—like the one I had last year, remember? It'll take about half the money, but don't worry, I'll earn some more. This shirt of mine is pretty shabby," he added, as if apologizing for his request.

"Why, of course I'll buy it for you," said his mother, "I'll get the material today, Pavlusha, and tomorrow I'll sew it. You really do need a new shirt." And she gazed tenderly at her son.

Pavel paused at the entrance to the barbershop and fingering the ruble in his pocket turned into the doorway.

The barber, a smart-looking young man, noticed him entering and signed toward the empty chair with his head.

"Next, please."

As he settled into the deep, soft chair, Pavel saw in the mirror before him a flustered, confused face.

"Clip it close?" the barber asked.

"Yes, that is, no—well, what I want is a haircut— how do you call it?" Pavel floundered, making a despairing gesture with his hand.

"I understand," the barber smiled.

A quarter of an hour later Pavel emerged, perspiring and exhausted by the ordeal, but with his hair neatly trimmed and combed. The barber had worked hard at the recalcitrant mop, but water and the comb had won out in the end and the bristling tufts now lay neatly in place.

Out in the street Pavel heaved a sigh of relief and pulled his cap down over his eyes.

"I wonder what mother'll say when she sees me?" he thought.

Tonya was vexed when Pavel did not keep his promise to go fishing with her.

"That stoker boy isn't very considerate," she

thought with annoyance, but when several more days passed and Pavel failed to appear she began to long for his company.

One day as she was about to go out for a walk, her mother looked into her room and said:

"A visitor to see you, Tonya. May he come in?"

Pavel appeared in the doorway, changed so much that Tonya barely recognized him at first.

He was wearing a brand-new blue sateen shirt and dark trousers. His boots had been polished until they shone, and, as Tonya noted at once, his bristly mop had been trimmed. The grimy young stoker was transformed.

Tonya was about to express her surprise, but checked herself in time for she did not want to embarrass the lad, who was uncomfortable enough as it was. So she pretended not to have noticed the striking change in his appearance and began scolding him instead.

"Why didn't you come fishing? You should be ashamed of yourself! Is that how you keep your promises?"

"I've been working at the sawmill these days and just couldn't get away."

He could not tell her that he had been working the last few days to the point of exhaustion in order to buy himself the shirt and trousers.

Tonya, however, guessed the truth herself and her annoyance with Pavel vanished.

"Let's go for a walk down to the pond," she suggested, and they went out through the garden onto the road.

Before long Pavel was telling Tonya about the revolver he had stolen from the Lieutenant, sharing his big secret with her as with a friend, and promising her that some day very soon they would go deep into the woods to do some shooting.

"But see that you don't give me away," Pavel said, abruptly.

"I shall never give you away," Tonya vowed.

CHAPTER FOUR

A fierce and merciless class struggle gripped the Ukraine. More and more people took to arms and each clash brought forth new fighters.

Gone were the days of peace and tranquillity for the respectable citizen.

The little tumbledown houses shook in the storm blasts of gun salvos, and the respectable citizen huddled against the walls of his cellar or took cover in his backyard trench.

An avalanche of Petlyura bands of all shades and hues overran the gubernia, led by little chieftains and big ones, all manner of Golubs, Archangels, Angels and Gordiuses and a host of other bandits.

Ex-officers of the tsarist army, Right and Left Ukrainian Socialist-Revolutionaries—any desperado who could muster a band of cutthroats, declared himself Ataman, and some raised the yellow-and-blue Petlyura flag and established their authority over whatever area was within the scope of their strength and opportunities.

Out of these heterogeneous bands reinforced by kulaks and the Galician regiments of Ataman Konovalets' siege corps, "Chief Ataman" Petlyura formed his regiments and divisions. And when Red partisan detachments struck at this Socialist-Revolutionary and kulak rabble the very earth trembled under the pounding of hundreds and thousands of hooves and the rumble of the wheels of machine-gun carts and gun carriages.

In April of that turbulent 1919, the respectable citizen, dazed and terrified, would open his shutters of a morning and, peering out with sleep-heavy eyes, greet his next-door neighbour with the anxious question:

"Avtonom Petrovich, do you happen to know who's in power today?"

And Avtonom Petrovich would hitch up his trousers and cast a frightened look around.

"Can't say, Afanas Kirillovich. Somebody did enter the town during the night. Who it was we'll find out soon enough: if they start robbing the Jews, we'll know they're Petlyura men, and if they're some of the 'comrades,' we'll be able to tell at once by the way they talk. I'm keeping an eye open myself so's to know what portrait to hang up. Wouldn't care to get into trouble like Gerasim Leontievich next door. You see, he didn't look out properly and had just gone and hung up a picture of Lenin when three men rushed in—Petlyura men as it turned out. They took one look at the picture and jumped on him—a good twenty strokes they gave him. 'We'll skin you alive, you Communist sonofabitch,' they shouted. And no matter how hard he tried to explain and how loud he yelled, nothing helped."

Noticing groups of armed men coming down the street the respectable citizen closes his windows and goes into hiding. Better to be on the safe side. . . .

As for the workers, they regarded the yellow-and-blue flags of the Petlyura thugs with suppressed hatred. They were powerless in the face of this wave of Ukrainian bourgeois chauvinism, and their spirits rose only when passing Red units, fighting fiercely against the yellow-and-blues that were bearing down on them from all sides, wedged their way into the town. For a day or two the red flag so dear to the worker's heart would fly over the town hall, but then the unit would move on again and the engulfing gloom return.

Now the town was in the hands of Colonel Golub, the "hope and pride" of the Transdnieper Division.

His band of two thousand cutthroats had made a triumphal entry into the town the day before. *Pan* the

119

Colonel had ridden at the head of the column on a splendid black stallion. In spite of the warm April sun he wore a Caucasian *bourka*, a lambskin Zaporozhye Cossack cap with a raspberry-red crown, a *cherkesska*, and the weapons that went with the outfit: dagger and sabre with chased-silver hilts. Between his teeth he held a curve-stem pipe.

A handsome fellow, *Pan* the Colonel Golub, with his black eyebrows and pallid complexion tinged slightly green from incessant carousals!

Before the revolution *Pan* the Colonel had been an agronomist at the beet plantations of a sugar refinery, but that was a dull life not to be compared with the position of an Ataman, and so on the crest of the murky waves that swept the land the agronomist emerged as *Pan* the Colonel Golub.

In the only theatre in town a gala affair was got up in honour of the new arrivals. The "flower" of the Petlyura intelligentsia was there in full force: Ukrainian teachers, the priest's two daughters, the beautiful Anya and her younger sister Dina, some ladies of lesser standing, former members of the household of Count Potocki, a handful of petty burghers, Ukrainian S.R. scum, who called themselves "free Cossacks."

The theatre was packed. Spur-clicking officers who might have been copied from old paintings of Zaporozhye Cossacks pranced around the teachers, the priest's daugters and the burghers' ladies who were decked out in Ukrainian national costumes ornamented with bright-coloured embroidered flowers and multi-hued beads and ribbons.

The regimental band blared. On the stage feverish preparations were under way for the performance of *Nazar Stodolya* scheduled for the evening.

There was no electricity, however, and the fact was reported in due course to *Pan* the Colonel at headquarters by his adjutant, Sublieutenant Polyantsev, who had now Ukrainianized his name and rank and styled himself Khorunzhy Palyanytsya. The Colonel, who intended to grace the evening with his presence, heard out Palyanytsya and said casually but imperiously:

"See that there is light. Find an electrician and start the electric power plant if you have to break your neck doing it."

"Very good, *Pan* Colonel."

Khorunzhy Palyanytsya found electricians without breaking his neck. Within two hours Pavel, an electrician and a mechanic were brought to the power plant by armed guards.

"If you don't have the lights on by seven I'll have all three of you strung up," Palyanytsya told them curtly, pointing to an iron beam overhead.

This blunt exposition of the situation had its effect and the lights came on at the appointed time.

The evening was in full swing when *Pan* the Colonel arrived with his lady, the buxom yellow-haired daughter of the barkeeper in whose house he was staying. Her father being a man of means, she had been educated at the Gymnasium in the biggest town in the gubernia.

When the two had taken the seats reserved for them as guests of honour in the front row, *Pan* the Colonel gave the signal and the curtain rose so suddenly that the audience had a glimpse of the stage director's back as he hurried off the stage.

During the play the officers and their ladies whiled away the time at the refreshment counter filling up on raw homemade liquor, supplied by the ubiquitous Palyanytsya and delicacies acquired by requisitioning. By the end of the performance they were all well under the weather.

After the final curtain Palyanytsya leaped on the stage.

"Ladies and gentlemen, the dancing will begin at once," he announced with a theatrical sweep of his arm.

There was general applause and the audience emptied out into the yard to give the Petlyura soldiers posted to guard the guests, a chance to carry out the chairs and clear the dance floor.

A half an hour later the theatre was the scene of wild revelry.

The Petlyura officers, flinging all restraint to the winds, furiously danced the *hopak* with local belles flushed from the heat, and the pounding of heavy boots rocked the walls of the ramshackle theatre building.

In the meantime a troop of armed horsemen was approaching the town from the direction of the flour mill. A Petlyura sentry-post stationed at the town limits sprang in alarm to their machine guns and there was a clicking of breech blocks in the night. Through the darkness came the sharp challenge:

"Halt! Who goes there?"

Two dark figures loomed out of the darkness. One of them stepped forward and roared out in a hoarse bass:

"Ataman Pavlyuk with his detachment. Who are you? Golub's men?"

"That's right," replied an officer who had also stepped forward.

"Where can I billet my men?" Pavlyuk asked.

"I'll phone headquarters at once," replied the officer and disappeared into a tiny hut on the roadside.

A minute later he came out and began issuing orders:

"Clear the machine gun off the road, men! Let the *Pan* Ataman pass."

Pavlyuk reined in his horse in front of the brightly illuminated theatre where a great many people were strolling out in the open air.

"Some fun going on here by the look of it," he said, turning to the esaul riding beside him. "Let's

123

dismount, Gukmach, and join the merrymaking. We'll pick ourselves a couple of girls—I see the place is thick with them. Hey, Stalezhko," he shouted. "You billet the lads with the townsfolk. We'll stop here. Escort, follow me." And he heaved himself heavily from his staggering mount.

At the entrance to the theatre Pavlyuk was stopped by two armed Petlyura men.

"Tickets?"

Pavlyuk gave them a derisive look and pushed one of them aside with his shoulder. The dozen men with him followed suit. All of them had horses outside, tethered to the fence.

The newcomers were noticed at once. Particularly conspicuous was the huge frame of Pavlyuk; he was wearing an officer's coat of good cloth, blue breeches of the kind worn in the guards, and a shaggy fur cap. A Mauser pistol hung from a strap slung over his shoulder and a hand grenade stuck out of his pocket.

"Who's that?" the whisper passed through the crowd around the dance floor where Golub's second in command was executing a wild dance.

His partner was the priest's elder daughter, who was whirling round with such abandon that her skirts flared out high enough to give the delighted warriors standing about a good view of her silk underthings.

Elbowing his way through the crowd, Pavlyuk went right out onto the dance floor.

Pavlyuk stared with glazed eyes at the priest's daughter's legs, passed his tongue over his dry lips, then strode across the dance floor to the orchestra platform, stopped, and flicked his plaited riding whip.

"Come on, give us the *hopak*!"

The conductor paid no attention to the order.

A sharp movement of Pavlyuk's hand and the whip cut down the conductor's back. The latter jumped as if stung and the music broke off, plunging the hall into silence.

"What insolence!" The barkeeper's daughter was furious. "You can't let him do that," she cried, clutching at the elbow of Golub seated at her side.

Golub heaved himself to his feet, kicked aside a chair, took three paces forward and stopped face to face with Pavlyuk. He had recognized the newcomer at once, and he had scores to settle with this rival claimant for local power. Only a week ago Pavlyuk had played the most scurvy trick on *Pan* the Colonel. At the height of a battle with a Red regiment which had mauled Golub's detachment on more than one occasion, Pavlyuk, instead of striking at the Bolsheviks from the rear, had broken into a town, overcome the resistance of the small pickets the Reds had left there, and, leaving a screening force to protect himself, sacked the place in the most thorough fashion. Of course, being a true Petlyura man, he saw to it that the Jewish population were the chief victims. In the meantime the Reds had smashed up Golub's right flank and made their way out of the trap.

And now this arrogant cavalry Captain had burst in here and had the audacity to strike *Pan* the Colonel's own bandmaster under his very eyes. No, this was too much. Golub knew that if he did not put the conceited petty Ataman in his place his prestige in the regiment would be gone.

For several seconds the two men stood there in silence glaring at each other.

Gripping the hilt of his sabre with one hand and feeling for the revolver in his pocket with the other, Golub rapped out:

"How dare you lay your hands on my men, you scoundrel!"

Pavlyuk's hand crept toward the grip of the Mauser.

"Easy there, *Pan* Golub, easy, or you may trip yourself up. Don't step on my pet corn. I'm liable to lose my temper."

This was more than Golub could stand.

"Throw them out and give them twenty-five lashes each!" he shouted.

The officers fell upon Pavlyuk and his men like a pack of hounds.

A shot crashed out with a report that sounded as if an electric bulb had been smashed against the floor, and the struggling men swirled and spun down the hall

126

like two packs of fighting dogs. In the wild melee men slashed at each other with sabres and dug their fingers into hair and throats, while the women, squealing with terror like stuck pigs, scattered away from the contestants.

In a few minutes Pavlyuk and his followers, disarmed and beaten, were dragged out of the hall, and thrown out into the street.

Pavlyuk himself lost his fur hat in the scrimmage, his face was bruised and his weapons were gone, and now he was beside himself with rage. He and his men leapt into the saddle and galloped down the street.

The evening was broken up. No one felt inclined to make merry after what had happened. The women refused to dance and insisted on being taken home, but Golub would not hear of it.

"Post sentries," he ordered. "Nobody is to leave the hall."

Palyanytsya hastened to carry out the orders.

"The dancing will continue until morning, ladies and gentlemen," Golub replied stubbornly to the protests that showered upon him. "I shall dance the first waltz myself."

The orchestra struck up again but there was to be no more frolicking that night nevertheless.

The Colonel had not circled the dance floor once with the priest's daughter when the sentries ran into the hall shouting:

"Pavlyuk's surrounding the theatre!"

At that moment a window facing the street crashed in and the snub-nosed muzzle of a machine gun was pushed in through the shattered window frame. It moved stupidly this way and that, as if picking out the figures scattering wildly away from it toward the centre of the hall as from the devil himself.

Palyanytsya fired at the thousand-candle-power lamp in the ceiling which exploded like a bomb, sending a shower of splintered glass down on everyone in the hall.

The hall was plunged in darkness. Someone shouted in the yard:

"Everybody get outside!" A stream of violent abuse followed.

The wild, hysterical screams of the women, the furious commands issued by Golub as he dashed about the hall trying to rally his officers who had completely lost their heads, the firing and shouting out in the yard all merged into an indescribable pandemonium. In the panic nobody noticed Palyanytsya slip through the back door into a deserted side street and run for all he was worth to Golub's headquarters.

A half an hour later a full-dress battle was raging in the town. The silence of the night was shattered by the incessant crackling of rifle fire interspersed with the rattle of machine guns. Completely stupefied, the townsfolk leapt up from their warm beds and pressed against window panes.

At last the firing abated, and only one machine gun somewhere in the outskirts kept up a sporadic shooting like the barking of a dog.

The fighting died down as the glimmer of dawn appeared on the horizon. . . .

Rumours that a pogrom was brewing crept through the town, finally reaching the tiny, low-roofed Jewish cottages with crooked windows that somehow managed to cling to the top of the muddy bluff overlooking the river. In these incredibly overcrowded hovels called houses lived the Jewish poor.

The compositors and other workers at the printshop where Sergei Bruzzhak had been working for more than a year were Jews. Strong bonds of friendship had sprung up between them and Sergei. Like a closely-knit family, they stood solid against their employer, the smug well-fed Mr. Blumstein. An incessant struggle went on between the proprietor and the printers. Blumstein did his best to grab more and pay his workers less. The printers had gone on strike several times and the printshop had stood idle for two or three weeks running. There were fourteen of them. Sergei, the youngest, spent twelve hours a day turning the wheel of a hand press.

Today Sergei noticed an ominous uneasiness among the workers. For the past several troubled months the shop had had little to do apart from printing occasional proclamations issued by the "Chief Ataman."

A consumptive compositor named Mendel called Sergei into a corner.

"Do you know there's a pogrom coming?" he said, looking at the boy with his sad eyes.

Sergei looked up in surprise.

"No, I hadn't the slightest idea."

Mendel laid a withered, yellow hand on Sergei's shoulder and spoke in a confiding, paternal tone.

"There's going to be a pogrom—that's a fact. The Jews are going to be beaten up. What I want to know is this—will you help your comrades in this calamity or not?"

"Of course I will, if I only can. What can I do, Mendel?"

The compositors were now listening to the conversation.

"You're a good boy, Seryozha, and we trust you. After all, your father's a worker like us. Now you run home and ask him whether he would agree to hide some old men and women at his place, and then we'll decide who they will be. Ask your people if there's anyone else they know willing to do the same. The Russians will be safe from these bandits for the time being. Run along, Seryozha, there's no time to waste."

"You can count on me, Mendel. I'll see Pavka and Klimka right away—their folks are sure to take in somebody."

"Just a minute," Mendel anxiously halted Sergei who was about to leave. "Who are Pavka and Klimka? Do you know them well?"

Sergei nodded confidently.

"Of course. They're my pals. Pavka Korchagin's brother is a mechanic."

"Ah, Korchagin," Mendel was reassured. "I know him—used to live in the same house. Yes, you can see the Korchagins. Go, Seryozha, and bring back an answer as soon as you can."

Sergei shot out into the street.

The pogrom began on the third day after the pitched battle between the Pavlyuk detachment and Golub's men.

Pavlyuk, routed and driven out of Shepetovka, had cleared out of the neighbourhood and seized a small town nearby. The night encounter in Shepetovka had cost him a score of men. Similar losses had been sustained by the Golub crowd.

The dead were hastily carted off to the cemetery and buried the same day without much ceremony, for there was nothing to boast about in the whole affair. The two Atamans had flown at each other's throats like two stray curs, and to make a fuss over the funeral would have been unseemly. True, Palyanytsya had wanted to make a big thing of it and declare Pavlyuk a Red bandit, but the Committee headed by the priest Vasili objected.

The skirmish evoked some grumbling in Golub's regiment, especially among his bodyguard which had sustained the heaviest losses, and to put an end to the dissatisfaction and bolster up spirits, Palyanytsya proposed staging a pogrom, to provide "a little diversion" for the men, was the cynical way he broached the subject to Golub. He argued that this was essential in view of the disaffection in the unit. And although the Colonel was loth to disturb the peace in the town on the eve of his marriage to the barkeeper's daughter, he finally gave in.

True, *Pan* the Colonel was somewhat reluctant to undertake the operation in view also of his recent admission into the S. R. Party. His enemies might again drag his name into disrepute and call him a pogrommonger, and without doubt would slander him to the "Chief Ataman." So far, however, Golub was not greatly dependent on the "Chief," since he foraged for himself. Besides, the "Chief" knew very well what riffraff he had serving under him, and himself had time and again demanded money for the Directory's needs from the so-called requisitions; as for the reputation of a pogrommonger, Golub already had quite a record in that respect. There was very little that he could add to it now.

The pogrom began early in the morning.

The town was still wrapped in the grey mist that precedes the break of day. The deserted streets which wound like wet strips of linen around the haphazardly built blocks of the Jewish quarter were lifeless. The tightly curtained and shuttered windows stared out with blind eyes.

Outwardly the quarter appeared to be immersed in sound early-morning slumber, but inside the houses there was no sleep. Entire families, fully dressed, huddled together in one room, preparing themselves for the impending disaster. Only children too young to realize what was happening slept peacefully in their mothers' arms.

Salomyga, the chief of Golub's bodyguard, a dark fellow with the swarthy complexion of a gypsy and a livid sabre-scar across his cheek, worked hard that morning to wake up Golub's aide. It was a painful awakening for Palyanytsya—he could not shake himself loose from the nightmare that had beset him all night; the grimacing, hunchbacked devil was still clawing at his throat. At last he raised his splitting head and saw Salomyga.

"Get up, you souse," Salomyga was shaking him by the shoulder. "It's high time to get down to business. You had one too many!"

Palyanytsya, now wide awake, sat up and, his face twisting from heartburn, spat out the bitter saliva that filled his mouth.

"What business?" he stared blankly at Salomyga.

"To rip up the sheenies, what else? You haven't forgotten, I hope."

It all came back to Palyanytsya. True enough, he had forgotten about it. The drinking bout at the farm where *Pan* the Colonel had retired with his fiancée and a handful of boon companions had been a heavy one.

Golub had found it convenient to leave town for the duration of the pogrom, for afterwards he could put it down to a misunderstanding in his absence, and in the meantime Palyanytsya would have ample opportunity to make a thorough job of it. Yes, Palyanytsya was an expert when it came to providing "diversion!"

Palyanytsya poured a pail of water over his head and, thus sobered, was soon striding about headquarters issuing orders.

The bodyguard hundred was already in the saddle. To avoid possible complications, the farsighted Palyanytsya ordered pickets posted between the town proper and the workers' quarters and the station. A machine gun was mounted in the Leszczinski garden facing the road in order to meet the workers with a squall of lead if they took it into their heads to interfere.

When all the preparations were complete, the aide and Salomyga leapt into the saddle.

"Halt, I nearly forgot," Palyanytsya said when they had already set out. "Get two carts to bring back Golub's wedding present. Ha-ha-ha! The first spoils as always to the commander, and the first girl, ha-ha-ha, for his aide—and that's me. Got it, you blockhead?"

The last remark was addressed to Salomyga, who glared back at him with jaundiced eyes.

"There'll be enough for everybody."

They spurred their horses down the highway, the aide and Salomyga leading the disorderly mob of mounted men.

The mist had lifted when Palyanytsya reined in his horse in front of a two-story house with a rusty sign reading "Fuchs, Draper."

His thin-shanked grey mare nervously stamped her hoof against the cobblestones.

"Well, with God's help we'll begin here," Palyanytsya said as he jumped to the ground.

"Off your horses, fellows," he turned to the men crowding around him. "The show's beginning. Now I don't want any heads bashed, there'll be a time for that. As for the girls, if you can manage it, hold out until evening."

One of the men bared his strong teeth and protested:

"Now then, *Pan* Khorunzhy, what if it's by mutual consent?"

There was loud guffawing all around. Palyanytsya eyed the man who had spoken with admiring approbation.

"Now that's another story—if they're willing, go right ahead, nobody can prohibit that."

Palyanytsya went up to the closed door of the store and kicked at it hard, but the sturdy oaken planks did not so much as tremble.

This was clearly the wrong place to begin. Palyanytsya rounded the corner of the house and headed for the door leading to Fuchs' apartment, supporting his sabre with his hand as he went. Salomyga followed.

The people inside the house had heard the clatter of hooves on the pavement outside and when the sound ceased in front of the shop and the men's voices carried through the walls their hearts seemed to stop beating and their bodies petrified.

The wealthy Fuchs had left town the day before with his wife and daughters, leaving his servant Riva, a gentle timid girl of nineteen, to look after his property. Seeing that she shrank from remaining alone in the deserted apartment he had suggested that she bring her old father and mother to stay with her until his return.

When Riva had tried meekly to protest, the cunning merchant had assured her that in all probability there would be no pogrom at all, for what could they expect to get from beggars? And he promised Riva to give her a piece of stuff for a dress when he returned.

Now the three waited in fear and trembling, hoping against hope that the men would ride past; perhaps they had been mistaken, perhaps it had only seemed that the horses had stopped in front of their house. But their hopes were dashed by the dull reverberation of a blow at the shop door.

Old, silvery-haired Peisakh stood in the doorway, his blue eyes wide open like a frightened child's, and he whispered a prayer to almighty Jehovah with all the passion of the fanatical believer. He prayed to God to protect this house from misfortune and for a while the old woman standing beside him could not hear the approaching footsteps for the mumble of his supplication.

Riva had fled to the farthest room where she hid behind the big oaken sideboard.

A shattering blow at the door sent a convulsive tremor through the two old people.

"Open the door!" Another blow, still more violent than the first, descended on the door, followed by furious curses.

But those within, numb with fright, could not lift a hand to unfasten the door.

Outside the rifle butts pounded until the bolts gave way and the splintering door crashed open.

The house filled with armed men who went through its every corner. A blow from a rifle butt smashed in the door leading into the store and the front door bolts were drawn from within.

The looting began.

When the carts had been piled high with bolts of cloth, shoes and other loot, Salomyga set out with the booty to Golub's quarters. When he returned he heard a shriek of terror issuing from the house.

Palyanytsya, leaving his men to sack the store, had walked into the proprietor's apartment and found the old folks and the girl standing there. Casting his green lynx-like eyes over them he snapped at the old couple:

"Get out of here!"

Neither mother nor father stirred.

Palyanytsya took a step forward and slowly drew his sabre.

"Mama!" the girl gave a heart-rending scream. It was this that Salomyga heard.

Palyanytsya turned to his men who had run in at the cry.

"Throw them out!" he barked, pointing at the two old people. When this had been done he told Salomyga who had now come on the scene: "You watch here at the door while I have a chat with the wench."

The girl screamed again. Old Peisakh made a rush for the door leading into the room, but a violent blow in the chest sent him reeling back against the wall, choking from the pain. Like a she-wolf fighting for her young, Toiba, the old mother, always so quiet and submissive, now flung herself at Salomyga.

"Let me in! What are you doing to my girl?"

She was struggling to get to the door and try as he might Salomyga could not break the convulsive grip of the aged fingers on his coat.

Peisakh, now recovered from the shock and pain, came to Toiba's assistance.

"Let us pass! Let us pass! Oh my daughter!"

Between them the old couple managed to push Salomyga away from the door. Enraged, he jerked his revolver from under his belt and brought the steel grip down hard upon the old man's grey head. Peisakh crumpled to the floor.

Inside the room Riva was screaming.

When Toiba was dragged out of the house she was out of her mind, and the street echoed to her wild shrieks and entreaties for help.

Inside the house everything was quiet.

Palyanytsya came out of the room. Without looking at Salomyga whose hand was already on the door handle, he stopped the latter from entering.

"No use going in—she choked when I tried to shut her up with a pillow." As he stepped over Peisakh's body he put his foot into a dark sticky mess.

"Not such a good beginning," he muttered as he went outside.

The others followed him without a word, leaving behind bloody footprints on the floor and the stairs.

Pillage was in full swing in the town. Brief savage clashes flared up between brigands who could not agree as to the division of the spoils, and here and there sabres flashed. And almost everywhere fists flailed without restraint. From the beer saloon twenty-five gallon kegs were being rolled out onto the sidewalk.

Then the looters began to break into Jewish homes.

There was no resistance. They went through the rooms, hastily turned every corner upside down, and went away laden with booty, leaving behind disordered heaps of clothing and the fluttering contents of ripped feather beds and pillows. The first day took a toll of only two victims: Riva and her father; but the oncoming night carried with it the unavoidable menace of death.

By evening the motley crew of scavengers was roaring drunk. The crazed Petlyura men were waiting for the night.

Darkness released them from the last restraint. It is easier to destroy man in the pit of night; even the jackal prefers the hours of gloom.

Few would ever forget these two terrible nights and three days. How many crushed and mangled lives they left behind, how many youthful heads turned grey in these bloody hours, how many bitter tears were shed! It is hard to tell whether those were the more fortunate who were left to live with souls desolated, in the agony of shame and humiliation, gnawed by indescribable grief, grief for near and dear ones who would never return. Indifferent to all this in the narrow alleys lay the lacerated, tormented, broken bodies of young girls with arms thrown back in convulsive gestures of agony.

Only at the very riverfront, in the house where Naum the blacksmith lived, the jackals who fell upon his young wife Sarah got a fierce rebuff. The smith, a man of powerful build in the prime of his twenty-four years and with the steel muscles of one who wielded the sledgehammer for a living, did not yield his mate.

In a brief but furious clash in the tiny cottage the skulls of two Petlyura men were crushed like so many rotten melons. With the terrible fury of despair, the smith fought fiercely for two lives, and for a long time the dry crackle of rifle fire could be heard from the river bank where the brigands now rushed, sensing the danger. With only one round of ammunition left, the smith mercifully shot his wife, and himself rushed out to his death, bayonet in hand. He was met by a squall of lead and his powerful body crashed to the ground outside his front door.

Prosperous peasants from nearby villages drove into town in carts drawn by well-fed horses, loaded their wagon boxes with whatever met their fancy, and, escorted by sons and relatives serving in Golub's force, hurried home so as to make another trip or two to town and back.

Seryozha Bruzzhak, who together with his father had hidden half of his printshop comrades in the cellar and attic, was crossing the garden on his way home when he saw a man in a long, patched coat running up the road, violently swinging his arms.

It was an old Jew, and behind the bareheaded, panting man whose features were paralyzed with mortal terror, galloped a Petlyura man on a grey horse. The distance between them dwindled fast and the mounted man leaned forward in the saddle to cut down his victim. Hearing the hoofbeats behind him, the old man threw up his hands as if to ward off the blow. At that moment Seryozha leapt onto the road and threw himself in front of the horse to protect the ancient.

"Leave him alone, you dog of a bandit!"

The rider, making no effort to stay the descending sabre, brought the flat of the blade down on the fair young head.

CHAPTER FIVE

The Red forces were pressing down hard on "Chief Ataman" Petlyura's units, and Golub's regiment was called to the front. Only a small rearguard detachment and the Commandant's detail were left in the town.

The people stirred. The Jewish section of the population took advantage of the temporary lull to bury their dead, and life returned once again to the tiny huts of the Jewish quarter.

On quiet evenings an indistinct rumble carried from the distance; somewhere not too far off the fighting was in progress.

At the station railwaymen were leaving their jobs to roam the countryside in search of work.

The Gymnasium was closed.

Martial law was declared in town.

It was a black, ugly night, one of those nights when the eyes, strain as they might, cannot pierce the gloom, and a man gropes about blindly expecting at any moment to fall into a ditch and break his neck.

The respectable citizen knows that at a time like this it is safer to sit at home in the dark; he will not light a lamp if he can help it, for light might attract unwelcome guests. Better the dark, much safer. There are of course those who are always restless—let them venture abroad if they wish, that's none of the respectable citizen's business. But he himself will not risk going out—not for anything.

It was one of those nights, yet there was a man abroad.

Making his way to the Korchagin house, he knocked cautiously at the window. There was no answer and he knocked again, louder and more insistently.

Pavel dreamt that a queer creature, anything but human, was aiming a machine gun at him; he wanted to flee, but there was nowhere to go, and the machine gun had broken into a terrifying chatter.

He woke up to find the window rattling. Someone was knocking.

Pavel jumped out of bed and went to the window to see who it was, but all he could make out was a vague dark shape.

He was all alone in the house. His mother had gone on a visit to his eldest sister, whose husband was a mechanic at the sugar refinery. And Artem was blacksmithing in a neighbouring village, wielding the sledge for his keep.

Yet it could only be Artem.

Pavel decided to open the window.

"Who's there?" he said into the darkness.

There was a movement outside the window and a muffled bass replied:

"It's me, Zhukhrai."

Two hands were laid on the window sill and then Fyodor's head came up until it was level with Pavel's face.

"I've come to spend the night with you. Any objections, mate?" Zhukhrai whispered.

"Of course not," Pavel replied warmly. "You know you're always welcome. Climb in."

Fyodor squeezed his great bulk through the opening.

He closed the window but did not move away from the window at once. He stood listening intently, and when the moon slipped out from behind a cloud and the road became visible he scanned it carefully. Then he turned to Pavel.

"We won't wake up your mother, will we?"

Pavel told him there was nobody home besides himself. The sailor felt more at ease and spoke in a louder voice.

"Those cutthroats are after my hide in earnest now, matey. They've got it in for me after what happened over at the station. If our fellows would stick together a bit more we could have given the greycoats a fine reception during the pogrom. But folks, as you see, aren't ready to plunge into the fire yet, and so nothing came of it. Now they're looking for me, twice they've had the dragnet out—today I got away by the skin of my teeth. I was going home, you see, by the back way of course, and had just stopped at the shed to look around, when I saw a bayonet sticking out from behind a tree trunk. I naturally cast off and headed for your place. If you've got nothing against it I'll drop anchor here for a few days. All right, mate? Good."

Zhukhrai, still breathing heavily, began pulling off his mud-splashed boots.

Pavel was glad he had come. The power plant had not been working latterly and Pavel found the deserted house a lonely place.

They went to bed. Pavel fell asleep at once, but Fyodor lay awake for a long time smoking. Presently he rose and, tiptoeing on bare feet to the window, stared out for a long time into the street. Finally, overcome by fatigue, he lay down and fell asleep, but his hand remained on the butt of the heavy Colt which he had tucked under the pillow, warming it with his body.

Zhukhrai's unexpected arrival that night and the eight days spent in his company influenced the whole course of Pavel's life. The sailor gave him his first insight into much that was new, stirring and significant.

The two ambushes laid for him had driven Zhukhrai into a mousetrap, and he now made use of his enforced idleness to pass on to the eager Pavel all his passionate fury and burning hatred for the Yellow-and-Blues who were throttling the area.

Zhukhrai spoke in language that was vivid, lucid and simple. He had no doubts, his path lay clearly before him, and Pavel came to see that all this tangle of political parties with high-sounding names—Social-ist-Revolutionaries, Social-Democrats, Polish Socialists

—was a collection of vicious enemies of the workers, and that the only revolutionary party which steadfastly fought against the rich was the Bolshevik Party.

Formerly Pavel had been hopelessly confused about all this.

And so this staunch, stout-hearted Baltic sailor weathered by sea squalls, a confirmed Bolshevik, who had been a member of the Russian Social-Democratic Labour Party (Bolsheviks) since 1915, taught Pavel the harsh truths of life, and the young stoker listened spellbound.

"I was something like you, matey, when I was young," he said. "Just didn't know what to do with my energy, a restless youngster always ready to kick over the traces. I was brought up in poverty. And at times the very sight of those pampered, well-fed sons of the town gentry made me see red. Often enough I beat them up badly, but all I got out of it was a proper trouncing from my father. You can't change things by carrying on a lone fight. You, Pavlusha, have all the makings of a good fighter in the workingman's cause, only you're still very young and you don't know much about the class struggle. I'll put you on the right road, matey, because I know you'll make good. I can't stand the quiet, smug sort. The whole world's afire now. The slaves have risen and the old life's got to be scuttled. But to do that we need stout fellows, no sissies, who'll go crawling into cracks like so many cockroaches when the fighting starts, but men with guts who'll hit out without mercy."

His fist crashed down on the table.

He got up, frowning, and paced up and down the room with hands thrust deep in his pockets.

His inactivity depressed him. He bitterly regretted having stayed behind in this town, and believing any further stay to be pointless, was firmly resolved to make his way through the front to meet the Red units.

A group of nine Party members would remain in town to carry on the work.

"They'll manage without me. I can't sit around any longer doing nothing. I've wasted ten months as it is," Zhukhrai thought irritably.

"What exactly are you, Fyodor?" Pavel once asked him.

Zhukhrai got up and shoved his hands into his pockets. He did not grasp the meaning of the question at first.

"Don't you know?"

"I think you're a Bolshevik or a Communist," Pavel said in a low voice.

Zhukhrai burst out laughing, slapping his massive chest in its tight-fitting striped jersey.

"Right enough, matey! It's as much a fact as that Bolshevik and Communist are one and the same thing." Suddenly he grew serious. "But now that you've grasped that much, remember it's not to be mentioned to anyone or anywhere, if you don't want them to draw and quarter me. Understand?"

"I understand," Pavel replied firmly.

Voices were heard from the yard and the door was pushed open without a preliminary knock. Zhukhrai's hand slipped into his pocket, but emerged again when Sergei Bruzzhak, thin and pale with a bandage on his head, entered the room, followed by Valya and Klimka.

"Hallo, old man," Sergei shook Pavel's hand and smiled. "Decided to pay you a visit, all three of us. Valya wouldn't let me go out alone, and Klimka is afraid to let her go by herself. He may be a redhead but he knows what he's about."

Valya playfully clapped her hand over his mouth.

"Chatterbox," she laughed. "He won't give Klimka any peace today."

Klimka revealed a row of white teeth in a good-natured grin.

"What can you do with a sick fellow? Brain pan's damaged, as you can see."

They all laughed.

Sergei, who had not yet recovered from the effects of the sabre blow, settled on Pavel's bed and soon the young people were engaged in a lively conversation. Sergei, usually so gay and cheerful, was now quiet and depressed. He told Zhukhrai of his encounter with the Petlyura man.

Zhukhrai knew the three young people, for he had visited the Bruzzhaks on several occasions. He liked these youngsters; they had not yet found their place in the vortex of the struggle, but the aspirations of their class were so clearly expressed in them. He listened with interest to the young people's account of how they had helped to shelter Jewish families in their homes to save them from the pogrom. That evening he told the young folk much about the Bolsheviks, about Lenin, helping them to understand what was happening.

It was quite late when Pavel saw off his guests.

Zhukhrai went out every evening and returned late at night; before leaving town he had to discuss with the comrades who would remain in town the work they would have to do.

This particular night Zhukhrai did not come back. When Pavel woke up in the morning he saw at a glance that the sailor's bed had not been slept in.

Seized by some vague premonition, Pavel dressed hurriedly and left the house. Locking the door and putting the key in the usual place, he went to Klimka's house hoping that the latter would have some news of Fyodor. Klimka's mother, a stocky woman with a broad face pitted with pockmarks, was doing the wash. To Pavel's question whether she knew where Fyodor was she replied curtly:

"You'd think I'd nothing else to do but keep an eye on your Fyodor. It's all through him—the devil take him—that Zozulikha had the house turned upside down. What've you got to do with him? A queer lot, if you ask me. Klimka and you and the rest of them. . . ." She turned back in anger to her washtub.

Klimka's mother was an ill-tempered woman, with a biting tongue. . . .

From Klimka's house Pavel went to Sergei's. There too he voiced his fears.

"Why should you be so worried?" Valya intervened. "Perhaps he stayed over at some friend's place." But her words lacked confidence.

Pavel was too restless to stop at the Bruzzhaks' for long and although they tried to persuade him to stay for dinner he took his leave.

He headed back home in hopes of finding Zhukhrai there.

The door was locked. Pavel stood outside for a while with a heavy heart; he couldn't bear the thought of going into the deserted house.

For a few minutes he stood in the yard deep in thought, then, moved by an impulse, he went into the shed. He climbed up under the roof and brushing away the cobwebs reached into his secret hiding place and brought out the heavy Mannlicher wrapped in rags.

He left the shed and went down to the station, strangely elated by the feel of the revolver weighing down his pocket.

But there was no news of Zhukhrai at the station.

On the way back his step slowed down as he drew alongside the now familiar garden of the forest warden. Hoping he knew not for what he looked up at the windows of the house, but it was as lifeless as the garden. When he had passed the garden he turned back to glance at the paths now covered with a rusty crop of last year's leaves. The place seemed desolate and neglected—no industrious hand had laid a visible imprint here—and the dead stillness of the big old house made Pavel feel sadder still.

His last quarrel with Tonya had been the most serious they had had. It had all happened quite unexpectedly, nearly a month ago.

As he slowly walked back to town, his hands shoved deep into his pockets, Pavel recalled how it had come about.

They had met quite by chance on the road and Tonya had invited him over to her place.

"Dad and mother are going to a birthday party at the Bolshanskys, and I'll be all alone. Why don't you come over, Pavlusha? I have a very interesting book we could read—Leonid Andreyev's *Sashka Zhigulyov*. I've already finished it, but I'd like to reread it with you. I'm sure it would be a nice evening. Will you come?"

Her big, wide-open eyes looked at him expectantly from under the white bonnet she wore over her thick chestnut hair.

"I'll come."

At that they parted.

Pavel hurried to his machines, and at the very thought that he had a whole evening with Tonya to look forward to, the flames in the firebox seemed to burn more brightly and the burning logs to crackle more merrily than usual.

When he knocked at the wide front door that evening it was a slightly disconcerted Tonya who answered.

"I have visitors tonight. I didn't expect them, Pavlusha. But you must come in," she said.

Pavel wanted to leave and turned to the door.

"Come on in," she took him by the arm. "It'll do them good to know you." And putting her arm around his waist, she led him through the dining room into her own room.

As they entered she turned to the young people seated there and smiled.

"I want you to meet my friend Pavel Korchagin."

There were three people sitting around the small table in the middle of the room: Liza Sukharko, a pretty, dark-complexioned Gymnasium student with a pouting little mouth and a fetching coiffure, a lanky youth wearing a well-tailored black jacket, his sleek hair shining with hair-oil, and a vacant look in his grey eyes, and between them, in a foppish school jacket, Victor Leszczinski. It was him Pavel saw first when Tonya opened the door.

153

Leszczinski too recognized Korchagin at once and his fine arched eyebrows lifted in surprise.

For a few seconds Pavel stood silent at the door, eyeing Victor with frank hostility. Tonya hastened to break the awkward silence by asking Pavel to come in and turning to Liza to introduce her.

Liza Sukharko, who was inspecting the new arrival with interest, rose from her chair.

Pavel, however, spun around sharply and strode out through the semidark dining room to the front door. He was already on the porch when Tonya overtook him and seized him by the shoulders.

"Why are you running off? I especially wanted them to meet you."

Pavel removed her hands from his shoulders and replied sharply:

"I'm not going to be put on a show before that dummy. I don't belong to that crowd—you may like them, but I hate them. If I'd known they were your friends I'd never have come."

Tonya, suppressing her rising anger, interrupted him:

"What right have you to speak to me like that? I don't ask you who your friends are and who comes to see you."

"I don't care whom you see, only I'm not coming here any more," Pavel shot 'back at her as he went down the front steps. He ran to the garden gate.

He had not seen Tonya since then. During the pogrom, when together with the electrician he had given shelter to Jewish families at the power station, he had forgotten about the quarrel, and today he wanted to see her again.

Zhukhrai's disappearance and the knowledge that there was no one at home depressed Pavel. The grey stretch of road swung to the right ahead of him. The spring mud had not yet dried, and the road was pitted with holes filled with brown mire. Beyond a house whose shabby, peeling façade jutted out onto the edge of the pavement the road forked off.

Victor Leszczinski was saying goodbye to Liza at the street intersection opposite a wrecked stand with a splintered door and an inverted "Mineral Water" sign.

He held her hand in his as he spoke, pleadingly gazing into her eyes.

"You will come? You won't deceive me?"

"Of course I shall come. You must wait for me," Liza replied coquettishly.

And as she left him she smiled at him with promise in her misty hazel eyes.

A few yards further down the street Liza saw two men emerge from behind a corner onto the roadway. The first was a sturdy, broadchested man in worker's clothes, his unbuttoned jacket revealing a striped jersey underneath, a black cap pulled down over his forehead, and brown, low-topped boots on his feet. There was a blue-black bruise under his eye.

The man walked with a firm, slightly rolling gait.

Three paces behind, his bayonet almost touching the man's back, came a Petlyura soldier in a grey coat and two cartridge pouches at his belt. From under his shaggy sheepskin cap two small, cautious eyes watched the back of his captive's head. Yellow, tobacco-stained moustaches bristled on either side of his face.

Liza slackened her pace slightly and crossed over to the other side of the road. Just then Pavel emerged onto the highway behind her.

As he passed the old house and turned to the right at the bend in the road, he too saw the two men coming toward him.

Pavel stopped with a start and stood as if rooted to the ground. The arrested man was Zhukhrai.

"So that's why he didn't come back!"

Zhukhrai was coming nearer and nearer. Pavel's heart pounded as if it would burst. His thoughts raced madly as his mind sought vainly to grasp the situation. There was not enough time for deliberation. Only one thing was clear: Zhukhrai was done for.

Stunned and bewildered Pavel watched the two approach. What was to be done?

At the last moment he remembered the pistol in his pocket. As soon as they passed him he would shoot the man with the rifle in the back, and Fyodor would be free. With that decision reached on the spur of the moment his mind cleared. After all, it was only yesterday that Fyodor had told him: "For that we need stout fellows...."

Pavel glanced quickly behind him. The street leading to town was deserted; there was not a soul in sight. Ahead a woman in a light coat was hurrying across the road. She would not interfere. The second street branching off at the intersection he could not see. Only far away on the road to the station some people were visible.

Pavel moved over to the edge of the road. Zhukhrai saw him when they were only a few paces apart.

Zhukhrai looked at him from the corner of his eye and his thick eyebrows quivered. The unexpectedness of the encounter made him slow down his step. The bayonet pricked him in the back.

"Lively, there, or I'll hurry you along with this butt!" the escort said in a screechy falsetto.

Zhukhrai quickened his pace. He wanted to speak to Pavel, but refrained; he only waved his hand as if in greeting.

Fearing to attract the attention of the yellow-moustached soldier, Pavel turned aside as Zhukhrai passed, as if completely indifferent to what was going on.

But in his head drilled the anxious thought: "What if I miss him and the bullet hits Zhukhrai...."

157

With the Petlyura man almost on him there was no time to think.

When the yellow-moustached soldier came abreast of him, Pavel made a sudden lunge at him and seizing hold of the rifle struck the barrel down.

The bayonet hit a stone with a grating sound.

The attack caught the soldier unawares, and for a moment he was dumbfounded. Then he violently jerked the rifle toward himself. Throwing the full weight of his body on it, Pavel managed to retain his grip. A shot crashed out, the bullet striking a stone and ricocheting with a whine into the ditch.

Hearing the shot, Zhukhrai leapt aside and spun around. The soldier was wrenching at the rifle fiercely in an effort to tear it out of Pavel's hands. Pavel's arms were painfully twisted, but he did not release his hold. Then with a sharp lunge the enraged Petlyura man threw Pavel down on the ground, but still he could not wrench the rifle loose. Pavel went down, dragging the soldier down with him, and there was no power on earth that could have made him relinquish the rifle at this crucial moment.

In two strides Zhukhrai was alongside the struggling pair. His iron fist described an arc in the air and descended on the soldier's head; a second later the Petlyura man had been wrenched off Pavel and, sagging under the impact of two leaden blows in the face, his limp body collapsed into the wayside ditch.

The same strong hands that had delivered those blows lifted Pavel from the ground and set him on his feet.

Victor, who by this time had gone a hundred paces or so from the intersection, walked on whistling *La donna è mobile*, his spirits soaring after his meeting with Liza and her promise to see him at the abandoned factory the next day.

Among the inveterate rakes at the Gymnasium rumour had it that Liza Sukharko was rather daring in her love affairs. Insolent and conceited Semyon Zalivanov had once actually said that Liza had surrendered to him, and although Victor did not quite believe Semyon, Liza nevertheless intrigued him. Tomorrow he would find out whether Zalivanov had spoken the truth or not.

"If she comes I'll not hesitate. After all, she lets you kiss her. And if Semyon is telling the truth. . . ." Here his thoughts were interrupted as he stepped aside to let two Petlyura soldiers pass. One of them was astride a docktailed horse, swinging a canvas bucket— evidently on his way to water the animal. The other, in a short jacket and loose blue trousers, was walking alongside, resting his hand on the rider's knee and telling him a funny story.

Victor let them pass and was about to continue on his way when a rifle shot on the highway made him stop in his tracks. He turned and he saw the mounted man spurring his horse toward the sound, while the other soldier ran behind, supporting his sabre with his hand.

Victor ran after them. When he had almost reached the highway another shot rang out, and from around the corner came the horseman galloping madly. He urged on the horse with his heels and the canvas bucket, and leaping to the ground at the first gateway shouted to the men in the yard:

"To arms! They've killed one of our men!"

A minute later several men dashed out of the yard, clicking the bolts of their rifles as they ran.

Victor was arrested.

Several people were now clustered on the road, among them Victor and Liza, who had been detained as a witness.

Liza had been rooted to the spot from fright, and hence had a good view of Zhukhrai and Korchagin when they ran past; much to her surprise she realized that the young man who had attacked the Petlyura soldier was the one whom Tonya had wanted to introduce to her.

The two had just vaulted over the fence into a garden when the horseman came galloping down the street. Noticing Zhukhrai running with a rifle in his hands and the stunned soldier struggling to get back on his feet, the rider spurred his horse toward the fence.

Zhukhrai, however, turned around, raised the rifle and fired at the pursuer, who swung around and beat a hasty retreat.

The soldier, barely able to speak through his battered lips, was now telling what had happened.

"You dunderhead, what do you mean by letting a prisoner get away from under your nose? Now you're in for twenty-five strokes on your backside."

"Smart, aren't you?" the soldier snapped back angrily. "From under my nose, eh? How was I to know the other bastard would jump on me like a madman?"

Liza too was questioned. She told the same story as the escort, but she omitted to say that she knew the assailant. Nevertheless they were all taken to the commandant's office, and were not released until evening.

The Commandant himself offered to see Liza home, but she refused. His breath smelled of vodka and the offer boded no good.

Victor escorted Liza home.

It was quite a distance to the station and as they walked along arm in arm Victor was grateful for the incident.

"You haven't any idea who it was that freed the prisoner?" Liza asked as they were approaching her home.

"Of course not. How could I?"

"Do you remember the evening Tonya wanted to introduce a certain young man to us?"

11—325   *161*

Victor halted.

"Pavel Korchagin?" he asked, surprised.

"Yes, I think his name was Korchagin. Remember how he walked out in such a funny way? Well, it was he."

Victor stood dumbfounded.

"Are you sure?" he asked Liza.

"Yes. I remember his face perfectly."

"Why didn't you tell this to the Commandant?"

Liza was indignant.

"Do you think I would do anything so vile?"

"Vile? You call it vile to tell who attacked the escort?"

"And do you consider it honourable? You seem to have forgotten what they've done. Have you any idea how many Jewish orphans there are at the Gymnasium, and yet you'd want me to tell them about Korchagin? I'm sorry, I didn't expect that of you."

Leszczinski was much surprised by Liza's reply. But since it did not fit in with his plans to quarrel with her, he tried to change the subject.

"Don't be angry, Liza, I was only joking. I didn't know you were so upright."

"The joke was in very bad taste," Liza retorted drily.

As he was saying goodbye to her outside the Sukharko house, Victor asked:

"Will you come then, Liza?"

"I don't know," she replied vaguely.

Walking back to town, Victor turned the matter over in his mind. "Well, mademoiselle, you may think it vile, but I happen to think differently. Of course it's all the same to me who freed whom."

To him as a Leszczinski, the scion of an old Polish family, both sides were equally obnoxious. The only government he recognized was the government of the Polish gentry, the Recz Pospolita, and that would soon come with the Polish legions. But here was an opportunity to get rid of that scoundrel Korchagin. They'd twist his neck sure enough.

Victor was the only member of the family to have remained in town. He was staying with an aunt, who was married to the assistant director of the sugar refinery. His family had been living for some time in Warsaw, where his father Sigismund Leszczinski occupied a position of some importance.

Victor walked up to the commandant's office and turned into the open door.

Shortly afterwards he was on his way to the Korchagin house accompanied by four Petlyura men.

"That's the place," he said quietly, pointing to a lighted window. "May I go now?" he asked the Khorunzhy beside him.

"Of course. We'll manage ourselves. Thanks for the tip."

Victor hurried away down the sidewalk.

The last blow in the back sent Pavel reeling into the dark room to which they had led him, and his outstretched arms collided with the opposite wall. Feeling around he found something like a bunk, and he sat down, bruised and aching in body and spirit.

The arrest had come as a complete surprise. How had the Petlyura crowd found out about him? He was sure no one had seen him. What would happen next? And where was Zhukhrai?

He had left the sailor at Klimka's place. From there he had gone to Sergei, while Zhukhrai remained to wait for the evening in order to slip out of town.

"Good thing I hid the revolver in the crow's nest," Pavel thought. "If they had found it, it would have been all up with me. But how did they find out?" There was no answer to the question that tormented him.

The Petlyura men had not got much out of the Korchagin house although they made a thorough search of its every corner. Artem had taken his best suit and the accordion to the village, and his mother had taken a trunk with her, so that there was little left for them to pick up.

The journey to the guardhouse, however, was something Pavel would never forget. The night was pitch black, the sky overcast with clouds, and he had blundered along, blindly and half-dazed, propelled by brutal kicks from all sides.

He could hear voices behind the door leading into the next room, which was occupied by the Commandant's guard. A bright strip of light showed under the door. Pavel got up and feeling his way along the wall walked around the room. Opposite the bunk he discovered a window with solid sharp-pointed bars. He tried them with his hand—they were firmly fixed in place. The place had obviously been a storeroom.

He made his way to the door and stood there for a moment listening. Then he pressed lightly on the handle. The door gave a sickening creak and Pavel swore violently under his breath.

Through the narrow slit that opened before him he saw a pair of calloused feet with crooked toes sticking out over the edge of a bunk. Another light push against the handle and the door protested louder still. A disheveled figure with a sleep-swollen face now rose up in the bunk and fiercely scratching his lousy head with all five fingers burst into a long tirade. When the obscene flow of abuse ended, the creature reached out to the rifle standing at the head of the bunk and added phlegmatically:

"Shut that door and if I catch you looking in here once more I'll bash in your . . ."

Pavel shut the door. There was a roar of laughter in the next room.

He thought a great deal that night. His initial attempt to take a hand in the fight had ended badly for him. The very first step had brought capture and now he was trapped like a mouse.

Still sitting up, he drifted into a restless half-sleep, and the image of his mother with her peaked, wrinkled features and the eyes he loved so well rose before him. And he thought: "It's a good thing she's away—that makes it less painful."

A grey square of light from the window appeared on the floor.

The darkness was gradually retreating. Dawn was approaching.

CHAPTER SIX

A light shone in only one window of the big old house; the curtains were drawn. Outside Tresor, now chained for the night, suddenly barked in his reverberating bass.

Through a sleepy haze Tonya heard her mother speaking in a low voice.

"No, she is not asleep yet. Come in, Liza."

The light footsteps of her friend and the warm, impulsive hug finally dispelled her drowsiness.

Tonya smiled wanly.

"I'm so glad you've come, Liza. Papa passed the crisis yesterday and today he has been sleeping soundly all day. Mama and I have had some rest too after so many sleepless nights. Tell me all the news." Tonya drew her friend down beside her on the couch.

"Oh, there's plenty of news, but some of it's for your ears only," Liza smiled with a sly look at Yekaterina Mikhailovna.

Tonya's mother smiled. She was a matronly woman of thirty-six with the vigorous movements of a young girl, clever grey eyes and a face that was pleasant though not beautiful.

"I will gladly leave you alone in a few minutes, but first I want to hear the news that is fit for everybody's ears," she joked, pulling a chair up to the divan.

"Well, to begin with we've finished with school. The board has decided to issue graduation certificates to the seventh-graders. I *am* glad. I'm so sick of all this algebra and geometry! What good is it to any one? The boys may possibly continue their studies although they don't know where, with all this fighting going on. It's simply terrible. . . . As for us, we'll be married off and wives don't need algebra," Liza laughed.

After sitting with the girls for a little while, Yekaterina Mikhailovna went to her own room.

Liza now moved closer to Tonya and with her arms about her gave her a whispered account of the encounter at the crossroads.

"You can imagine my surprise, Tonechka, when I realized that the lad who was running away was . . . guess who?"

Tonya, who was listening with interest, shrugged her shoulders.

"Korchagin!" Liza blurted out breathlessly.

Tonya started and winced.

"Korchagin?"

Liza, pleased with the impression she had made, went on to describe her quarrel with Victor.

Carried away by her story, Liza did not notice Tonya's face grow pale and her fingers pluck nervously at her blue blouse. Liza did not know how Tonya's heart constricted with anxiety, nor did she realize why the long lashes framing her pretty eyes trembled so.

Tonya paid scant heed to Liza's story of the drunken Khorunzhy. A single thought bored into her mind: "So Victor Leszczinski knows who attacked the soldier. Oh, why did Liza tell him?" And in spite of herself the words broke from her lips.

"What did you say?" Liza could not grasp her meaning at once.

"Why did you tell Leszczinski about Pavlusha. . . . I mean Korchagin? He's sure to betray him. . . ."

"Oh, surely not!" Liza protested. "I don't think he would do such a thing. After all, why should he?"

Tonya sat up sharply and hugged her knees so hard that it hurt.

"You don't understand, Liza! He and Korchagin are enemies, and besides there is something else. . . ."

You made a big mistake when you told Victor about Pavlusha."

Only now did Liza notice Tonya's agitation, and her inadvertant use of Korchagin's first name opened Liza's eyes to something she had but vaguely guessed at.

She could not help feeling guilty and lapsed into an embarrassed silence.

"So it's true," she thought. "Fancy Tonya falling in love with an ... a plain workman." Liza wanted to talk about it very much, but out of consideration for her friend she refrained. Anxious to atone for her guilt in some way, she gripped Tonya's hands.

"Are you very worried, Tonya?"

"No, perhaps Victor is more honourable than I think," Tonya replied absently.

The awkward silence that ensued was broken by the arrival of a schoolmate of theirs, a bashful, gawky lad named Demianov.

After seeing her friends off, Tonya stood for a long time leaning against the wicket gate and staring at the dark strip of road leading to town. That eternal vagrant, the wind, laden with a chill dampness and the dank odour of the wet spring soil fanned her face. Dull red lights blinked in the windows of the houses over in the town. There it was, that town that lived a life apart from hers, and somewhere there, under one of those roofs, unaware of the danger that threatened him, was her rebellious friend Pavel. Perhaps he had forgotten her—how many days had flown by since their last meeting? He had been in the wrong that time, but all that had long been forgotten. Tomorrow she would see him and their friendship would be restored, a moving, warming friendship. It was sure to return—of that Tonya had not the slightest doubt. If only the night did not betray him, the night that seemed to harbour evil, as if lying in wait for him.... It was chilly, and after a last look at the road, Tonya went in. The thought, "If only the night does not betray him," still drilled in her head as she dozed off wrapped up in the blankets of her bed.

Tonya woke up early in the morning before anyone else was about, and dressed quickly. She slipped out of the house quietly so as not to wake up the family, untied the big shaggy Tresor and set out for town with the dog. She hesitated for a moment in front of the Korchagin house, then pushed the gate open and walked into the yard. Tresor dashed ahead wagging his tail....

Artem had returned from the village early that same morning. The blacksmith he had worked for had given him a lift into town on his cart. On reaching home he threw the sack of flour he had earned on his shoulders and walked into the yard, followed by the blacksmith carrying the rest of his belongings. Outside the open door Artem set the sack down on the ground and called out:

"Pavka!"

There was no answer.

"What's the hitch there? Why not go right in?" said the smith as he came up.

Setting his belongings down in the kitchen, Artem went into the next room. The sight that met his eyes there dumbfounded him: the place was turned upside down and old clothes littered the floor.

"What the devil is this?" Artem muttered completely at a loss.

"It's a mess all right," agreed the blacksmith.

"Where's the boy gone to?" Artem was getting angry. But the place was deserted and there was no one about to supply an answer.

The blacksmith said goodbye and left.

Artem went into the yard and looked around.

"I can't make head or tail of this! All the doors wide open and no Pavka."

Then he heard footsteps behind him. Turning around he saw a huge dog with ears pricked standing before him. A girl was walking toward the house from the gate.

"I must see Pavel Korchagin," she said in a low voice, surveying Artem.

"I've got to see him too. But the devil knows where he's gone. When I got here the house was unlocked and no Pavka anywhere about. So you're looking for him too?" he addressed the girl.

The girl answered with a question:

"Are you Korchagin's brother Artem?"

"I am. Why?"

Instead of replying, the girl stared in alarm at the open door. "Why didn't I come last night?" she thought. "It can't be, it can't be. . . ." And her heart grew heavier still.

"You found the door open and Pavel gone?" she asked Artem, who was staring at her in surprise.

"And what would you be wanting of Pavel may I ask?"

Tonya came closer to him and casting a look around spoke jerkily:

"I don't know for sure, but if Pavel isn't at home he must have been arrested."

Artem started nervously. "Arrested. What for?"

"Let's go inside," Tonya said.

Artem listened in silence while Tonya told him all she knew. By the time she had finished he was despairing.

"Damn it all! As if there wasn't enough trouble without this mess," he muttered gloomily. "Now I see why the place was turned upside down. What the hell did the boy have to get mixed up in this business for. . . . Where can I find him now? And who may you be, miss?"

"My father is forest warden Tumanov. I'm a friend of Pavel's."

"I see," Artem drawled out vaguely. "Here I was bringing flour to feed the boy up, and now this. . . ."

172

Tonya and Artem looked at each other in silence.

"I must go now," Tonya said softly as she prepared to go. "Perhaps you'll be able to find him. I'll come back in the evening to hear what you have learned."

Artem gave her a silent nod.

A lean fly just awakened from its winter sleep buzzed in a corner of the window. On the edge of an old threadbare couch sat a young peasant woman, her elbows resting on her knees and her eyes fixed blankly on the filthy floor.

The Commandant, chewing a cigarette stuck in the corner of his mouth, finished writing on a sheet of paper with a flourish, and, obviously pleased with himself, added an ornate signature ending in a curlicue under the title "Commandant of the town of Shepetovka, Khorunzhy." From the door came the clinking of spurs. The Commandant looked up.

Before him stood Salomyga with a bandaged arm.

"Hullo, what's blown you in?" the Commandant greeted him.

"Not a good wind, at any rate. Got my hand sliced to the bone by a *Bogunets*."*

Ignoring the woman's presence Salomyga cursed violently.

* *Bogunets*—a fighting man of the Bogun Regiment of the Red Army, thus named after the hero of the national-liberation struggle waged by the Ukrainian people in the 17th century.

173

"So what are you doing here? Convalescing?"

"We'll have time to convalesce in the next world. They're pressing down pretty hard on us at the front."

The Commandant interrupted him, nodding toward the woman.

"We'll talk about that later."

Salomyga sat down heavily on a stool and removed his cap, which bore a cockade with an enamel trident, the emblem of the UNR (Ukrainian National Republic).

"Golub sent me," he began in a low tone. "A division of regulars is going to be transferred here soon. In general there's going to be some doings in town, and it's my job to put things straight. The 'Chief' himself may come here with some foreign bigwig or other, so there's to be no talk about any 'diversions.' What're you writing?"

The Commandant shifted the cigarette to the other corner of his mouth.

"I've got a damn nuisance of a boy here. Remember that chap Zhukhrai, the one who stirred up the railwaymen against us? Well, he was caught at the station."

"He was, eh? Go on," Salomyga pulled his stool closer, highly interested.

"Well, that blockhead Omelchenko, the Station Commandant, sent him over escorted by a Cossack, and on the way the lad I've got in here took the prisoner away from him in broad daylight. The Cossack was disarmed and got his teeth knocked out, and was left to whistle for his prisoner. Zhukhrai got away, but we managed to grab this fellow. Here you have it all down on paper," and he pushed a sheaf of sheets covered with writing toward Salomyga.

The latter scanned through the report, turning over the sheets with his left hand.

When he had finished, he looked at the Commandant.

"And so you got nothing out of him?"

The Commandant pulled nervously at the peak of his cap.

"I've been at him for five days now, but all he says is, 'I don't know anything and I didn't free him.' The young scoundrel! You see, the escort recognized him—practically choked the life out of him as soon as he saw him. I could hardly pull the Cossack off—the fellow had good reason to be sore because Omelchenko at the station had given him twenty-five strokes with the cleaning rod for losing his prisoner. There's no sense in keeping him any more so I'm sending this off to headquarters for permission to finish him off."

Salomyga spat in disdain.

"If I had him he'd speak up sure enough. You're not much at conducting enquiries. Whoever heard of a theology student making a Commandant! Did you try the rod?"

The Commandant was furious.

"You're going a bit too far. Keep your sneers to yourself. I'm the Commandant here and I'll ask you not to interfere."

Salomyga looked at the bristling Commandant and roared with laughter.

"Ha-ha-ha. . . . Don't puff yourself up too much, priest's son, or you'll burst. To hell with you and your problems. Better tell me where a fellow can get a couple of bottles of *samogon*?"

The Commandant grinned.

"Can be done."

"As far as this is concerned," Salomyga jabbed at the sheaf of papers with his finger, "if you want to fix him properly put him down as eighteen years instead of sixteen. Round the top of the six off like that. Otherwise they mightn't pass it."

There were three of them in the storeroom. A bearded old man in a threadbare coat lay on his side on the bunk, his spindle legs, encased in wide linen trousers, drawn up under him. He had been arrested because the horse of the Petlyura men billeted with him had been missing from the shed. An elderly woman with small shifty eyes and a pointed chin was sitting on the floor. She made her living by selling *samogon* and had been thrown in here on a charge of stealing a watch and other valuables. Korchagin lay semiconscious in the corner under the window, his head resting on his crushed cap.

A young woman, wearing a coloured kerchief, her eyes dilated with terror, was led into the storeroom.

She stood for a moment or two and then sat down next to the *samogon* woman.

"Got caught, eh, wench?" the latter spoke rapidly, inspecting the newcomer with curious eyes.

There was no answer, but the *samogon* woman would not give up.

"Why'd they pick you up, eh? Nothing to do with *samogon* by any chance?"

The peasant girl got up and looked at the persistent hag.

"No, it's because of my brother," she replied quietly.

"And who's he?" the old woman persisted.

The old man spoke up.

"Why don't you leave her alone? She's probably got enough to worry about without your chattering away."

The woman turned quickly toward the bunk.

"Who are you to tell me what to do? I'm not talking to you, am I?"

The old man spat.

"Leave her alone, I tell you."

Silence descended again on the storeroom. The peasant girl spread out a big shawl and lay down, resting her head on her arm.

The *samogon* woman began to eat. The old man sat up, setting his feet on the floor, slowly rolled himself a cigarette and lit it. Clouds of acrid smoke spread out.

"A person can't eat in peace with that stink," the woman grumbled, her jaws working busily. "You've smoked the whole place up."

The old man returned with a sneer:

"Afraid of losing weight, eh? You won't be able to get through the door soon. Why don't you give the boy something to eat instead of stuffing it all into yourself."

The woman made an angry gesture.

"I tried, but he doesn't want anything. And as for that you can keep your mouth shut—it's not your food I'm eating."

The girl turned to the *samogon* woman and, nodding toward Korchagin, asked:

"Do you know why he's in here?"

The woman brightened up at being addressed and readily replied.

"He's a local lad—Korchagina's younger boy. His mother's a cook."

Leaning over to the girl, she whispered in her ear:

178

"He freed a Bolshevik—a sailor we had hereabouts who used to lodge with my neighbour Zozulikha."

The young woman remembered the words she had overheard: "I'm sending this off to headquarters for permission to finish him off."

One after the other troop trains pulled in at the junction, and battalions of regulars poured out in a disorderly mob. The armoured train *Zaporozhets*, four cars long, its steel sides ribbed with rivets, crawled along a side track. Guns were unloaded from flatcars and horses were led out of closed freight cars. The horses were saddled on the spot and mounted men jostled their way through the milling crowds of infantrymen to the station yard where the cavalry unit was lining up.

Officers ran up and down, calling the numbers of their units.

The station buzzed like a wasps' nest. Gradually the regular squares of platoons were hammered out of the shapeless mass of vociferous, swirling humanity and soon a stream of armed men was pouring into town. Until late in the evening carts creaked and rattled and the stragglers bringing up the rear of the rifle division trailed along the highway.

The procession finally ended with the headquarters company marching briskly by, bellowing the while from a hundred and twenty throats:

> *What's this hue, what's this cry*
> *All about?*
> *'Tis Petlyura and his boys,*
> *Without doubt....*

Pavel Korchagin got up to look out of the window.
Through the early twilight he could hear the rumbling
of wheels on the street, the tramping of many feet, and
a multitude of voices raised in song.

From behind him came a soft voice.

"The troops have come to town."

Korchagin turned round.

The speaker was the girl who had been brought
in the day before.

He had already heard her story—the *samogon*
woman had wormed it out of her. She came from a
village seven versts from the town, where her elder
brother, Gritsko, now a Red partisan, had headed a
poor peasants' committee when the Soviets were in
power.

When the Reds left, Gritsko girded himself with
a machine-gun belt and went with them. Now the
family was being hounded incessantly. Their only
horse had been taken away from them. The father had
been imprisoned for a while and had a rough time of
it. The village elder—one of those on whom Gritsko
had clamped down—was always billeting strangers in
their house, out of sheer spite. The family was completely ruined. And when the Commandant had come

to the village the day before to make a search, the elder had brought him to the girl's place. She struck his fancy and the next morning he brought her to town with him "for interrogation."

Korchagin could not fall asleep, try as he might he could not find rest, and in his brain drilled one insistent thought which he could not dispel: "What next?"

His bruised body ached painfully, for the escort had beaten him with bestial fury.

To escape the hateful thoughts crowding his mind he listened to the whispering of the two women.

In a barely audible voice the girl was telling how the Commandant had badgered her, threatening and coaxing, and when she rebuffed him, turning on her in fury. "I'll lock you up in a cellar where you can't get away from me," he had said.

Darkness lurked in the corners of the cell. There was another night ahead, a stifling, restless night. It was the seventh night in captivity, but it seemed to Pavel that he had been there for months. The floor was hard, and pain racked his body. There were three of them now in the storeroom. The *samogon* woman had been released by the Khorunzhy to procure some vodka. Grandpa was snoring on the bunk as if he were at home on his Russian stove; he bore his misfortune with stoic calm and slept soundly through the night. Khristina and Pavel lay on the floor, almost side by side. Yesterday Pavel had seen Sergei through the window—he had stood for a long time out in the street, looking sadly at the windows of the houses.

"He knows I'm here," Pavel had thought.

For three days running someone had brought sour black bread for him—who it was the guards would not tell. And for two days the Commandant had repeatedly questioned him.

What could it all mean?

During the questioning he had given nothing away; on the contrary he had denied everything. Why he had kept silent, he did not know himself. He wanted to be brave and strong, like those of whom he had read in books, yet that night when he was being taken to prison and one of his captors had said, "What's the use of dragging him along, *Pan* Khorunzhy? A bullet in the back will fix him," he had been afraid. Yes, the thought of dying at sixteen was terrifying! To die meant not to be alive any more.

Khristina was also thinking. She knew more than the young man. Most likely he did not know yet what was in store for him ... what she had overheard.

He tossed about restlessly at night unable to sleep. Khristina pitied him, oh, how she pitied him, though her own plight weighed down heavily upon her—it was impossible to forget the menace of the Commandant's words: "I'll fix you up tomorrow—if you won't have me it's the guardhouse for you. The Cossacks won't let you off. So take your choice."

Oh how hard it was, and no mercy to be expected anywhere! Was it her fault that Gritsko had joined the Reds? How cruel life was!

A dull pain choked her and in the agony of helpless despair and fear her body was racked by soundless sobs.

A shadow moved in the corner by the wall.

"Why are you crying?"

In a passionate whisper Khristina poured out her woes to her silent cell mate. He did not speak, but laid his hand lightly on hers.

"They'll torture me to death, curse them," she whispered in terror, gulping down her tears. "Nothing can save me."

What could Pavel say to this girl? There was nothing to say. Life was crushing them both in an iron ring.

Perhaps he ought to put up a fight when they came for her tomorrow? They'd only beat him to death, or a sabre blow on the head would end it all. Wishing to comfort somehow the distraught girl, he stroked her hand tenderly. The sobbing ceased. At intervals the sentry at the entrance could be heard challenging a passer-by with the usual "Who goes there?" and then everything was quiet again. Grandpa was fast asleep. The interminable minutes crawled slowly by. Then, to his utter surprise, Pavel felt the girl's arms go around him and pull him toward her.

"Listen," hot lips were whispering, "there is no escape for me: if it isn't the officer, it'll be those others. Take me, love, so that dog won't be the first to have me."

"What are you saying, Khristina!"

But the strong arms did not release him. Full, burning lips pressed down on his—they were hard to escape. The girl's words were simple, tender—and he knew why she uttered them.

Then he was oblivious to his surroundings. The lock on the door, the red-headed Cossack, the Commandant, the brutal beatings, the seven stifling, sleepless nights—all were forgotten, and for a moment there existed only the burning lips and the face moist with tears.

Suddenly he remembered Tonya.

How could he forget her? Those dear, wonderful eyes.

He mustered his strength and broke away from Khristina's embrace. He staggered to his feet like a drunken man and seized hold of the grill. Khristina's hands found him.

"Why, what is the matter?"

All her heart was in that question! He bent down to her and pressing her hands said:

"I can't, Khristina. You are so ... good." He did not know himself what he said besides.

He straightened up again to break the intolerable silence and went over to the bunk. Sitting down on the edge he woke up the old man.

"Give me a smoke, please, Granddad."

The girl, huddled in her shawl, wept in the corner.

The next day the Commandant came with some Cossacks and took Khristina away. Her eyes sought Pavel's in farewell, and there was reproach in them. And when the door slammed behind her his soul was more desolate and dreary than ever.

All day long Granddad could not get a word out of Pavel. The sentries and the commandant's guard were changed. Toward evening a new prisoner was brought in. Pavel recognized him: it was Dolinnik, a carpenter from the sugar refinery. He was a solidly built man of squat build wearing a faded yellow shirt under a threadbare jacket. He surveyed the storeroom with a keen eye.

Pavel had seen him in 1917, in February, when the reverberations of the revolution reached their town. He had heard only one Bolshevik speak during the noisy demonstrations held then and that Bolshevik was Dolinnik. He had climbed onto a roadside fence and addressed the troops. Pavel remembered his closing words:

"Follow the Bolsheviks, soldiers, they will not betray you!"

He had not seen the carpenter since.

Granddad was glad to have a new cell mate, for he obviously found it hard to sit silent all day long. Dolinnik settled down next to him on the edge of the bunk, smoked a cigarette with him and questioned him about everything.

Then the newcomer moved over to Korchagin.

"Well, young man?" he asked Pavel. "And how did *you* get in here?"

Pavel replied in monosyllables and Dolinnik saw that it was suspicion that made the young man so sparing of words. When the carpenter learned of the charge laid against Pavel his intelligent eyes widened with amazement and he sat down next to the lad.

"So you say you got Zhukhrai away? That's interesting. I didn't know they'd nabbed you."

Pavel, taken by surprise, raised himself on his elbow.

"I don't know any Zhukhrai. They can pin anything on you here."

Dolinnik, smiling, moved closer to him.

"That's all right, my boy. You don't need to be cautious with me. I know more than you do."

Quietly, so that the old man should not overhear, he continued:

"I saw Zhukhrai off myself, he's probably reached his destination by now. Fyodor told me all about what happened."

186

After thinking for a moment in silence, Dolinnik added:

"I see you're made of the right stuff, boy. Though the fact that they caught you and know everything is bad, very bad, I should say."

He took off his jacket and spreading it on the floor, sat down on it with his back against the wall, and began to roll another cigarette.

Dolinnik's last remark made everything clear to Pavel. There was no doubt about it that Dolinnik was all right. He had seen Zhukhrai off, and that meant. . . .

That evening he learned that Dolinnik had been arrested for agitation among Petlyura's Cossacks. Moreover, he had been caught distributing an appeal issued by the gubernia revolutionary committee calling on the troops to surrender and go over to the Reds.

Dolinnik was careful not to tell Pavel much.

"Who knows," he thought to himself, "they may use the ramrod on the boy. He's still too young."

Late at night when they were settling themselves for sleep, he voiced his apprehensions in the brief remark:

"Well, Korchagin, we seem to be in a pretty bad fix. Let's see what's going to come out of it."

The next day a new prisoner was brought in—the flop-eared, scraggy-necked barber Shlyoma Zeltser whom everybody in town knew.

"Fuchs, Bluvstein and Trachtenberg are going to

welcome him with bread and salt," he was telling
Dolinnik with much spirit and gesticulation. "I said
that if they want to do that, they can, but will the rest
of the Jewish population back them up? No they won't,
you can take it from me. Of course they have their own
fish to fry. Fuchs has a store and Trachtenberg's got
the flour mill. But what've I got? And the rest of the
hungry lot? Nothing—paupers, that's what we are.
Well, I've got a loose tongue, and today when I was
shaving an officer—one of the new ones who came
recently—I said: 'Do you think Ataman Petlyura
knows about these pogroms or not? Will he see the
delegation?' Oi, how many times I've got into trouble
through this tongue of mine. So what do you think
this officer did when I had shaved him and powdered
his face and done all in fine style too? He gets up and
instead of paying me arrests me for agitating against
the authorities." Zeltser struck his chest with his fist.
"Now what sort of agitation was that? What did I say?
I only asked the fellow.... And to lock me up for
that. ..."

In his excitement Zeltser twisted a button on Dolinnik's shirt and tugged at his arms.

Dolinnik smiled in spite of himself as he listened
to the indignant Shlyoma.

"Yes, Shlyoma," he said gravely when the barber
had finished, "that was a stupid thing for a clever fellow
like you to do. You chose the wrong time to let your

tongue run away with you. I wouldn't have advised you to get in here."

Zeltser nodded understandingly and made a gesture of despair with his hand. Just then the door opened and the *samogon* woman was pushed in. She staggered in, heaping foul curses on the Cossack who brought her.

"You and your Commandant ought to be roasted on a slow fire! I hope he shrivels up and croaks from that booze of mine!"

The guard slammed the door shut and they heard him locking it on the outside.

As the woman settled down on the edge of the bunk the old man addressed her good-humouredly.

"So, you're back with us again, you old chatter-box? Sit down and make yourself at home."

The *samogon* woman darted a hostile glance at him and picking up her bundle sat down on the floor next to Dolinnik.

It turned out that she had been released just long enough for her captors to get some bottles of *samogon* out of her.

Suddenly shouts and the sound of running feet could be heard from the guardroom next door. Somebody was barking out orders. The prisoners stopped talking to listen.

Strange things were happening on the commons in front of the ungainly church with the ancient belfry.

On three sides the square was lined with rectangles of troops—units of the division of regular infantry mustered in full battle kit.

In front, facing the entrance to the church stood three regiments of infantry in squares placed in checkerboard fashion, their ranks buttressed against the school fence.

This grey, rather dirty mass of Petlyura soldiers standing there with rifles at rest, wearing absurd Russian helmets like pumpkins cut in half, and heavily laden down with bandoliers, was the best division the "Directory" had.

Well-uniformed and shod from the stores of the former tsarist army and consisting mainly of kulaks who were consciously fighting the Soviets, the division had been transferred here to defend this strategically important railway junction. The shining steel ribbons of railway tracks ran in five different directions from Shepetovka, and for Petlyura the loss of the junction would have meant the end of everything. As it was, the "Directory" had very little territory left in its hands, and the small town of Vinnitsa was now Petlyura's capital.

The "Chief Ataman" himself had decided to inspect the troops and now everything was in readiness for his arrival.

Back in a far corner of the square where they were least likely to be seen stood a regiment of new

recruits—barefoot youths in shabby civilian clothes
of all descriptions. These were farm lads picked up
from their beds by midnight raiding parties or seized
on the streets and none of them had the least intention
of doing any fighting.

"We're not crazy," they said among themselves.

The most the Petlyura officers could do was to
bring the recruits to town under escort, divide them
into companies and battalions and issue them arms.
The very next day, however, a third of the recruits
thus herded together would disappear and with each
passing day their numbers dwindled.

It would have been more than foolhardy to issue
them boots, particularly since the boot stocks were far
from plentiful. Nevertheless an order was issued for
everyone to report for conscription shod. The result
was an astonishing collection of dilapidated footwear
tied on with bits of string and wire.

They were marched out for parade barefoot.

Behind the infantry stood Golub's cavalry regiment.

Mounted men held back the dense crowds of
curious townsfolk who had come to see the parade.

After all, the "Chief Ataman" himself was to be
present! Events like this were rare enough in town
and no one wanted to miss the free entertainment it
promised.

On the church steps gathered the colonels and
captains, the priest's two daughters, a handful of

Ukrainian teachers, a group of "free Cossacks," and the slightly hunchbacked mayor—in a word, the elite representing the "public," and among them the Inspector-General of Infantry wearing a Caucasian *cherkesska*. It was he who was in command of the parade.

Inside the church Vasili the priest was garbing himself in his Easter service vestments.

Petlyura was to be received in grand style. For one thing, the newly mobilized recruits were to take the oath of allegiance, and for this purpose a yellow-and-blue flag had been brought out.

The Division Commander set out for the station in a rickety old Ford car to meet Petlyura.

When he had gone, the Inspector of Infantry called over Colonel Chernyak, a tall, well-built officer with a foppishly twirled moustache.

"Take someone along with you and see that the commandant's office and the rear services are in proper shape. If you find any prisoners there look them over and get rid of the riffraff."

Chernyak clicked his heels, took along the first Cossack captain his eye lighted on and galloped off.

The Inspector turned politely to the priest's elder daughter.

"What about the banquet, everything in order?"

"Oh yes. The Commandant's doing his best," she replied, gazing avidly at the handsome Inspector.

Suddenly a stir passed through the crowd: a rider was coming down the road at a mad gallop, bending low over the neck of his horse. He waved his hand and shouted:

"They're coming!"

"Fall in!" barked the Inspector.

The officers ran to their places.

As the Ford chugged up to the church the band struck up *The Ukraine Lives On*.

Following the Division Commander, the "Chief Ataman" heaved himself laboriously out of the car. Petlyura was a man of medium height, with an angular head firmly planted on a red bull neck; he wore a blue tunic of fine wool cloth girded tight with a yellow belt to which a small Browning in a chamois holster was attached. On his head was a peaked khaki uniform cap with a cockade bearing the enamel trident.

There was nothing especially warlike about the figure of Simon Petlyura. As a matter of fact, he did not look like a military man at all.

He heard out the Inspector's report with an expression of displeasure on his face. Then the mayor addressed him in greeting.

Petlyura listened absently, staring at the assembled regiments over the mayor's head.

"Let us begin," he nodded to the Inspector.

Mounting the small platform next to the flag, Petlyura delivered a ten-minute speech to the troops.

The speech was unconvincing. Petlyura, evidently tired from the road, spoke without enthusiasm. He finished to the accompaniment of the regulation shouts of "*Slava! Slava!*" from the soldiers and climbed down from the platform dabbing his perspiring forehead with a handkerchief. Then, together with the Inspector and the Division Commander, he inspected the units.

As he passed the ranks of the newly mobilized recruits his eyes narrowed in a disdainful scowl and he bit his lips in annoyance.

Toward the end of the inspection, when the new recruits platoon by platoon marched in uneven ranks to the flag, where the priest Vasili was standing Bible in hand, and kissed first the Bible and then the hem of the flag, an unforeseen incident occurred.

A delegation which had contrived by some unknown means to reach the square approached Petlyura. At the head of the group came the wealthy timber merchant Bluvstein with an offering of bread and salt, followed by Fuchs, the draper, and three other respectable businessmen.

With a servile bow Bluvstein extended the tray to Petlyura. It was taken by an officer standing alongside.

"The Jewish population wishes to express its sincere gratitude and respect for you, the head of the state. Please accept this address of greeting."

"Good," muttered Petlyura, quickly scanning the sheet of paper.

Fuchs stepped forward.

"We most humbly beg you to allow us to open our enterprises and we ask for protection against pogroms." Fuchs stumbled over the last word.

An angry scowl darkened Petlyura's features.

"My army does not engage in pogroms. You had better remember that."

Fuchs spread out his arms in a gesture of resignation.

Petlyura's shoulder twitched nervously. The untimely appearance of the delegation irritated him. He turned to Golub, who was standing behind chewing his black moustache.

"Here's a complaint against your Cossacks, *Pan* Colonel. Investigate the matter and take measures accordingly," said Petlyura. Then, addressing the Inspector, he said drily:

"You may begin the parade."

The ill-starred delegation had not expected to run up against Golub and they now hastened to withdraw.

The attention of the spectators was now wholly absorbed by the preparations for the ceremonial march-past. Sharp commands were rapped out.

Golub, his features outwardly calm, walked over to Bluvstein and said in a loud whisper:

"Get out of here, you heathen souls, or I'll make mincemeat out of you!"

The band struck up and the first units marched through the square. As they drew alongside Petlyura, the troops bellowed a mechanical "*Slava!*" and then swung down the highway to disappear into the side-streets. At the head of the companies uniformed in brand-new khaki outfits the officers marched at an easy gait as if they were simply taking a stroll, swinging their swagger sticks. The swagger stick mode, like cleaning rods for the soldiers, had just been introduced in the division.

The new recruits brought up the rear of the parade. They came in a disorderly mass, out of step and jostling one another.

There was a low rustle of bare feet as the mobilized men shuffled by, prodded on by the officers who worked hard but in vain to bring about some semblance of order. When the second company was passing a peasant lad in a linen shirt on the side nearest the reviewing stand gaped in such wide-eyed amazement at the "Chief" that he stepped into a hole in the road and fell flat on the ground. His rifle slid over the cobble-stones with a loud clatter. He tried to get up but was knocked down again by the men behind him.

Some of the spectators burst out laughing. The company broke ranks and passed through the square in complete disorder. The luckless lad picked up his rifle and ran after the others.

Petlyura turned away from this sorry spectacle and walked over to the car without waiting for the end of the review. The Inspector, who followed him, asked diffidently:

"*Pan* the Ataman will not stay for dinner?"

"No," Petlyura flung back curtly.

Sergei Bruzzhak, Valya and Klimka were watching the parade in the crowd of spectators pressed against the high fence surrounding the church. Sergei, gripping the bars of the grill, looked at the faces of the people below him with hatred in his eyes.

"Let's go, Valya, they've shut up shop," he said in a deliberately loud defiant voice, and turned away from the fence. People stared at him in astonishment.

Ignoring everyone, he walked to the gate, followed by his sister and Klimka.

Colonel Chernyak and the Captain galloped up to the commandant's office and dismounted. Leaving the horses in the charge of a dispatch rider they strode rapidly into the guardhouse.

"Where's the Commandant?" Chernyak asked the dispatch rider sharply.

"Dunno," the man stammered. "Gone off somewhere."

Chernyak looked around the filthy, untidy room, the unmade beds and the Cossacks of the commandant's guard who sprawled on them and made no attempt to rise when the officers entered.

"What sort of a pigsty is this?" Chernyak roared. "And who gave you permission to wallow about like hogs?" he lashed at the men lying flat on their backs.

One of the Cossacks sat up, belched and growled:

"What're you squawking for? We've got our own squawker here."

"What!" Chernyak leapt toward the man. "Who do you think you're talking to, you bastard? I'm Colonel Chernyak. D'you hear, you swine! Up, all of you, or I'll have you flogged!" The enraged Colonel dashed about the guardhouse. "I'll give you one minute to sweep out the filth, straighten out the bedding and make your filthy mugs presentable. You look like a band of brigands, not Cossacks!"

Beside himself with rage, the Colonel violently kicked at a slop pail obstructing his path.

The Captain was no less violent, and, adding emphasis to his curses by wielding his three-thonged whip, drove the men out of their bunks.

"The Chief Ataman's reviewing the parade. He's liable to drop in here any minute. Get a move on there!"

Seeing that things were taking a serious turn and that they really might be in for a flogging—they knew

Chernyak's reputation well enough—the Cossacks sprang into feverish activity.

In no time work was in full swing.

"We ought to have a look at the prisoners," the Captain suggested. "There's no telling whom they've got locked up here. Might be trouble if the Chief looks in."

"Who has the key?" Chernyak asked the sentry. "Open the door at once."

A Sergeant jumped up and opened the lock.

"Where's the Commandant? How long do you think I'm going to wait for him? Find him at once and send him in here," Chernyak ordered. "Muster the guard in the yard! Why are the rifles without bayonets?"

"We only took over yesterday," the Sergeant tried to explain, and hurried off in search of the Commandant.

The Captain kicked the storeroom door open. Several of the people inside got up from the floor, the others remained motionless.

"Open the door wider," Chernyak commanded. "Not enough light here."

He scrutinized the prisoners' faces.

"What are you in for?" he snapped at the old man sitting on the edge of the bunk.

The old man half rose, hitched up his trousers and, frightened by the sharp order, mumbled:

"Dunno myself. They just locked me up and here I am. There was a horse disappeared from the yard, but I've got nothing to do with it."

"Whose horse?" the Captain interrupted him.

"An army horse, of course. My billets sold him and drank the proceeds and now they're blaming me."

Chernyak ran his eye swiftly over the old man and with an impatient jerk of his shoulder shouted: "Pick up your things and get out of here!" Then he turned to the *samogon* woman.

The old man could not believe his ears. Blinking his shortsighted eyes, he turned to the Captain:

"Does that mean I can go?"

The Cossack nodded as much as to say: the faster you get out the better.

Hurriedly the old man seized his bundle which hung over the edge of the bunk and dashed through the door.

"And what are you in for?" Chernyak was questioning the *samogon* woman.

Swallowing the mouthful of pie she had been chewing, the woman rattled off a ready answer:

"It's an injustice it is that I should be in here, *Pan* Chief. Just think of it, to drink a poor widow's *samogon* and then lock her up."

"You're not in the *samogon* business, are you?" Chernyak asked.

"Business? Nothing of the kind," said the woman with an injured air. "The Commandant came and took four bottles and didn't pay a kopek. That's how it is: they drink your booze and never pay. You wouldn't call that business, would you?"

"Enough. Now go to the devil!"

The woman did not wait for the order to be repeated. She picked up her basket and backed to the door, bowing in gratitude.

"May God bless you with good health, your honours."

Dolinnik watched the comedy with wide-open eyes. None of the prisoners could make out what it was all about. The only thing that was clear was that the arrivals were chiefs of some kind who had the power to dispose of them as they saw fit.

"And you there?" Chernyak spoke to Dolinnik.

"Stand up when *Pan* the Colonel speaks to you!" barked the Captain.

Slowly Dolinnik raised himself to his feet from the floor.

"What are you in for?" Chernyak repeated.

For a few seconds Dolinnik's eyes rested on the Colonel's neatly twirled moustache and his clean-shaven face, then on the peak of his new cap with the enamel cockade and a wild thought flashed through his mind: Maybe it'll work!

"I was arrested for being out on the streets after

eight o'clock," he said the first thing that came into his head.

He awaited the answer in an agony of suspense.

"What were you doing out at night?"

"It wasn't night, only about eleven o'clock."

As he spoke he no longer believed that this shot in the dark would succeed.

His knees trembled when he heard the brief command:

"Get out."

Dolinnik walked hurriedly out of the door, forgetting his jacket; the Captain was already questioning the next prisoner.

Korchagin was the last to be interrogated. He sat on the floor completely dumbfounded by the proceedings. At first he could not believe that Dolinnik had been released. Why were they letting everyone off like this? But Dolinnik... Dolinnik had said that he had been arrested for breaking the curfew.... Then it dawned upon him.

The Colonel began questioning the scraggy Zeltser with the usual "What are you in for?"

The barber, pale with nervousness, blurted out:

"They tell me I was agitating, but I haven't any idea what my agitation consisted of."

Chernyak pricked up his ears.

"What's that? Agitation? What were you agitating about?"

Zeltser spread out his arms in bewilderment.

"I don't know myself, I only said that they were collecting signatures to a petition to the Chief Ataman from the Jewish population."

"What sort of petition?" both Chernyak and the Captain moved menacingly toward Zeltser.

"A petition asking that pogroms be prohibited. You know, we had a terrible pogrom. The whole population's afraid."

"That's enough," Chernyak interrupted him. "We'll give you a petition you won't forget, you dirty Jew." Turning to the Captain, he snapped: "Put this one away properly. Have him taken to headquarters—I'll have a talk with him there personally. We'll see who's behind this petition business."

Zeltser tried to protest but the Captain struck him sharply across the back with his riding whip.

"Shut up, you bastard!"

His face twisted with pain, Zeltser staggered back into a corner. His lips trembled and he barely restrained the sobs that choked him.

While this was going on, Pavel rose to his feet. He was now the only prisoner besides Zeltser in the storeroom.

Chernyak stood in front of the boy and inspected him with his piercing black eyes.

"Well, what are you doing here?"

The Colonel's question elicited a quick reply:

"I cut off a saddle skirt for soles."

"Whose saddle was it?" the Colonel asked.

"We've got two Cossacks billeted at our place and I cut off the skirt of an old saddle for soles. So the Cossacks hauled me in here." Seized by a wild hope to regain his freedom, he added: "I didn't know it wasn't allowed...."

The Colonel eyed Pavel with disgust.

"Of all the things this Commandant thought of, damn his hide! Look at the prisoners he picked up!" As he turned to the door, he shouted: "You can go home, and tell your father to give you the thrashing you deserve. Out with you!"

Still unable to believe his ears, his heart pounding as if it would burst, Pavel snatched up Dolinnik's jacket from the floor and rushed for the door. He ran through the guardroom and slipped out into the open air behind the back of the Colonel as he walked out into the yard. In a moment Pavel was through the wicket gate and in the street.

The unlucky Zeltser remained alone in the store-room. He looked round with harassed eyes, instinctively took a few steps toward the exit, but just then a sentry entered the guardhouse, closed the door, inserted the padlock, and sat down on a stool next to the door.

Out on the porch Chernyak, pleased with himself, said to the Captain:

"It's a good thing we looked in. Think of the rubbish we found there—we'll have to lock up that Commandant for a couple of weeks. Well, it's time we were going."

The Sergeant had mustered his detail in the yard. When he saw the Colonel, he ran over and reported:

"Everything's in order, *Pan* Colonel."

Chernyak inserted a boot into a stirrup and sprang lightly into the saddle. The Captain was having some trouble with his restive horse. Reining in his mount, the Colonel said to the Sergeant:

"Tell the Commandant that I let out all the rubbish he'd collected in there. And tell him I'll give him two weeks in the guardhouse for the way he ran things here. As for the fellow in there now, transfer him to headquarters at once. Let the guard be in readiness."

"Very good, *Pan* Colonel," the Sergeant saluted.

Spurring on their horses, the Colonel and the Captain galloped back to the square where the parade was already coming to an end.

Pavel swung himself over the seventh fence and stopped exhausted. He could go no further. Those days cooped up in the stifling storeroom without food had sapped his strength.

Where should he go? Home was out of the question, and to go to the Bruzzhaks' might bring disaster upon the whole family if anyone discovered him there.

He did not know what to do, and ran on again blindly, leaving behind the vegetable patches and back gardens at the edge of the town. Colliding heavily with a fence, he came to himself with a start and looked about him in amazement: there behind the tall fence was the forest warden's garden. So this was where his weary legs had brought him! He could have sworn that he had had no thought of coming this way. How then did he happen to be here? For that he could find no answer.

Yet rest awhile he must; he had to consider the situation and decide on the next step. He remembered that there was a summerhouse at the end of the garden. No one would see him there.

Hoisting himself to the top of the fence, he clambered over and dropped into the garden below. With a brief glance at the house, barely visible among the trees, he made for the summerhouse. To his dismay he found that it was open on nearly all sides. The wild vine that had walled it in during the summer had withered and now all was bare.

He turned to go back, but it was too late. There was a furious barking behind him. He wheeled round and saw a huge dog coming straight at him down the leaf-strewn path leading from the house. Its fierce growls rent the stillness of the garden.

Pavel made ready to defend himself. The first attack he repulsed with a heavy kick. But the animal crouched to spring a second time. There is no saying how the encounter would have ended had a familiar voice not called out at that point: "Come here, Tresor! Come here!"

Tonya came running down the path. She dragged Tresor back by the collar and turned to address the young man standing by the fence.

"What are you doing here? You might have been badly mauled by the dog. It's lucky I..."

She stopped short and her eyes widened in surprise. How extraordinarily like Korchagin was this stranger who had wandered into her garden.

The figure by the fence stirred.

"Tonya!" said the young man softly. "Don't you recognize me?"

Tonya cried out and rushed impulsively over to him.

"Pavel, you?"

Tresor, taking the cry as a signal for attack, sprang forward.

"Down, Tresor, down!" A few cuffs from Tonya and he slunk back with an injured air toward the house, his tail between his legs.

"So you're free?" said Tonya, clinging to Pavel's hands.

"You knew then?"

"I know everything," replied Tonya breathlessly. "Liza told me. But however did you get here? Did they let you go?"

"Yes, but only by mistake," Pavel replied wearily. "I ran away. I suppose they're looking for me now. I really don't know how I got here. I thought I'd rest a bit in your summerhouse. I'm awfully tired," he added apologetically.

She gazed at him for a moment or two and a wave of pity and tenderness mingled with anxiety and joy swept over her.

"Pavel, my darling Pavel," she murmured holding his hands fast in hers. "I love you.... Do you hear me? My stubborn boy, why did you go away that time? Now you're coming to us, to me. I shan't let you go for anything. It's nice and quiet in our house and you can stay as long as you like."

Pavel shook his head.

"What if they find me here? No, I can't stay in your place."

Her hands squeezed his fingers, her eyelids fluttered and her eyes flashed.

"If you refuse I shall never speak to you again. Artem isn't here, he was marched off under escort to the locomotive. All the railwaymen are being mobilized. Where will you go?"

Pavel shared her anxiety, and only his fear of endangering this girl who had grown so dear to him held him back. But at last worn out by his harrowing experiences, hungry and exhausted, he gave in.

While he sat on the sofa in Tonya's room, the

following conversation ensued between mother and daughter in the kitchen.

"Listen, Mama, Korchagin is in my room. He was my pupil, you remember? I don't want to hide anything from you. He was arrested for helping a Bolshevik sailor to escape. Now he has run away from prison, but he has nowhere to go." Her voice trembled. "Mother dear, please let him stay here for a while."

The mother looked into her daughter's pleading eyes with a searching gaze.

"Very well, I have no objection. But where do you intend to put him?"

Tonya flushed scarlet.

"He can sleep in my room on the sofa," she said in deep confusion. "We needn't tell Papa anything for the time being."

Her mother looked straight into her eyes.

"Is this what you have been fretting about so much lately?" she asked.

"Yes."

"But he is scarcely more than a boy."

"I know," replied Tonya, nervously fingering the sleeve of her blouse. "But if he hadn't escaped they would have shot him just the same."

Yekaterina Mikhailovna was clearly alarmed by Korchagin's presence in her home. His arrest and her daughter's obvious infatuation with a lad she scarcely knew disturbed her.

But Tonya, considering the matter settled, was already thinking of attending to her guest's comfort.

"He must have a bath, first thing, Mama. I'll see to it at once. He is awfully dirty, like a chimney sweep. It must be ages since he had a wash."

And she bustled off to heat the water for the bath and find some clean linen for Pavel. When all was ready she rushed into the room, seized Pavel by the arm and avoided unnecessary explanation by hurrying him off to the bathroom.

"You must have a complete change of clothes. Here is a suit for you to put on. Your things will have to be washed. You can wear that in the meantime," she said pointing to the chair where a blue sailor blouse with striped white collar and a pair of bell-bottomed trousers were neatly laid out.

Pavel looked surprised. Tonya smiled.

"I wore it at a masquerade ball once," she explained. "It will be just right for you. Now, hurry. While you're washing, I'll get you something to eat."

She went out and shut the door, leaving Pavel with no alternative but to undress and climb into the tub.

An hour later all three, mother, daughter and Pavel, were dining in the kitchen.

Pavel, who was ravenously hungry, consumed three helpings before he was aware of it. He was rather shy of Yekaterina Mikhailovna at first but soon thawed out when he saw how friendly she was.

After dinner they retired to Tonya's room and at Yekaterina Mikhailovna's request Pavel related his experiences.

"What do you intend doing now?" Yekaterina Mikhailovna asked when he had finished.

Pavel pondered the question a moment. "I should like to see Artem first, and then I shall have to get away from here."

"But where will you go?"

"I think I could make my way to Uman or perhaps to Kiev. I don't know myself yet, but I must get away from here as soon as possible."

Pavel could hardly believe that everything had changed so quickly. Only that morning he had been in the filthy cell and now here he was sitting beside Tonya, wearing clean clothes, and what was most important, he was free.

What queer turns life can take, he thought: one moment the sky seems black as night, and then the sun comes shining through again. Had it not been for the danger of being arrested again he would have been the happiest lad alive at this moment.

But he knew that even as he sat here in this large, silent house he was liable to be caught. He must go away from here, anywhere, rather than remain. And yet he did not at all welcome the idea of going away. How thrilling it had been to read about the heroic Garibaldi! How he had envied him! But when you came to think of it, Garibaldi's must have been a hard life, hounded as he was from place to place. He, Pavel, had only lived through seven days of misery and torment, yet it had seemed like a whole year.

No, clearly he was not cut out to be a hero.

"What are you thinking about?" Tonya asked, bending over toward him. The deep blue of her eyes seemed fathomless.

"Tonya, shall I tell you about Khristina?"

"Yes, do," Tonya urged him.

He told her the sad story of his fellow-captive.

The clock ticked loudly in the silence as he ended his story. "... and that was the last we saw of her," his words came with difficulty. Tonya's head dropped and she had to bite her lips to force back the tears that choked her.

Pavel looked at her. "I must go away tonight," he said with finality.

"No, no, I shan't let you go anywhere tonight."

She stroked his bristly hair tenderly with her slim warm fingers. . . .

"Tonya, you must help me. Someone must go to the station and find out what has happened to Artem and take a note to Seryozha. I have a revolver hidden in a crow's nest. I daren't go for it, but Seryozha can get it for me. Will you be able to do this for me?"

Tonya got up.

"I'll go to Liza Sukharko right away. She and I will go to the station together. Write your note and I'll take it to Seryozha. Where does he live? Shall I tell him where you are if he should want to see you?"

Pavel considered for a moment before replying. "Tell him to bring it to your garden this evening."

It was very late when Tonya returned. Pavel was fast asleep. The touch of her hand awoke him and he opened his eyes to find her standing over him, smiling happily.

"Artem is coming here soon. He has just come back. Liza's father has agreed to vouch for him and they're letting him go for an hour. The engine is standing at the station. I couldn't tell him you are here. I just told him I had something very important to tell him. There he is now!"

Tonya ran to open the door. Artem stood in the doorway dumb with amazement, unable to believe his eyes. Tonya closed the door behind him so that her father, who was lying ill with typhus in the study, might not overhear them.

Another moment and Artem was giving Pavel a bear's hug that made his bones crack and crying: "Pavel! My little brother!"

And so it was decided; Pavel was to leave the next day. Artem would arrange for Bruzzhak to take him on a train bound for Kazatin.

Artem, usually grave and reserved, was now almost beside himself with joy at having found his brother after so many anxious days of worrying about his fate.

"Then it's settled. Tomorrow morning at five you'll be at the warehouse. While they're loading on fuel you can slip in. I wish I could stay and have a chat with you but I must be getting back. I'll see you off tomorrow. They're making up a battalion of railwaymen. We go about under an armed escort just like when the Germans were here."

Artem said goodbye to his brother and left.

Dusk gathered fast, Sergei would be arriving soon with the pistol. While he waited, Pavel paced nervously up and down the dark room. Tonya and her mother were with the forest warden.

He met Sergei in the darkness by the fence and the two friends shook hands warmly. Sergei had brought Valya with him. They conversed in low tones.

"I haven't brought the gun," Sergei said. "That backyard of yours is thick with Petlyura men. There are carts standing all over the place and they had a bonfire going. So I couldn't climb the tree to get the gun. It's a damn shame." Sergei was much put out.

"Never mind," Pavel consoled him. "Perhaps it's just as well. It would be worse if I happened to be caught on the way with the gun. But make sure you get hold of it."

Valya moved closer to Pavel.

"When are you leaving?"

"Tomorrow, at daybreak."

"How did you manage to get away? Tell us."

In a rapid whisper Pavel told them his story. Then he took leave of his comrades. Sergei's unusual gravity betrayed his emotion.

"Good luck, Pavel, don't forget us," Valya said in a choking voice.

And with that they left him, the darkness swallowing them up in an instant.

Inside the house all was quiet. The measured ticking of the clock was the only sound in the stillness.

For two of the house's inmates there was no thought of sleep that night. How could they sleep when in six hours they were to part, perhaps never to meet again. Was it conceivable in that brief space of time to give utterance to the myriad of ideas and thoughts that seethed within them?

Youth, sublime youth, when passion, as yet unknown, is only dimly felt in a quickening of the pulse; when your hand coming in chance contact with your sweetheart's breast trembles as if affrighted and falters, and when the sacred friendship of youth guards you from the final step! What can be sweeter than to feel her arm about your neck and her burning kiss on your lips!

215

It was the second kiss they had exchanged throughout their friendship. Pavel, who had experienced many a beating but never a caress except from his mother, was stirred to the depths of his being. Hitherto life had shown him its most brutal side, and he had not known it could be such a glorious thing; now this girl had taught him what happiness could mean.

He breathed the perfume of her hair and seemed to see her eyes in the darkness.

"I love you so, Tonya, I can't tell you how much, for I don't know how to say it."

His brain was in a whirl. How responsive her supple body.... But youth's friendship is a sacred trust.

"Tonya, when all this mess is over I'm bound to get a job as a mechanic, and if you really want me, if you're really serious and not just playing with me, I'll be a good husband to you. I'll never beat you, never do anything to hurt you, I swear it."

Fearing to fall asleep in each other's arms—lest Tonya's mother find them and think ill of them—they separated.

Day was breaking when they fell asleep after having made a solemn compact never to forget one another.

Yekaterina Mikhailovna woke Pavel early. He jumped quickly out of bed. While he was in the bathroom, putting on his own clothes and boots, with Dolinnik's jacket on top, Yekaterina Mikhailovna woke Tonya.

They hurried through the grey morning mist to the station. When they reached the timber yards by the back way they found Artem waiting impatiently for them beside the loaded tender.

A powerful locomotive moved up slowly, enveloped in clouds of hissing steam. Bruzzhak looked out of the cab.

Pavel bid Tonya and Artem a hasty farewell, then gripped the iron rail and climbed up into the locomotive. Looking back he saw two familiar figures at the crossing—the tall figure of Artem and the small graceful form of Tonya beside him. The wind tore angrily at the collar of her blouse and tossed her chestnut hair. She waved to him.

Artem glanced at Tonya out of the corner of his eye and noticing that she was on the verge of tears, he sighed.

"I'll be damned if there isn't something up between these two," he said to himself. "And me thinking Pavel is still a little boy!"

When the train disappeared behind the bend he turned to Tonya and said: "Well, are we going to be friends?" And Tonya's tiny hand was lost in his huge paw.

From the distance came the rumble of the train gathering speed.

CHAPTER SEVEN

For a whole week the town, belted with trenches and enmeshed in barbed-wire entanglements, went to sleep at night and woke up in the morning to the pounding of guns and the rattle of rifle fire. Only in the small hours of the morning would the din subside, and even then the silence would be shattered from time to time by bursts of fire as the outposts probed out each other. At dawn men busied themselves around the battery at the railway station. The black snout of a gun belched savagely and the men hastened to feed it another portion of steel and explosive. Each time a gunner pulled at a lanyard the earth trembled under-foot. Three versts from town the shells whined over the village occupied by the Reds, drowning out all other sounds, and sending up geysers of earth.

The Red battery was stationed on the grounds of an old Polish monastery standing on a high hill in the centre of the village.

The Military Commissar of the battery, Comrade Zamostin, leapt to his feet. He had been sleeping with his head resting on the trail of a gun. Now, tightening his belt from which a heavy Mauser was suspended, he listened to the flight of the shell and waited for the explosion. Then the yard echoed to his resonant voice.

"We'll catch up on our sleep tomorrow, Comrades. Time to get up!"

The gun crews slept beside their guns, and they were on their feet as quickly as the Commissar. All but Sidorchuk, who raised his head reluctantly and looked around with sleep-heavy eyes.

"The swine—hardly light yet and they're at it again. Just out of spite, the bastards!"

Zamostin laughed.

"Unsocial elements, Sidorchuk, that's what they are. They don't care whether you want to sleep or not."

The artilleryman grumblingly roused himself.

A few minutes later the guns in the monastery yard were in action and shells were exploding in the town.

On a platform of planks rigged up on top of the tall smoke stack of the sugar refinery, a Petlyura officer and a telephonist were stationed. They had climbed up the iron ladder inside the chimney.

From this vantage point, which gave them a perfect view of the entire town, they directed the fire of their artillery. Through their field glasses they could see every movement made by the Red troops besieging the town. Today the Bolsheviks were particularly active. An armoured train was slowly edging in on the Podolsk station, keeping up an incessant fire as it came. Beyond it the attack lines of the infantry could be seen. Several times the Red forces tried to take the town by storm, but the Petlyura troops were firmly entrenched on the approaches. The trenches erupted a squall of fire, filling the air with a maddening din which mounted into an unintermittent roar, reaching its highest pitch during the attacks. Swept by this leaden hailstorm, unable to stand the inhuman strain, the Bolshevik lines fell back, leaving motionless bodies behind on the field.

Today the blows delivered at the town were more persistent and frequent than before. The air quivered from the reverberations of the gunfire. From the height of the smoke stack you could see the steadily advancing Bolshevik lines, the men throwing themselves on the ground only to rise again and press irresistibly forward. Now they had all but taken the station. The Petlyura division's available reserves were sent into action, but they could not close the breach driven in their positions. Filled with a desperate resolve, the Bolshevik attack lines spilled into the streets adjoining the station, whose defenders, the third regiment of the Petlyura division, routed from their last positions in the gardens and orchards at the edge of the town by a brief but terrible thrust, scattered into the town. Before they could recover enough to make a new stand, the Red Army men poured into the streets, sweeping away in bayonet charges the Petlyura pickets left behind to cover the retreat.

Nothing could induce Sergei Bruzzhak to stay down in the basement where his family and the nearest neighbours had taken refuge. And in spite of his mother's entreaties he climbed out of the chilly cellar. An armoured car with the name *Sagaidachny* on its side clattered past the house, firing wildly as it went. Behind it ran panic-stricken Petlyura men in complete disorder. One of them slipped into Sergei's yard, where with feverish haste he tore off his cartridge belt, helmet and rifle and then vaulted over the fence and disappeared in the truck gardens beyond. Sergei looked out into the street. Petlyura soldiers were running down the road leading to the Southwestern Station, their retreat covered by an armoured car. The highway leading to town was deserted. Then a Red Army man dashed into sight. He threw himself down on the ground and began firing down the road. A second and a third Red Army man came into sight behind him.... Sergei watched them coming, crouching down and firing as they ran. A bronzed Chinese with bloodshot eyes, clad in an undershirt and girded with machine-gun belts, was running full height, a grenade in each hand. And ahead of them all came a Red Army man, hardly more than a boy, with a light machine gun. The sight of the first Red troops to enter the town filled Sergei with joy. He dashed out onto the road and shouted as loud as he could:

"Long live the comrades!"

So unexpectedly did he rush out that the Chinese all but knocked him off his feet. The Red Army man's first reaction was to throw himself upon the boy, but the exultation on the latter's face stayed him.

"Where is Petlyura?" the Chinese shouted at him, panting heavily.

But Sergei did not hear him. He ran back into the yard, picked up the cartridge belt and rifle abandoned by the Petlyura man and hurried after the Red Army men. They did not notice him until they had stormed the Southwestern Station. Here, after cutting off several trainloads of munitions and supplies and hurling the enemy into the woods, they stopped to rest and regroup. The young machine gunner came over to Sergei and asked in surprise:

"Where are you from, Comrade?"

"I'm from this town. I've been waiting for you to come."

Sergei was soon surrounded by Red Army men.

"I know him," the Chinese said in broken Russian. "He yelled 'Long live comrades!' He's a Bolshevik, he's with us, a good fellow!" he added with a broad smile, slapping Sergei on the shoulder approvingly.

Sergei's heart leapt with joy. He had been accepted at once, accepted as one of them. And together with them he had taken the station in a bayonet charge.

The town bestirred itself. The townsfolk, exhausted by their ordeal, emerged from the cellars and basements and came out to the front gates to see the Red Army units enter the town. Thus it was that Sergei's mother and his sister Valya saw Sergei marching along with the others in the ranks of the Red Army men. He was hatless, but girded with a cartridge belt and with a rifle slung over his shoulder.

Antonina Vasilievna threw up her hands in indignation.

So her Seryozha had got mixed up in the fight. He would pay for this! Fancy him parading with a rifle in front of the whole town! There was bound to be trouble later on. Antonina Vasilievna could no longer restrain herself:

"Seryozha, come home this minute!" she shouted. "I'll show you how to behave, you scamp! I'll teach you to fight!" And at that she marched out to the road with the firm intention of bringing her son back.

But this time Sergei, her Seryozha, whose ears she had so often boxed, turned a stern pair of eyes at his mother and burning with shame and a sense of injury snapped at her:

"Stop shouting! I'm staying where I am." And he marched past without stopping.

Antonina Vasilievna was beside herself with anger.

"So that's how you treat your mother! Don't you dare come home after this!"

"I won't!" Sergei cried, without turning around.

Antonina Vasilievna remained standing on the road in utter confusion. Past her moved the ranks of weatherbeaten, dust-covered fighting men.

"Don't cry, mother! We'll make sonny a commissar," a strong, jovial voice rang out. A burst of jolly laughter rippled through the platoon. Up at the head of the company voices struck up a song in unison:

> *Comrades, the bugles are sounding,*
> *Shoulder your arms for the fray.*
> *On to the kingdom of liberty*
> *Boldly shall we fight our way...*

The ranks joined in a mighty chorus and Sergei's ringing voice merged in the swelling melody. He had found a new family. In it one bayonet was his, Sergei's.

On the gates of the Leszczinski house hung a strip of white cardboard with the brief inscription: "Revcom." Beside it was an arresting poster of a Red Army man looking into your eyes and pointing his finger straight at you over the words: "Have *you* joined the Red Army?"

The Political Department people had been at work during the night putting up these posters all over the town. Nearby hung the Revolutionary Committee's first proclamation to the toiling population of Shepetovka:

> "Comrades! The proletarian troops have taken this town. Soviet power has been restored. We call on you to maintain order. The bloody cutthroats have been thrown back, but if you want them never to return, if you want to see

224

them destroyed once and for all, join the ranks of the Red Army. Give all your support to the power of the working folk. Military authority in this town is in the hands of the chief of the garrison. Civilian affairs will be administered by the Revolutionary Committee.

"Signed: *Dolinnik*

"Chairman of the Revolutionary Committee."

People of a new sort appeared in the Leszczinski house. The word "comrade," for which only yesterday people had paid with their life, was now heard on all sides. That indescribably moving word, "comrade!"

For Dolinnik there was no sleep or rest these days. The carpenter was busy establishing revolutionary government.

In a small room on the door of which hung a slip of paper with the pencilled words "Party Committee" sat Comrade Ignatieva, calm and imperturbable as always. The Political Department entrusted her and Dolinnik with the task of setting up the organs of Soviet power.

One more day and office workers were seated at desks and a typewriter was clicking busily. A Commissariat of Supplies was organized under nervous, dynamic Pyzycki. Now that Soviet power was firmly established in the town, Pyzycki, formerly a mechanic's helper at the local sugar refinery, proceeded with grim determination to wage war on the bosses of the sugar refinery who, nursing a bitter hatred for the Bolsheviks, were lying low and biding their time.

At a meeting of the refinery workers he summed up the situation in harsh, unrelenting terms.

"The past is gone never to return," he declared, speaking in Polish and banging his fist on the edge of the tribune to drive home his words. "It is enough that our fathers and we ourselves slaved all our lives for the Potockis. We built palaces for them and in return His Highness the Count gave us just enough to keep us from dying of starvation.

"How many years did the Potocki counts and the Sanguszko princes ride our backs? Are there not any number of Polish workers whom Potocki ground down just as he did the Russians and Ukrainians? And yet the count's henchmen have now spread the rumour among these very same workers that the Soviet power will rule them all with an iron hand.

"That is a foul lie, Comrades! Never have workingmen of different nationalities had such freedom as now. All proletarians are brothers. As for the gentry, we are going to curb them, you may depend on that." His hand swung down again heavily on the barrier of the rostrum. "Who is it that has made brothers spill each other's blood? For centuries kings and nobles have sent Polish peasants to fight the Turks. They have

…ways incited one nation against another. Think of all
…he bloodshed and misery they have caused! And who
benefited by it all? But soon all that will stop. This
is the end of those vermin. The Bolsheviks have flung
out a slogan that strikes terror into the hearts of the
bourgeoisie: 'Proletarians of all lands, unite!' There
lies our salvation, there lies our hope for a better future, for the day when all workingmen will be brothers. Comrades, join the Communist Party!

"There will be a Polish republic too one day but
it will be a Soviet republic without the Potockis, for
they will be rooted out and we shall be the masters
of Soviet Poland. You all know Bronik Ptaszinski,
don't you? The Revolutionary Committee has appointed
him commissar of our factory. 'We were naught, we
shall be all.' We shall have cause for rejoicing, Comrades. Only take care not to give ear to the hissing of
those hidden reptiles! Let us place our faith in the
workingman's cause and we shall establish the broth-
erhood of all peoples throughout the world!"

These words were uttered with a sincerity and
fervour that came from the bottom of this simple workingman's heart. He descended the platform amid shouts
of enthusiastic acclaim from the younger members of
the audience. The older workers, however, hesitated to
speak up. Who knew but what tomorrow the Bolsheviks
might have to give up the town and then those who
remained would have to pay dearly for every rash

word. Even if you escaped the gallows, you would lo
your job for sure.

The Commissar of Education, the slim, well-kni
Chernopyssky, was so far the only schoolteacher in the
locality who had sided with the Bolsheviks.

Opposite the premises of the Revolutionary Committee the Special Duty Company was quartered; its
men were on duty at the Revolutionary Committee. At
nights a Maxim gun stood ready in the garden at the
entrance to the Revcom, a sinewy ammunition belt
trailing from its breech. Two men with rifles stood
sentry duty beside it.

Comrade Ignatieva on her way to the Revcom went
up to one of them, a young Red Army man, and asked:

"How old are you, Comrade?"

"Going on seventeen."

"Do you live here?"

The Red Army man smiled. "Yes, I only joined
the army the day before yesterday during the fighting."

Ignatieva studied his face.

"What does your father do?"

"He's an engine driver's assistant."

At that moment Dolinnik appeared, accompanied
by a man in uniform.

"Here you are," said Ignatieva, turning to Dolinnik, "I've found the very lad to put in charge of
the district committee of the Komsomol. He's a local
man."

228

Dolinnik glanced quickly at Sergei—for it was he.

"Ah yes. You're Zakhar's boy, aren't you? All right, go ahead and stir up the young folk."

Sergei looked at them in surprise. "But what about the company?"

"That's all right, we'll attend to that," Dolinnik, already mounting the steps, threw over his shoulder.

By evening two days later the local committee of the Young Communist League of the Ukraine had been formed.

Sergei plunged into the vortex of the new life that had burst suddenly and swiftly upon the town. It filled his entire existence so completely that he forgot his family although it was so near at hand.

He, Sergei Bruzzhak, was now a Bolshevik. For the hundredth time he pulled out of his pocket the document issued by the Committee of the Ukrainian Communist Party, certifying that he, Sergei, was a Komsomol and Secretary of the Komsomol Committee. And should anyone entertain any doubts on that score there was the impressive Mannlicher—a gift from dear old Pavel—in its makeshift canvas holster hanging from the belt of his tunic. A most convincing credential that! Too bad Pavlushka wasn't around!

Sergei's days were spent on assignments given by the Revcom. Today too Ignatieva was waiting for him. They were to go down to the station to the Division Political Department to get newspapers and books for the Revolutionary Committee. Sergei hurried out of the building to the street, where a man from the Political Department was waiting for them with an automobile.

During the long drive to the station where the Headquarters and Political Department of the First Soviet Ukrainian Division were located in railway cars, Ignatieva plied Sergei with questions.

"How has your work been going? Have you formed your organization yet? You ought to persuade your friends, the workers' children, to join the Komsomol. We shall need a group of Communist youth very soon. Tomorrow we shall draw up and print a Komsomol leaflet. Then we'll hold a big youth rally in the theatre. When we get to the Political Department I'll introduce you to Ustinovich. She is working with the young people, if I'm not mistaken."

Ustinovich turned out to be a girl of eighteen with dark bobbed hair, in a new khaki tunic with a narrow leather belt. She gave Sergei a great many pointers in his work and promised to help him. Before he left she gave him a large bundle of books and newspapers, including one of particular importance, a booklet containing the program and rules of the Komsomol.

When he returned late that night to the Revcom Sergei found Valya waiting for him outside.

"You ought to be ashamed of yourself!" she cried. "What do you mean by staying away from home like this? Mother is crying her eyes out and father is very angry with you. There's going to be an awful row."

"No there isn't," he reassured her. "I haven't any time to go home, honest I haven't. I won't be coming tonight either. But I'm glad you've come because I want to have a talk with you. Let's go inside."

Valya could hardly recognize her brother. He was quite changed. He fairly bubbled with energy.

As soon as she was seated Sergei went straight to the point.

"Here's the situation, Valya. You've got to join the Komsomol. You don't know what that is? The Young Communist League. I'm running things here. You don't believe me? All right, look at this!"

Valya read the paper and looked at her brother in bewilderment.

"What will I do in the Komsomol?"

Sergei spread out his hands. "My dear girl, there's heaps to do! Look at me, I'm so busy I don't sleep nights. We've got to make propaganda. Ignatieva says we're going to hold a meeting in the theatre soon and talk about the Soviet power. She says I'll have to make a speech. I think it's a mistake because I don't know how to make speeches. I'm bound to make a hash of it. Now, what about your joining the Komsomol?"

"I don't know what to say. Mother would be wild with me if I did."

231

"Never mind mother, Valya," Sergei urged. "She doesn't understand. All she cares about is to have her children beside her. But she has nothing against the Soviet power. On the contrary, she's all for it. But she would rather other people's sons did the fighting. Now is that fair? Remember what Zhukhrai told us? And look at Pavel, he didn't stop to think about his mother. The time has come when we young folk must fight for our right to make something of our lives. Surely you won't refuse, Valya? Think how fine it will be. You could work with the girls, and I would be working with the fellows. That reminds me, I'll tackle that red-headed devil Klimka this very day. Well, Valya, what do you say? Are you with us or not? I have a little booklet here that will tell you all about it."

He took the booklet of Komsomol rules out of his pocket and handed it to her.

"But what if Petlyura comes back again?" Valya asked him in a low voice, her eyes glued to her brother's face.

This thought had not yet occurred to Sergei and he pondered it for a moment.

"I would have to leave with all the others, of course," he said. "But what would happen to you? Yes, it would make mother very unhappy." He lapsed into silence.

"Seryozha, couldn't you enroll me without mother

232

or anyone else knowing? Just you and me? I could help just the same. That would be the best way."

"I believe you're right, Valya."

Ignatieva entered the room at that point.

"This is my little sister Valya, Comrade Ignatieva. I've just been talking to her about joining the Komsomol. She would make a suitable member, but you see, our mother might make difficulties. Could we enroll Valya so that no one would know about it? You see, we might have to give up the town. I would leave with the army, of course, but Valya is afraid it would go hard with mother."

Ignatieva, sitting on the edge of a chair, listened gravely.

"Yes," she agreed. "That is the best course."

The packed theatre buzzed with the excited chatter of the youth who had come in response to notices posted all over town. A brass band of workers from the sugar refinery was playing. The audience, consisting mainly of students of the local high school and Gymnasium, was less interested in the meeting than in the concert that was to follow it.

At last the curtain rose and Comrade Razin, Secretary of the Uyezd Committee, who had just arrived, appeared on the platform.

All eyes were turned to this short, slenderly built man with the small, sharp nose, and his speech was listened to with keen attention. He told them about the struggle that had swept the entire country and called on the youth to rally to the Communist Party. He spoke like an experienced orator but made excessive use of terms like "orthodox Marxists," "social-chauvinists" and the like, which his hearers did not understand. Nevertheless, when he finished they applauded him warmly, and after introducing the next speaker, who was Sergei, he left.

It was as he had feared: now that he was face to face with the audience, Sergei did not know what to say. He fumbled painfully for a while until Ignatieva came to his rescue by whispering from her seat at the presidium table: "Tell them about organizing a nucleus."

Sergei at once went straight to the point.

"Well, Comrades, you've heard all there is to be said. What we've got to do now is to form a nucleus. Who is in favour?"

A hush fell on the gathering. Ustinovich stepped into the breach. She got up and told the audience how the youth was being organized in Moscow. Sergei in the meantime stood aside in confusion.

He raged inwardly at the meeting's reaction to the question of organizing a nucleus and he scowled down at the audience. They hardly listened to Ustinovich. Sergei saw Zalivanov whisper something to Liza Sukharko with a contemptuous look at the speaker on the platform. In the front row the senior Gymnasium girls with powdered faces were casting coy glances about them and whispering among themselves. Over in the corner near the door leading backstage was a group of young Red Army men. Among them Sergei saw the young machine gunner. He was sitting on the edge of the stage fidgeting nervously and gazing with undisguised hatred at the flashily dressed Liza Sukharko and Anna Admovskaya who, totally unabashed, were carrying on a lively conversation with their escorts.

Realizing that no one was listening to her, Ustinovich quickly wound up her speech and sat down. Ignatieva took the floor next, and her calm compelling manner quelled the restless audience.

"Comrades," she said, "I advise each of you to think over what has been said here tonight. I am sure that some of you will become active participants in the revolution and not merely spectators. The doors are open to receive you, the rest is up to you. We should like to hear you express your opinion. We invite anyone who has anything to say to step up to the platform."

Once more silence reigned in the hall. Then a voice spoke up from the back.

"I'd like to speak!"

Misha Levchukov, a lad with a slight squint and the burly figure of a young bear, made his way to the stage.

"The way things are," he said, "we've got to help the Bolsheviks. I'm for it. Seryozhka knows me. I'm joining the Komsomol."

Sergei beamed. He sprang forward to the centre of the stage.

"You see, Comrades!" he cried. "I always said Misha was one of us: his father was a switchman and he was crushed by a car, and that's why Misha couldn't get an education. But he didn't need to go to Gymnasium to understand what's wanted at a time like this."

There was an uproar in the hall. A young man with carefully brushed hair asked for the floor. It was Okushev, a Gymnasium student and the son of the local apothecary. Tugging at his tunic, he began:

"I beg your pardon, Comrades. I don't understand what is wanted of us? Are we expected to go in for politics? If so, when are we going to study? We've got to finish the Gymnasium. If it was some sport society, or club that was being organized where we could gather and read, that would be another matter. But to go in for politics means taking the risk of getting hanged afterwards. Sorry, but I don't think anybody will agree to that."

There was laughter in the hall as Okushev jumped off the stage and resumed his seat. The next speaker was the young machine gunner. Pulling his cap down over his forehead with a furious gesture and glaring down at the audience, he shouted:

"What're you laughing at, you vermin!"

His eyes were two burning coals and he trembled all over with fury. Taking a deep breath he began:

"Ivan Zharky is my name. I'm an orphan. I never knew my mother or my father and I never had a home. I grew up on the street, begging for a crust of bread and starving most of the time. It was a dog's life, I can tell you, something you mama's boys know nothing about. Then the Soviet power came along and the Red Army men picked me up and took care of me. A whole platoon of them adopted me. They gave me clothes and taught me to read and write. But what's most important, they taught me what it was to be a human being. Because of them I became a Bolshevik and I'll be a Bolshevik till I die. I know damn well what we're fighting for, we're fighting for us poor folk, for the workers' government. You sit there cackling but you don't know that two hundred comrades were killed fighting for this town. They perished..." Zharky's voice vibrated like a taut string. "They gave up their lives gladly for our happiness, for our cause.... People are dying all over the country, on all the fronts, and you're playing at merry-go-rounds here. Comrades," he went on, turning suddenly to the presidium table, "you're wasting your time talking to them there," he jabbed a finger toward the hall. "Think they'll understand you? No! A full stomach is no comrade to an empty one. Only one man came forward here and that's because he's one of the poor, an orphan. Never mind," he roared furiously at the gathering, "we'll get along without you. We're not going to beg you to join us, you can go to the devil, the lot of you! The only way to talk to the likes of you is with a machine gun!" And with this parting thrust he stepped off the stage and made straight for the exit, glancing neither to right or left.

None of those who had presided at the meeting stayed on for the concert.

"What a mess!" said Sergei with chagrin as they were on their way back to the Revcom. "Zharky was right. We couldn't do anything with that Gymnasium crowd. It just makes you wild!"

"There's nothing to be surprised about," Ignatieva interrupted him. "There were hardly any proletarian youth there at all. Most of them were either sons of the petty bourgeois or local intellectuals—philistines all of them. You will have to work among the sawmill and sugar refinery workers. But that meeting was not altogether wasted. You'll find there are some very good comrades among the students."

Ustinovich agreed with Ignatieva.

"Our task, Seryozha," she said, "is to bring home our ideas, our slogans to everyone. The Party will focus the attention of all working people on every new event. We shall hold many meetings, conferences and congresses. The Political Department is opening a summer theatre at the station. A propaganda train is due to arrive in a few days and then we'll get things going in real earnest. Remember what Lenin said—we won't win unless we draw the masses, the millions of working people into the struggle."

Late that evening Sergei escorted Ustinovich to the station. On parting he clasped her hand firmly and held it a few seconds longer than absolutely necessary. A faint smile flitted across her face.

On his way back Sergei dropped in to see his people. He listened in silence to his mother's scolding, but when his father chimed in, Sergei took up the offensive and soon had Zakhar Vasilievich at a disadvantage.

"Now listen, dad, when you went on strike under the Germans and killed that sentry on the locomotive, you thought of your family, didn't you? Of course you did. But you went through with it just the same because your workingman's conscience told you to. I've also thought of the family. I know very well that if we retreat you folks will be persecuted because of me. And I couldn't sit at home anyway. You know how it is yourself, dad, so why all this fuss? I'm working for a good cause and you ought to back me up instead of kicking up a row. Come on, dad, let's make it up and then ma will stop scolding me too." He regarded

239

his father with his clear blue eyes and smiled affectionately, confident that he was in the right.

Zakhar Vasilievich stirred uneasily on the bench and through his thick bristling moustache and untidy little beard his yellowish teeth showed in a smile.

"Dragging class consciousness into it, eh, you young rascal? You think that revolver you're sporting is going to stop me from giving you a good hiding?"

But his voice held no hint of anger, and mastering his confusion, he held out his horny hand to his son. "Carry on, Seryozha. Once you've started up the gradient I'll not be putting on the brakes. But you mustn't forget us altogether, drop in once in a while."

It was night. A shaft of light from the slightly open door lay on the steps. Behind the huge lawyer's desk in the large room with its upholstered plush furniture sat five people: Dolinnik, Ignatieva, Cheka chief Timoshenko, looking like a Kirghiz in his Cossack fur cap, the giant railwayman Shudik and flat-nosed Ostapchuk from the railway yards. A meeting of the Revcom was in progress.

Dolinnik, leaning over the table and fixing Ignatieva with a stern look, hammered out hoarsely:

"The front must have supplies. The workers have to eat. As soon as we came the shopkeepers and market profiteers raised their prices. They won't take Soviet money. Old tsarist money or Kerensky notes are the only kind in circulation here. Today we must sit down and work out fixed prices. We know very well that none of the profiteers are going to sell their goods at the fixed price. They'll hide what they've got. In that case we'll make searches and confiscate the bloodsuckers' goods. This is no time for niceties. We can't let the workers starve any longer. Comrade Ignatieva warns us not to go too far. That's the reaction of a faint-hearted intellectual, if you ask me. Now don't take offence, Zoya, I know what I'm talking about. And in any case it isn't a matter of the petty traders. I have received information today that Boris Zon, the innkeeper, has a secret cellar in his house. Even before the Petlyura crowd came, the big shopowners had huge stocks of goods hidden away there." He paused to throw a sly, mocking glance at Timoshenko.

"How did you find that out?" the latter inquired, taken aback. He was annoyed at Dolinnik's being ahead of him with information which it was his, Timoshenko's, job to obtain.

Dolinnik chuckled. "I know everything, brother. Besides learning about the cellar, I happen to know that you and the Division Commander's chauffeur polished off half a bottle of *samogon* between you yesterday."

Timoshenko fidgeted in his chair and a flush spread over his sallow features.

"Good for you!" he exclaimed in unwilling admiration. But catching sight of Ignatieva's disapproving frown, he went no further. "That blasted carpenter has his own Cheka!" he thought to himself as he eyed the Chairman of the Revcom.

"Sergei Bruzzhak told me," Dolinnik went on. "He knows someone who used to work in the refreshment bar. Well, that lad heard from the cooks that Zon used to supply them with all they needed in unlimited quantities. Yesterday Sergei found out definitely about that cellar. All that has to be done now is to locate it. Get the boys on the job, Timoshenko, at once. Take Sergei along. If we strike lucky we'll be able to supply the workers and the division."

Half an hour later eight armed men entered the innkeeper's home. Two remained outside to guard the entrance.

The proprietor, a short stout man as round as a barrel, with a wooden leg and a face covered with a bristly growth of red hair, met the newcomers with obsequious politeness.

"What is it, Comrades?" he inquired in a husky bass. "Aren't you a bit late?"

Behind Zon, stood his daughters in hastily donned dressing-gowns, blinking in the glare of Timoshenko's flashlight. From the next room came the sighs and groans of Zon's buxom wife who was hurriedly dressing.

"We've come to search the house," Timoshenko explained curtly.

Every square inch of the floor was thoroughly examined. A spacious barn piled high with sawn wood, several pantries, the kitchen and a roomy cellar—all were inspected with the greatest care. But not a trace of the secret cellar was found.

In a tiny room off the kitchen the servant girl lay fast asleep. She slept so soundly that she did not hear them come in. Sergei wakened her gently.

"You work here?" he asked. The bewildered sleepy-eyed girl drew the blanket over her shoulders and shielded her eyes from the light.

"Yes," she replied. "Who are you?"

Sergei told her and, instructing her to get dressed, left the room.

In the spacious dining room Timoshenko was questioning the innkeeper who spluttered and fumed in great agitation:

"What do you want of me? I haven't got any more cellars. You're just wasting your time, I assure you. Yes, I did keep a tavern once but now I'm a poor man. The Petlyura crowd cleaned me out and very nearly killed me too. I am very glad the Soviets have come to power, but all I own is here for you to see," and he spread out his short pudgy hands, the while his bloodshot eyes darted from the face of the Cheka chief to Sergei and from Sergei to the corner and the ceiling.

Timoshenko bit his lips.

"So you won't tell, eh? For the last time I order you to show us where that cellar is."

"But, Comrade Officer, we've got nothing to eat ourselves," the innkeeper's wife wailed. "They've taken all we had." She made an attempt to weep but nothing came of it.

"You say you're starving, but you keep a servant," Sergei put in.

"That's not a servant. She's just a poor girl who's living with us, because she has nowhere to go. Khristina'll tell you that herself."

Timoshenko's patience snapped. "All right then," he shouted, "now we'll set to work in earnest!"

Morning dawned and the search was still going on. Exasperated after thirteen hours of fruitless efforts, Timoshenko had already decided to abandon the quest when Sergei, on the point of leaving the servant girl's room he had been examining, heard the girl's faint whisper behind him: "Look inside the stove in the kitchen."

Ten minutes later the dismantled Russian stove revealed an iron trapdoor. And within an hour a two-ton truck loaded with barrels and sacks drove away from the inn now surrounded by a crowd of gaping onlookers.

Maria Yakovlevna Korchagina came home one hot day carrying her small bundle of belongings. She wept bitterly when Artem told her what had happened to Pavel. Her life now seemed empty and drear. She had to look for work, and after a time she began taking in washing from Red Army men who arranged for her to receive soldiers' rations by way of payment.

One evening she heard Artem's footsteps outside the window sounding more hurried than usual. He pushed open the door and announced from the threshold: "I've brought a letter from Pavka."

"Dear Brother Artem," wrote Pavel. "This is to let you know, that I am alive although not altogether well. I got a bullet in my hip but I am getting better now. The doctor says the bone is uninjured. So don't worry about me, I'll be all right. I may get leave after I'm discharged from hospital and I'll come home for a while. I didn't manage to get to mother's, what happened was that I joined the cavalry brigade commanded by Comrade Kotovsky, whom I'm sure you've heard about because he's famous for his bravery. I have never seen anyone like him before and I have the greatest respect for our commander. Has mother come home yet? If she has, give her my best love. Forgive me for all the trouble I have caused you. Your brother Pavel.

"Artem, please go to the forest warden's and tell them about this letter."

Maria Yakovlevna shed many tears over Pavel's letter. The scatterbrained lad had not even given the address of his hospital.

Sergei had become a frequent visitor at the green railway coach down at the station bearing the sign: "Agitprop Div. Pol. Dept." In one of the compartments of the Agitation and Propaganda Car, Ustinovich and Ignatieva had their office. The latter with the inevitable cigarette between her lips smiled knowingly whenever he appeared.

The Secretary of the Komsomol District Committee had grown quite friendly with Rita Ustinovich, and besides the bundles of books and newspapers, he carried away with him from the station a vague sense of happiness after every brief encounter with her.

Every day the open-air theatre of the Division Political Department drew big audiences of workers and Red Army men. The agit-train of the Twelfth Army, swathed in bright coloured posters, stood on a siding, seething with activity twenty-four hours a day. A printing plant had been installed inside and newspapers, leaflets and proclamations poured out in a steady stream. The front was near at hand.

One evening Sergei chanced to drop in at the theatre and found Rita there with a group of Red Army men. Late that night as he was seeing her home to the station where the Political Department staff was quartered, he blurted out: "Why do I always want to be seeing you, Comrade Rita?" And added: "It's so nice to be with you! After seeing you I always feel I could go on working without stopping."

Rita halted. "Now look here, Comrade Bruzzhak," she said, "let's agree here and now that you won't ever wax lyrical any more. I don't like it."

Sergei blushed like a reprimanded schoolboy.

"I didn't mean anything," he said, "I thought we were friends ... I didn't say anything counterrevolutionary, did I? Very well, Comrade Ustinovich, I shan't say another word!"

And leaving her with a hasty handshake he all but ran back to town.

Sergei did not go near the station for several days. When Ignatieva asked him to come he refused on the grounds that he was too busy. As a matter of fact he was.

Shudik was fired at as he was passing on his way home one night through a street inhabited mainly by Poles in managerial positions at the sugar refinery. The searches that followed brought to light weapons and documents belonging to a Pilsudski organization known as the Strelets.

A conference was called at the Revcom. Ustinovich, who was present, took Sergei aside and said in a calm voice: "So your philistine vanity was hurt, was it? You're letting personal matters interfere with your work? That won't do, Comrade."

And so Sergei resumed his visits to the green railway car.

He attended a district conference and participated in the heated debates that lasted for two days. On the third day he went off with the rest of the conference delegates to the forest beyond the river and spent a day and a night fighting bandits led by Zarudny, one of Petlyura's officers still at large.

On his return he went to see Ignatieva and found Ustinovich there. Afterwards he saw her home to the station and on parting held her hand tightly. She drew it away angrily. Again Sergei kept away from the agitprop car for many days and avoided seeing Rita even on business. And when she would demand an explanation of his behaviour he would reply curtly: "What's the use of talking to you? You'll only accuse me of being a philistine or a traitor to the working class or something."

Trains carrying the Caucasian Red Banner Division pulled in at the station. Three swarthy-complexioned commanders came over to the Revcom. One of them, a tall slim man wearing a belt of chased silver, went straight up to Dolinnik and demanded in a tone that brooked no refusal: "No argument now. Fork out one hundred cartloads of hay. My horses are dying."

And so Sergei was sent with two Red Army men to procure hay. In one village they were attacked by a band of kulaks. The Red Army men were disarmed and beaten unmercifully. Sergei got off lightly because of his youth. All three were carted back to town by people from the Poor Peasants' Committee.

An armed detachment was sent out to the village and the hay was delivered the following day.

Not wishing to alarm his family, Sergei stayed at Ignatieva's place until he recovered from the effects of his misadventure. Rita Ustinovich came to visit him there and for the first time she pressed Sergei's hand with a warmth and tenderness he himself would never have risked.

One hot afternoon Sergei dropped in at the agitcar to see Rita. He read her Pavel's letter and told her something about his friend. On his way out he threw over his shoulder: "I think I'll go to the woods and take a dip in the lake."

Rita looked up from her work. "Wait for me. I'll come with you."

The lake was as smooth and placid as a mirror. Its warm translucent water exhuded an inviting freshness.

"Wait for me over by the road. I'm going in," Rita ordered him.

Sergei sat down on a boulder by the bridge and lifted his face to the sun. He could hear her splashing in the water behind him.

Presently through the trees he caught sight of Tonya Tumanova and Chuzhanin, the Military Commissar of the agit-train, coming down the road arm-in-arm. Chuzhanin, in his well-made officer's uniform with its smart leather belt and numberless straps and squeaking chrome-leather boots, cut a dashing figure. He was in earnest conversation with Tonya.

Sergei recognized Tonya as the girl who had brought him the note from Pavel. She too looked hard at him as they approached. She seemed to be trying to place him. When they came abreast of him Sergei took Pavel's last letter out of his pocket and went up to her.

"Just a moment, Comrade. I have a letter here which concerns you partly."

Pulling her hand free Tonya took the letter. The slip of paper trembled slightly in her hand as she read.

"Have you had any more news from him?" she asked, handing the letter back to Sergei.

"No," he replied.

At that moment the pebbles crunched under Rita's feet and Chuzhanin, who had been unaware of her presence, bent over and whispered to Tonya: "We'd better go."

But Rita's mocking, scornful voice stopped him.

"Comrade Chuzhanin! They've been looking for you over at the train all day."

Chuzhanin eyed her with dislike.

"Never mind," he said surlily. "They'll manage without me."

Rita watched Tonya and the Military Commissar go.

"It's high time that good-for-nothing was sent packing!" she observed drily.

The forest murmured as the breeze stirred the mighty crowns of the oaks. A delicious freshness was wafted from the lake. Sergei decided to go in.

When he came back from his swim he found Rita sitting on a treetrunk not far from the road. They wandered, talking, into the depths of the woods. In a small glade with tall thick grass they paused to rest. It was peaceful in the forest. The oaks whispered to one another. Rita threw herself down on the soft grass and clasped her hands under her head. Her shapely legs in their old patched boots were hidden in the tall grass.

Sergei's eye chanced to fall on her feet. He noticed the neatly patched boots, then looked down at his own boot with the toe sticking out of a hole, and he laughed.

251

"What are you laughing at?" she asked.

Sergei pointed to his boot. "How are we going to fight in boots like these?"

Rita did not reply. She was chewing a blade of grass and her thoughts were obviously elsewhere.

"Chuzhanin is a rotten Party member," she said at last. "All our political workers go about in rags but he doesn't think of anybody but himself. He does not belong in the Party.... As for the front, the situation there is really very serious. Our country has a long and bitter fight before it." She paused, then added. "We shall have to fight with both words and rifles, Sergei. Have you heard about the Central Committee's decision to draft one-fourth of the Komsomol into the army? If you ask me, Sergei, we shan't be here for long."

Listening to her, Sergei was surprised to detect some new note in her voice. With her black limpid eyes upon him, he was ready to throw discretion to the winds and tell her that her eyes were like mirrors, but he checked himself in time.

Rita raised herself on her elbow. "Where's your pistol?"

Sergei fingered his belt ruefully. "That kulak band took it away from me."

Rita put her hand into the pocket of her tunic and brought out a gleaming automatic pistol.

"See that oak, Sergei?" she pointed the muzzle at

a furrowed trunk about twenty-five paces from where they lay. And raising the weapon to the level of her eyes she fired almost without taking aim. The splintered bark showered down.

"See?" she said much pleased with herself and fired again. And again the bark splintered and fell in the grass.

"Here," she handed him the weapon with a mocking smile. "Now let's see what you can do."

Sergei muffed one out of three shots. Rita smiled condescendingly. "I thought you'd do worse."

She put down the pistol and stretched out on the grass. Her tunic stretched tightly over her firm breasts.

"Sergei," she said softly. "Come here."

He moved closer.

"Look at the sky. See how blue it is. Your eyes are that colour. And that's bad. They ought to be grey, like steel. Blue is much too soft a colour."

And suddenly clasping his blond head, she kissed him on the lips.

Two months passed. Autumn arrived.

Night crept up stealthily, enveloping the trees in its dark shroud. The telegraphist at Division Headquarters bent over his apparatus which was ticking out Morse and gathering up the long narrow ribbon that wound itself snakily beneath his fingers rapidly translated the dots and dashes into words and phrases:

"Chief of Staff First Division Copy to Chairman Revcom Shepetovka. Evacuate all official institutions in town within ten hours after receipt of this wire. Leave one battalion in town at disposal of commander N. regiment in command sector of front. Division Headquarters, Political Department, all military institutions to be moved to Baranchev station. Report execution of order to Division Commander.

"(Signed)"

Ten minutes later a motorcycle was hurtling through the slumbering streets of the town, its acetylene headlight stabbing the darkness. It stopped, spluttering, outside the gates of the Revcom. The rider hurried inside and handed the telegram to the chairman, Dolinnik. At once the place was seething with activity. The special-duty company lined up. An hour later carts loaded with Revcom property were rumbling through the town to the Podolsk station where it was loaded into railway cars.

When he learned the contents of the telegram Sergei ran out after the motorcyclist.

"Can you give me a lift to the station, Comrade?" he asked the rider.

"Climb on behind, but mind you hold on fast."

A dozen paces from the agitcar which had already been attached to the train Sergei saw Rita. He seized her by the shoulders and, conscious that he was about to lose something that had grown ineffably dear and precious to him, whispered: "Goodbye, Rita, dear comrade! We'll meet again sometime. Don't forget me."

To his horror he felt the tears choking him. He must go at once. Not trusting himself to speak, he wrung her hand until it hurt.

Morning found the town and station desolate and deserted. The last train had blown its whistle as if in farewell and pulled out, and now the rearguard battalion which had been left behind took up positions on either side of the tracks.

Yellow leaves fluttered down from the trees leaving the branches bare. The wind caught the fallen leaves and swept them rustling along the paths.

Sergei in a Red Army greatcoat, with canvas cartridge belts slung over his shoulders, occupied the crossing opposite the sugar refinery with a dozen Red Army men. The Poles were approaching.

Avtonom Petrovich knocked at the door of his neighbour Gerasim Leontievich. The latter, not yet dressed, poked his head out of the door.

"What's up?"

Avtonom Petrovich pointed to the Red Army men moving down the street, and winked: "They're clearing out."

Gerasim Leontievich looked at him with a worried air: "What sort of emblem do the Poles have, do you know?"

"A single-headed eagle, I believe."

"Where the devil can you find one?"

Avtonom Petrovich scratched his head in consternation.

"It's all right for them," he said after a moment or two of reflection. "They just get up and go. But you have to worry your head about getting in right with the new authorities."

The rattle of a machine gun tore into the silence. A locomotive whistle sounded unexpectedly from the station followed by the detonation of a gun from the same quarter. A heavy shell bored its way high into the air with a loud whine and fell on the road beyond the refinery, enveloping the roadside shrubs in a cloud of blue smoke. Silent and grim the retreating Red Army troops marched through the street, turning frequently to look back as they went.

A tear traced a chill path down Sergei's cheek. Quickly he wiped it away, glancing furtively at his comrades to make sure that no one had seen it. Beside Sergei marched Antek Klopotowski, a lanky sawmill worker. His finger rested on the trigger of his rifle. Antek was gloomy and preoccupied. His eyes meeting Sergei's, he confided the thoughts that were tormenting him.

"They'll come down hard on our folks, especially mine because we're Poles. You, a Pole, they'll say, opposing the Polish Legion. They're sure to kick my old man out of the sawmill and flog him. I told him to come with us, but he didn't have the heart to leave the family. Hell, I can't wait to get my hands on those accursed swine!" And Antek angrily pushed back the helmet that had slipped down over his eyes.

...Farewell dear old town, unsightly and dirty though you are with your ugly little houses and your crooked roads. Farewell dear ones, farewell. Farewell Valya and the comrades who have remained to work in the underground. The Polish Whiteguard legions, alien, vicious and merciless, are approaching.

Sadly the railway workers in their oil-stained shirts watched the Red Army men go.

"We'll be back, Comrades!" Sergei cried out with aching heart.

CHAPTER EIGHT

The river gleams dully through the early morning haze; softly its waters gurgle against the smooth pebbles of the banks. In the shallows by the banks the river is calm, its silvery surface almost unruffled; but out in midstream it is dark and restless, hurrying swiftly onward. A thing of majestic beauty, this river immortalized by Gogol. The tall right bank drops steeply down to the water, like a mountain halted in its advance by the broad sweep of the waters. The flat left bank below is covered with sandy spots left when the water receded after the spring floods.

Five men lay beside a snub-nosed Maxim gun in a tiny trench dug into the river bank. This was a forward outpost of the Seventh Rifle Division. Nearest the gun and facing the river lay Sergei Bruzzhak.

The day before, worn out by the endless battles and swept back by a hurricane of Polish artillery fire, they had given up Kiev, withdrawn to the left bank of the river, and dug in there.

The retreat, the heavy losses and finally the surrender of Kiev to the enemy had been a bitter blow to the men. The Seventh Division had heroically fought its way through enemy encirclement and, advancing through the forests, had emerged on the railway line at Malin Station, and with one furious blow had hurled back the Polish forces and cleared the road to Kiev.

But the lovely city had been given up and the Red Army men mourned its loss.

The Poles, having driven the Red units out of Darnitsa, now occupied a small bridgehead on the left bank of the river beside the railway bridge. But furious counterattacks had frustrated all their efforts to advance beyond that point.

As he watched the river flowing past, Sergei could not but think of what had happened the previous day.

Yesterday, at noon, his unit had met the Poles with a furious counterattack; yesterday he had had his first hand-to-hand engagement with the enemy. A beardless Polish legionary had come swooping down upon him, his rifle with its long, sabre-like French bayonet thrust forward; he bounded toward Sergei like a hare, shouting something unintelligible. For a fraction of a second Sergei saw his eyes dilated with frenzy. The next instant Sergei's bayonet clashed with the Pole's, and the shining French blade was thrust aside. The Pole fell. . . .

Sergei's hand did not falter. He knew that he would have to go on killing, he, Sergei, who was capable of such tender love, such steadfast friendship. He was not vicious or cruel by nature, but he knew that he must fight these misguided soldiers whom the world's parasites had whipped up into a frenzy of bestial hatred and sent against his native land. And he, Sergei, would kill in order to hasten the day when men would no longer kill one another.

Paramonov tapped him on the shoulder. "We'd better be moving on, Sergei, or they'll spot us."

For a year now Pavel Korchagin had travelled up and down his native land, riding on machine-gun carriages and gun caissons or astride a small grey mare with a nick in her ear. He was a grown man now, matured and hardened by suffering and privation. The tender skin chafed to the raw by the heavy cartridge belt had long since healed and a hard callous had formed under the rifle strap on his shoulder.

Pavel had seen much that was terrible in that year. Together with thousands of other fighting men as ragged and ill-clad as himself but afire with the indomitable determination to fight for the power of their class, he had marched over the length and breadth of his native land and only twice had the storm swept on without him: the first time when he was wounded in the hip, and the second, when in the bitterly cold February of 1920 he sweltered in the sticky heat of typhus.

The typhus took a more fearful toll of the regiments and divisions of the Twelfth Army than Polish machine guns. By that time the Twelfth Army was operating over a vast territory stretching across nearly the whole of the Northern Ukraine blocking the further advance of the Poles.

Pavel had barely recovered from his illness when he returned to his unit which was now holding the station of Frontovka, on the Kazatin-Uman branch line. Frontovka stood in the forest and consisted of a small station building with a few wrecked and abandoned cottages around it. Three years of intermittent battles had made civilian life in these parts impossible. Frontovka had changed hands times without number.

Big events were brewing again. At the time when the Twelfth Army, its ranks fearfully depleted and partly disorganized, was falling back to Kiev under the pressure of the Polish armies, the proletarian republic was mustering its forces to strike a crushing blow at the victory-drunk Polish Whites.

The battle-seasoned divisions of the First Cavalry Army were being transferred to the Ukraine all the way from the North Caucasus in a campaign unparalleled in military history. The Fourth, Sixth, Eleventh and Fourteenth Cavalry divisions moved up one after another to the Uman area, concentrating in the rear of the front and sweeping away the Makhno bandits on their way to the scene of decisive battles.

Sixteen and a half thousand sabres, sixteen and a half thousand fighting men tanned and weathered by the blazing steppe sun.

To prevent this decisive blow from being thwarted by the enemy was the primary concern of the Supreme Command of the Red Army and the Command of the Southwestern Front at this juncture. Everything was done to ensure the successful concentration of this huge mounted force. Active operations were suspended on the Uman sector. The direct telegraph lines from Moscow to the front headquarters in Kharkov and thence to the headquarters of the Fourteenth and Twelfth armies hummed incessantly. Telegraph operators tapped out coded orders: "Divert attention Poles from concentration cavalry army." The enemy was actively engaged only when the Polish advance threatened to involve the Budyonny cavalry divisions.

The campfire shot up red tongues of flame. Dark spirals of smoke curled up from the fire, driving off the swarms of restless buzzing midges. The men lay in a semicircle around the fire whose reflection cast a coppery glow on their faces. The water bubbled in messtins set in the bluish-grey ashes.

A stray tongue of flame leaped out suddenly from beneath a burning log and licked at someone's tousled head. The head was jerked away with a growl: "Damnation!" And a gust of laughter rose from the men grouped around the fire.

A middle-aged man with clipped moustache wearing a serge tunic examined the muzzle of his rifle in the firelight and boomed:

"The lad's so full of book-learning he don't feel the heat of the fire."

"You might tell the rest of us what you're reading there, Korchagin?" someone suggested.

The young Red Army man fingered his singed locks and smiled.

"A real good book, Comrade Androshchuk. Just can't tear myself away from it."

"What's it about?" inquired a snub-nosed lad sitting next to Korchagin, laboriously repairing the

262

strap of his pouch. He bit off the coarse thread, wound the remainder round the needle and stuck it inside his helmet. "If it's about love I'm your man."

A loud guffaw greeted this remark. Matveichuk raised his close-cropped head and winked slyly at the snub-nosed lad: "Love's a fine thing, Sereda," he said. "And you're such a handsome lad, a regular picture. Wherever we go the girls fairly wear their shoes out running after you. Too bad a handsome phiz like yours should be spoiled by one little defect: you've got a five-kopek piece instead of a nose. But that's easily remedied. Just hang a Novitsky 10-pounder* on the end of it overnight and in the morning it'll be all right."

The roar of laughter that followed this sally caused the horses tethered to the machine-gun carriers to whinny in fright.

Sereda glanced nonchalantly over his shoulder. "It's not your face but what you've got in your noodle that counts," he tapped himself on the forehead expressively. "Take you, you've got a tongue like a stinging nettle but you're no better than a donkey, and your ears are cold."

"Now then lads, what's the sense in getting riled?" Tatarinov, the Section Commander, admonished the two who were ready to fly at each other. "Better let

---

* The Novitsky grenade weighing about four kilograms and used to demolish wire entanglements.

263

Korchagin read to us if he's got something worth listening to."

"That's right. Go to it, Pavlushka!" the men urged from all sides.

Pavel moved a saddle closer to the fire, settled himself on it and opened the small thick volume resting on his knees.

"The book is called *The Gadfly*, Comrades. The Battalion Commissar gave it to me. It's got me, Comrades. If you'll sit quietly I'll read it to you."

"Fire away! And don't worry, we won't let anyone disturb us."

When some time later Comrade Puzyrevsky, the Regimental Commander, rode up unnoticed to the campfire with his Commissar he saw eleven pairs of eyes glued to the reader. He turned to the Commissar:

"There you have half of the regiment's scouts," he said, pointing to the group of men. "Four of them are raw young Komsomols, but they're good soldiers all of them. The one who's reading is Korchagin, and that one there with eyes like a wolfcub is Zharky. They're friends, but they're always competing with each other on the quiet. Korchagin used to be my best scout. Now he has a very serious rival. What they're doing just now is political work, and very effective it is too. I hear these youngsters are called 'the young guard.' Most appropriate, in my opinion."

"Is that the political instructor reading?" the Commissar asked.

"No. Kramer is the political instructor." Puzyrevsky spurred his horse forward.

"Greetings, Comrades!" he called.

All heads turned toward the commander as he sprang lightly from the saddle and went up to the group.

"Warming yourselves, friends?" he said with a broad smile and his strong face with the narrow, slightly Mongolian eyes lost its severity. The men greeted their commander warmly as they would a good comrade and friend. The Commissar, who intended to ride on, did not dismount.

Pushing aside his pistol in its holster, Puzyrevsky sat down next to Korchagin.

"Shall we have a smoke?" he suggested. "I have some first-rate tobacco here."

He rolled a cigarette, lit it and turned to the Commissar: "You go ahead, Doronin, I'll stay here for a while. If I'm needed at headquarters you can let me know."

"Go on reading, I'll listen too," Puzyrevsky said to Korchagin when Doronin had gone.

Pavel read to the end, laid the book down on his knees and gazed pensively at the fire. For a few moments no one spoke. All brooded on the tragic fate of the Gadfly. Puzyrevsky puffed on his cigarette, waiting for the discussion to begin.

"A grim story that," said Sereda, breaking the silence. "So there are people like that in the world. Few men could stand what he did. But when a man has an idea to fight for he's strong enough to stand anything." Sereda was visibly moved. The book had made a deep impression on him.

"If I could lay my hands on that priest who tried to shove a cross down his throat I'd finish the swine off on the spot!" Andryusha Fomichev, a shoemaker's apprentice from Belaya Tserkov, cried wrathfully.

"A man doesn't mind dying if he has something to die for," Androshchuk, pushing one of the pots closer to the fire with a stick, said in a tone of conviction. "That's what gives a man strength. You can die without regrets if you know you're in the right. That's how heroes are made. I knew a lad once. Poraika was his name. Well, when the Whites cornered him in Odessa, he tackled a whole platoon singlehanded and before they could get at him with their bayonets he blew himself and the whole lot of them up with a grenade. And he wasn't anything much to look at. Not the kind of a fellow you read about in books, though he'd be well worth writing about. There's plenty of fine lads to be found among our kind."

He stirred the contents of the messtin with a spoon, tasted it with pursed-up lips and continued:

"There are some who die a dog's death, a mean, dishonourable death. I'll tell you something that happened during the fighting at Izyaslav. That's an old town on the Goryn River built back in the time of the princes. There was a Polish church there, built like a fortress. Well, we entered that town and advanced single file along the crooked alleys. A company of Letts were holding our right flank. When we get to the highway what do we see but three saddled horses tied to the fence of one of the houses. Aha, we think, here's where we bag some Poles! About ten of us rushed into the yard. In front of us ran the commander of that Lettish company, waving his Mauser.

"The front door was open and we ran in. But instead of Poles we found our own men in there. A mounted patrol it was. They'd got in ahead of us. It wasn't a pretty sight we laid eyes on there. They were abusing a woman, the wife of the Polish officer who lived there. When the Lett saw what was going on he shouted something in his own language. His men grabbed the three and dragged them outside. There were only two of us Russians, the rest were Letts. Their commander was a man by the name of Bredis. I don't understand their language but I could see he'd given orders to finish those fellows off. They're tough lot those Letts, unflinching. They dragged those three out to the stables. I could see their goose was cooked. One of them, a great hulking fellow with a mug that just asked for a brick, was kicking and struggling for all he was worth. They couldn't put him up against the wall just because of a wench, he yelped. The others were begging for mercy too.

"I broke out into a cold sweat. I ran over to Bredis and said: 'Comrade Company Commander,' I said, 'let the tribunal try them. What do you want to dirty your hands with their blood for? The fighting isn't over in the town and here we are wasting time with this here scum.' He turned on me with eyes blazing like a tiger's. Believe me, I was sorry I spoke. He points his gun at me. I've been fighting for seven years but I admit I was properly scared that minute. I see he's ready to shoot first and ask questions afterwards. He yells at me in bad Russian so I could hardly understand what he was saying: 'Our banner is dyed with our blood,' he says. 'These men are a disgrace to the whole army. The penalty for banditry is death.'

"I couldn't stand it any more and I ran out of that yard into the street as fast as I could and behind me I heard them shooting. I knew those three were done for. By the time we got back to the others the town was already ours.

"That's what I mean by a dog's death, the way those fellows died. The patrol was one of those that'd joined us at Melitopol. They'd been with Makhno at one time. Riffraff, that's what they were."

Androshchuk stood his messtin beside him and proceeded to untie his bread bag.

"You do come across scum like that on our side sometimes. You can't account for everyone. On the face of it they're all for the revolution. And through them we all get a bad name. But that was a nasty thing to see, I tell you. I shan't forget it in a hurry," he wound up, sipping his tea.

Night was well advanced by the time the camp was asleep. Sereda's whistling snores could be heard in the silence. Puzyrevsky slept with his head resting on the saddle. Kramer, the political instructor, sat scribbling in his notebook.

Returning the next day from a scouting detail, Pavel tethered his horse to a tree and called over Kramer, who had just finished drinking tea.

"Look, Kramer, what would you say if I switched over to the First Cavalry Army, eh? There's going to be big doings there by the looks of it. They're not being massed in such numbers just for fun, are they? And we here won't be seeing much of it."

Kramer looked at him in surprise.

"Switch over? Do you think you can change units in the army the way you change seats in a cinema?"

"But what difference does it make where a man fights?" Pavel interposed. "I'm not deserting to the rear, am I?"

But Kramer was categorically opposed to the idea.

269

"What about discipline? You're not a bad young-ster, Pavel, on the whole, but in some things you're a bit of an anarchist. You think you can do as you please? You forget, my lad, that the Party and the Komsomol are founded on iron discipline. The Party must come first. And each one of us must be where he is most needed and not where he wants to be. Puzyrevsky turned down your application for a trans-fer, didn't he? Well, there's your answer."

Kramer spoke with such agitation that he was seized with a fit of coughing. This tall, gaunt man was a printer by profession and the lead dust had lodged itself firmly in his lungs and often a hectic flush would appear on his waxen cheeks.

When he had calmed down, Pavel said in a low but firm voice:

"All that is quite correct but I'm going over to the Budyonny army just the same."

The next evening Pavel was missing at the camp-fire.

In the neighbouring village a group of Budyonny cavalrymen had formed a wide circle on a hill outside the schoolhouse. One giant of a fellow, seated on the back of a machine-gun carrier, his cap pushed to the back of his head, was playing an accordion. The instru-ment wailed and blared out of time under his inept fingers like a thing in torment, confusing the dashing cavalryman in unbelievably wide red riding breeches who was dancing a mad hopak in the centre of the ring.

Eager-eyed village lads and lasses clambered on to the gun carrier and fences to watch the antics of these troopers whose brigade had just entered their village.

"Go it, Toptalo! Kick up the earth! Ekh, that's the stuff, brother! Come on there, you with the accordion, make it hot!"

But the player's huge fingers that could bend an iron horseshoe with the utmost ease sprawled clumsily over the keys.

"Too bad Makhno got Afanasi Kulyabka," remarked one bronzed cavalryman regretfully. "That lad was a first-class accordion player. He rode on the right flank of our squadron. Too bad he was killed. A good soldier and the best accordion player we ever had!"

Pavel, who was standing in the circle, overheard this last remark. He pushed his way over to the machine-gun carrier and laid his hand on the accordion bellows. The music subsided.

"What d'you want?" the accordionist demanded with a scowl.

Toptalo stopped short and an angry murmur rose from the crowd: "What's the trouble there?"

Pavel reached out for the instrument. "Let's have a try," he said.

The Budyonny cavalryman looked at the Red infantryman with some mistrust and reluctantly slipped the accordion strap off his shoulder.

With an accustomed gesture Pavel laid the instrument on his knee, spread the sinuous bellows out fanwise and let go with a rollicking melody that poured forth with all the lusty vigour of which the accordion is capable:

> *Ekh, little apple,*
> *Whither away?*
> *Get copped by the Cheka*
> *And that's where you stay!*

Toptalo caught up the familiar tune and swinging his arms like some great bird he swept into the ring, executing the most incredible twists and turns, and slapping himself smartly on the thighs, knees, head, forehead, the shoe soles, and finally on the mouth in time with the music.

Faster and faster played the accordion in a mad intoxicating rhythm, and Toptalo, kicking his legs out wildly, spun around the circle like a top until he was quite out of breath.

On June 5, 1920, after a few brief but furious encounters Budyonny's First Cavalry Army broke through the Polish front between the Third and Fourth Polish armies, smashed a cavalry brigade under General Sa-

wicki stationed on its path and swept on toward Ruzhiny.

The Polish command hastily formed a striking force and threw it into the breach. Five tanks were rushed from Pogrebishche Station to the scene of the fighting. But the Cavalry Army by-passed Zarudnitsy from where the Poles planned to strike and came out in the Polish rear.

General Kornicki's Cavalry Division was dispatched in pursuit of the First Cavalry Army with orders to strike at the rear of the force, which the Polish command believed to be headed for Kazatin, one of the most important strategic points in the Polish rear. This move, however, did not improve the position of the Poles. Although they succeeded in closing the breach and cutting off the Cavalry Army, the presence of a strong mounted force behind their lines which threatened to destroy their rear bases and swoop down on their army group at Kiev was far from reassuring. As they advanced, the Red cavalry divisions destroyed small railway bridges and tore up railway track to hamper the Polish retreat.

On learning from prisoners that the Poles had an army headquarters in Zhitomir (actually the headquarters of the whole front was located there), the commander of the First Cavalry Army decided to take Zhitomir and Berdichev, both important railway junctions and administrative centres. At dawn on June 7 the Fourth Cavalry Division was already on its way at full speed to Zhitomir.

Korchagin now rode on the right flank of one of the squadrons in place of Kulyabko, the lamented accordionist. He had been enrolled in the squadron on the collective request of the men, who had not wanted to part with such an excellent accordion player.

Without checking their foam-flecked horses they fanned out at Zhitomir and bore down on the city with naked steel flashing in the sun.

The earth groaned under the pounding hooves, the mounts breathed hoarsely, and the men rose in their stirrups.

Underfoot the ground sped past and ahead the large city with its gardens and parks hurried to meet the division. The mounted avalanche flashed by the gardens and poured into the centre of the city, and the air was rent by a fear-inspiring battlecry as inexorable as death itself.

The Poles were so stunned that they offered little resistance. The local garrison was crushed.

Bending low over the neck of his mount, Korchagin sped along side by side with Toptalo astride his thin-shanked black. Pavel saw how the dashing cavalryman cut down with an unerring blow a Polish legionary before the man had time to raise his rifle to his shoulder.

The iron-shod hooves grated on the paving stones as they careered down the street. Then, at an intersection they found themselves face to face with a machine gun planted in the very middle of the road and three men in blue uniforms and rectangular Polish caps bending over it. There was also a fourth, with coils of gold braid on his collar, who levelled a Mauser at the mounted men.

Neither Toptalo nor Pavel could check their horses and they galloped toward the machine gun, straight into the jaws of death. The officer fired at Korchagin, but missed. The bullet whanged past Pavel's cheek, and the next moment the Lieutenant had struck his head against the paving stones and was lying limp on his back, thrown off his feet by the horse's onrush.

That very moment the machine gun crackled in savage, feverish haste, and stung by a dozen leaden wasps Toptalo and his black crumpled to the ground.

Pavel's mount reared up on its hind legs, snorting with terror, and leapt with its rider over the prone bodies to the men at the machine gun. His sabre described a flashing arc in the air and sank into the blue rectangle of one of the army caps.

Again the sabre flashed upwards ready to descend upon a second head, but the frantic horse leapt aside.

Like a turbulent mountain stream the squadron now poured in at the street intersection and scores of sabres gleamed in the air.

The long narrow corridors of the prison echoed with cries.

The cells packed with men and women with gaunt, tormented faces were in a turmoil. They knew there was fighting going on in the city, and they could hardly believe that this meant freedom, that the attackers that had so suddenly descended on the place were their own people.

There was firing in the prison yard. Men running down the corridors. And then the cherished, poignantly familiar words: "You are free, Comrades!"

Pavel ran to a locked door with a tiny window to which dozens of pairs of eyes were glued, and brought his rifle butt down fiercely against the lock again and again.

"Wait, let me crack it with a bomb," Mironov pushed Pavel aside and produced a hand grenade from a pocket.

Platoon commander Tsygarchenko tore the grenade from his hands.

"Stop, you fool, are you mad! They'll bring the keys in a jiffy. What we can't break down we'll open with keys."

The prison guards were already being led down the corridor, prodded along with revolvers. Then the passage filled with ragged and unwashed men and women wild with joy.

Throwing the cell door wide open, Pavel ran inside.

"Comrades, you're free! We're Budyonny's men—our division's taken the town!"

A woman her eyes brimming with tears ran to Pavel and throwing her arms around him as if she had found someone near and dear to her, broke into sobs.

The liberation of five thousand and seventy-one Bolsheviks whom the Polish Whites had driven into these stone dungeons to await shooting or the gallows and of two thousand Red Army political workers, was more important to the division's fighting men than all the trophies they had captured, a greater reward than victory itself. For seven thousand revolutionaries the impenetrable gloom of night had been supplanted by the bright sun of a hot June day.

One of the prisoners, with skin as yellow as a lemon, rushed at Pavel in a transport of joy. It was Samuel Lekher, one of the compositors from the Shepetovka printshop.

Pavel's face turned grey as he listened to Samuel's account of the bloody tragedy enacted in his native town and the words seered his heart like drops of molten metal.

"They took us at night, all of us at once. Some scoundrel had betrayed us to the military gendarmerie. And once they had us in their clutches they showed no

277

mercy. They beat us terribly, Pavel. I suffered less than the others because after the first few blows I dropped down unconscious. But the others were stronger than me.

"We had nothing to hide. The gendarmes knew everything better than we did. They knew every step we had taken, and no wonder for there had been a traitor among us! I can't talk about those days, Pavel. You know many of those who were taken. Valya Bruzzhak, and Rosa Gritsman, a fine girl just turned seventeen—such trusting eyes she had, Pavel! Then there was Sasha Bunshaft, you know him, one of our typesetters, a merry lad, always drawing caricatures of the boss. They took him and two Gymnasium students, Novoselsky and Tuzhits—you remember them too most likely. The others too were local people or from the district centre. Altogether twenty-nine were arrested, six of them women. They were all brutally tortured. Valya and Rosa were raped the first day. Those swine outraged the poor things in every possible way, then dragged them back to the cell more dead than alive. Soon after that Rosa began to rave and a few days later she was completely out of her mind.

"They didn't believe that she was insane, they said she was shamming and beat her unmercifully every time they questioned her. She was a terrible sight when they finally shot her. Her face was black with bruises, her eyes were wild, she looked like an old woman.

278

"Valya Bruzzhak was splendid to the very end. They all died like real fighters. I don't know how they had the strength to endure it all. Ah, Pavel, how can I describe their death to you? It was too horrible.

"Valya had been doing the most dangerous kind of work: she was the one who kept in touch with the wireless operators at the Polish headquarters and with our people in the district centre, besides which they found two grenades and a pistol when they searched her place. The grenades had been given to her by the provocateur. Everything had been framed so as to charge them with intending to blow up the headquarters.

"Ah, Pavel, it is painful for me to speak of those last days, but since you insist I shall tell you. The military court sentenced Valya and two others to be hanged, the rest to be shot. The Polish soldiers who had worked with us were tried two days earlier. Corporal Snegurko, a young wireless operator who had worked in Lodz as an electrician before the war, was charged with treason and with conducting Communist propaganda among the soldiers and sentenced to be shot. He did not appeal, and was shot twenty-four hours after the sentence.

"Valya was called in to give evidence at his trial. She told us afterwards that Snegurko pleaded guilty to the charge of conducting Communist propaganda but vigorously denied that he had betrayed his country.

279

'My fatherland,' he said, 'is the Polish Soviet Socialist Republic. Yes, I am a member of the Communist Party of Poland. I was drafted into the army against my will, and once there I did my best to open the eyes of other men like myself who had been driven off to the front. You may hang me for that, but not for being a traitor to my fatherland, for that I never was and never will be. Your fatherland is not my fatherland. Yours is the fatherland of the gentry, mine is the workers' and peasants' fatherland. And in my fatherland, which will come—of that I am deeply convinced—no one will ever call me a traitor.'

"After the trial we were all kept together. Just before the execution we were transferred to the jail. During the night they set up the gallows opposite the prison beside the hospital. For the shooting they chose a place near a big ditch over by the forest not far from the road. A common grave was dug for us.

"The sentence was posted up all over town so that everyone should know of it. The Poles decided to hold a public execution to frighten the population. From early morning they began driving the townsfolk to the place of execution. Some went out of curiosity, terrible though it was. Before long they had a big crowd collected outside the prison wall. From our cell we could hear the hum of voices. They had stationed machine guns on the street behind the crowd, and brought up mounted and foot gendarmes from all parts of the area.

A whole battalion of them surrounded the streets and vegetable fields beyond. A pit had been dug beside the gallows for those who were to be hanged.

"We waited silently for the end, now and then exchanging a few words. We had talked everything over the night before and said our goodbyes. Only Rosa kept whispering to herself over in one corner of the cell. Valya, after all the beatings and outrages she had endured, was too weak to move and lay still most of the time. Two local Communist girls, sisters they were, could not keep back the tears as they clung to one another in their last farewell. Stepanov, a young man from the country, a strapping lad who had knocked out two gendarmes when they came to arrest him, told them to stop. 'No tears, Comrades! You may weep here, but not out there. We don't want to give those bloody swine a chance to gloat. There won't be any mercy anyway. We've got to die, so we might as well die decently. We won't crawl on our knees. Remember, Comrades, we're going to die well.'

"Then they came for us. In the lead was Szwarkowski, the counterintelligence chief, a mad dog of a sadist if there ever was one. When he didn't do the raping himself he amused himself by watching his gendarmes do it. We were marched to the gallows across the road between two rows of gendarmes, 'canaries' we called them on account of their yellow shoulder-knots. They stood there with their sabres bared.

"They hurried us through the prison yard with their rifle butts and made us form fours. Then they opened the gates and led us out into the street and stood us up facing the gallows so that we should see our comrades die as we waited for our turn to come. It was a tall gallows made of thick logs. Three nooses of heavy rope hung down from the crosspiece and under each noose was a platform with steps supported by a block of wood that could be kicked aside. A faint murmur rose from the sea of people which rocked and swayed. All eyes were fixed on us. We recognized some of our people in the crowd.

"On a porch some distance away stood a group of Polish gentry and officers with binoculars. They had come to see the Bolsheviks hanged.

"The snow was soft underfoot. The forest was white with it, and it lay thick on the trees like cotton fluff. The whirling snowflakes fell slowly, melting on our burning faces, and the steps of the gallows were carpeted with snow. We were scantily dressed but none of us felt the cold. Stepanov did not even notice that he was walking in his stocking feet.

"Beside the gallows stood the military prosecutor and senior officers. At last Valya and the two other comrades who were to be hanged were led out of the jail. They walked all three arm in arm, Valya was in the middle supported by the other two for she had no strength to walk alone. But she did her best to hold

282

herself erect, remembering Stepanov's words: 'We must die well, Comrades!' She wore a woollen jacket but no coat.

"Szwarkowski evidently didn't like the idea of them walking arm-in-arm for he pushed them from behind. Valya said something and one of the mounted gendarmes slashed her full force across the face with his whip. A woman in the crowd let out a frightful shriek and began struggling madly in an effort to break through the cordon and reach the prisoners, but she was seized and dragged away. It must have been Valya's mother. When they were close to the gallows Valya began to sing. Never have I heard a voice like that— only a person going to his death could sing with such feeling. She sang the *Warszawianka,* and the other two joined in. The mounted guards lashed out in a blind fury with their whips, but the three did not seem to feel the blows. They were knocked down and dragged to the gallows like sacks. The sentence was quickly read and the nooses were slipped over their heads. At that point we began to sing:

Arise, ye prisoners of starvation . . .

"Guards rushed at us from all sides and I just had time to see the blocks knocked out from under the platforms with rifle butts and the three bodies jerking in the nooses. . .

"The rest of us had already been put to the wall

283

when it was announced that ten of us had had our sentences commuted to 20 years imprisonment. The other sixteen were shot."

Samuel clutched convulsively at the collar of his shirt as if he were choking.

"For three days the bodies hung there in the nooses. The gallows were guarded day and night. After that a new batch of prisoners were brought to jail and they told us that on the fourth day the rope that held the corpse of Comrade Toboldin, the heaviest of the three, had given way. After that they removed the other two and buried them all.

"But the gallows was not taken down. It was still standing when we were brought to this place. It stands there with the nooses waiting for fresh victims."

Samuel fell silent staring with unseeing eyes before him, but Pavel was unaware that the story had ended. The three bodies with the heads twisted horribly to one side swayed silently before his eyes.

The bugle sounding the assembly outside brought Pavel to himself with a start.

"Let's go, Samuel," he said in a barely audible voice.

A column of Polish prisoners was being marched down the street lined with cavalry. At the prison gates stood the Regimental Commissar writing an order on his notepad.

"Comrade Antipov," he said, handing the slip of

paper to a stalwart squadron commander, "take this, and have all the prisoners taken under cavalry escort to Novgorod-Volynsky. See that the wounded are given medical attention. Then put them on carts, drive them about twenty versts from the town and let them go. We have no time to bother with them. But there must be no maltreatment of prisoners."

Mounting his horse, Pavel turned to Samuel. "Hear that?" he said. "They hang our people, but we have to escort them back to their own side and treat them nicely besides. How can we do it?"

The Regimental Commander turned and looked sternly at the speaker. "Cruelty to unarmed prisoners," Pavel heard him say as if speaking to himself, "will be punished by death. We are not Whites!"

As he rode off, Pavel recalled the final words of the order of the Revolutionary Military Council which had been read out to the regiment:

"The land of the workers and peasants loves its Red Army. It is proud of it. And on that Army's banners there shall not be a single stain."

"Not a single stain," Pavel's lips formed the words.

At the time the Fourth Cavalry Division took Zhitomir, the 20th Brigade of the Seventh Rifle Division forming part of a shock corps under Comrade Golikov was crossing the Dnieper River in the area of Okuninovo village.

The corps, which consisted of the 25th Rifle Division and a Bashkir cavalry brigade, had orders to cross the Dnieper and straddle the Kiev-Korosten railway at Irsha Station. This maneouvre would cut off the Poles' last avenue of retreat from Kiev.

It was during the crossing of the river that Misha Levchukov of the Shepetovka Komsomol organization perished. They were running over the shaky pontoon bridge when a shell fired from somewhere beyond the steep bank opposite whined viciously overhead and plunged into the water, ripping it to shreds. The same instant Misha disappeared under one of the pontoons. The river swallowed him up and did not give him back. Yakimenko, a fair-haired soldier in a battered cap, cried out: "Mishka! Hell, that was Mishka! Went down like a stone, poor lad!" For a moment he stared horrified into the dark water, but the men running up from behind pushed him on: "What're you gaping there for, you fool. Get on with you!" There was no time to worry about anyone. The brigade had fallen behind the others who had already occupied the right bank of the river.

It was not until four days later that Sergei learned of Misha's death. By that time the brigade had captured Bucha Station and swinging round to face Kiev was repulsing furious attacks by the Poles who were attempting to break through to Korosten.

Yakimenko threw himself down beside Sergei in

the firing line. He had been firing steadily for some time and now he had difficulty forcing back the bolt of his overheated rifle. Keeping his head carefully lowered he turned to Sergei and said: "Got to give her a rest. She's red hot!"

Sergei barely heard him above the din of the shooting.

When the noise subsided somewhat Yakimenko remarked as if casually: "Your comrade got drowned in the Dnieper. He was gone before I could do anything." That was all he said. He tried the bolt of his rifle, took out another clip and applied himself to the task of reloading.

The Eleventh Division sent to take Berdichev encountered fierce resistance from the Poles. A bloody battle was fought in the streets of the town. The Red Cavalry advanced through a squall of machine-gun fire. The town was captured and the remnants of the routed Polish forces fled. Trains were seized intact in the railway yards. But the most terrible disaster for the Poles was the exploding of an ammunition dump which served the whole front. A million shells went up in the air. The explosion shattered window panes into tiny fragments and caused the houses to tremble as if made of cardboard.

The capture of Zhitomir and Berdichev took the Poles in the rear and they came pouring out of Kiev in two streams, desperately fighting to make their way out of the steel ring encircling them.

Swept along by the maelstrom of battle Pavel lost all sense of self these days. His individuality merged with the mass and for him, as for every fighting man, the word "I" was forgotten; only the word "we" remained: our regiment, our squadron, our brigade.

Events developed with the speed of a hurricane. Each day brought something new.

Budyonny's cavalry army swept forward like an avalanche, striking blow after blow until the entire Polish rear was smashed to pieces. Drunk with the excitement of their victories, the mounted divisions hurled themselves with passionate fury at Novograd-Volynsky, the heart of the Polish rear. As the ocean wave dashes itself against the rockbound shore, recedes and rushes on again, so they fell back only to press on again and again with awesome shouts of "Forward! Forward!"

Nothing could save the Poles—neither the barbed-wire entanglements, nor the desperate resistance put up by the garrison entrenched in the city. And on the morning of June 27 Budyonny's cavalry forded the Sluch River without dismounting, entered Novograd-Volynsky and drove the Poles out of the city in the direction of Korets. At the same time the Forty-Fifth Division crossed the Sluch at Novy Miropol, and the Kotovsky cavalry brigade swooped down upon the settlement of Lyubar.

The radio station of the First Cavalry Army received an order from the commander-in-chief of the front to concentrate the entire cavalry force for the capture of Rovno. The irresistible onslaught of the Red divisions sent the Poles scattering in demoralized panic-stricken groups.

It was in these hectic days that Pavel Korchagin had a most unexpected encounter. He had been sent by the Brigade Commander to the station where an armoured train was standing. Pavel took the steep railway embankment at a canter and reined in at the steel-grey head carriage. With the black muzzles of guns protruding from the turrets, the armoured train looked grim and formidable. Several men in oil-stained clothes were at work beside it raising the heavy steel armour plating that protected the wheels.

"Where can I find the commander of the train?" Pavel inquired of a leather-jacketed Red Army man carrying a pail of water.

"Over there," the man replied pointing to the loco-motive.

Pavel rode up to the engine. "I want to see the commander!" he said. A man with a pock-marked face, clad in leather from head to foot, turned. "I'm the commander."

Pavel pulled an envelope from his pocket.

"Here is an order from the Brigade Commander. Sign on the envelope."

The commander rested the envelope on his knee and scribbled his signature on it. Down on the tracks a man with an oil can was working on the middle wheel of the locomotive. Pavel could only see his broad back and the pistol-butt sticking out of the pocket of his leather trousers.

The train commander handed the envelope back to Pavel who picked up the reins and was about to set off when the man with the oil can straightened up and turned round. The next moment Pavel had leapt off his horse as though swept down by a violent gust of wind.

"Artem!"

The man dropped his oil can and caught the young Red Army man in a bear's embrace.

"Pavka! You rascal! It's you!" he cried unable to believe his eyes.

The commander of the armoured train and several gunners standing by looked on with broad smiles.

"Fancy brothers bumping into each other like that!" they said.

It happened on August 19 during a battle in the Lvov area. Pavel had lost his cap in the fighting and had reined in his horse. The squadrons ahead had already cut into the Polish positions. At that moment Demidov came galloping through the bushes on his way down to the river. As he flew past Pavel he shouted:

"The Division Commander's been killed!"

Pavel started. Letunov, his heroic commander, that man of sterling courage dead! A savage fury seized Pavel.

With the blunt edge of his sabre he urged on his exhausted Gnedko whose bit dripped with a bloody foam and tore into the thick of the battle.

"Kill the vermin, kill 'em! Cut down the Polish *szlachta*! They've killed Letunov!" And blindly he slashed at a figure in a green uniform. Enraged at the death of their Division Commander, the cavalrymen wiped out a whole platoon of Polish legionaries.

They galloped headlong over the battlefield in pursuit of the enemy, but now a Polish battery went into action. Shrapnel rent the air spattering death on all sides.

Suddenly there was a blinding green flash before Pavel's eyes, thunder smote his ears and red-hot iron seared into his skull. The earth spun strangely and horribly about him and began to turn slowly upside down.

Pavel was thrown from the saddle like a straw. He flew right over Gnedko's head and fell heavily to the ground.

Instantly black night descended.

CHAPTER NINE

The octopus has a bulging eye the size of a cat's head, a glazed reddish eye green in the centre with a pulsating phosphorescent glow. The octopus is a loathsome mass of tentacles, which writhe and squirm like a tangled knot of snakes, the dry scaly skin rustling hideously as they move. The octopus stirs. He sees it next to his very eyes. And now the tentacles creep over his body; they are cold and they sting like nettles. The octopus shoots out its sting, and it bites into his head like a leech, and, wriggling convulsively, it sucks at his blood. He feels the blood draining out of his body into the swelling body of the octopus. And the sting goes on sucking and the pain of its sucking is unbearable.

Somewhere far far away he can hear human voices: "How is his pulse now?"

And another voice, a woman's, replies softly:

"His pulse is a hundred and thirty-eight. His temperature 103.1. He is delirious all the time."

The octopus disappeared, but the pain lingered. Pavel felt someone touch his wrist. He tried to open his eyes, but his lids were so heavy he had not the strength to lift them. Why was it so hot? Mother must have heated the stove. And again he hears those voices:

"His pulse is one hundred and twenty-two now."

He tries to open his eyelids. But a fire burns within him. He is suffocating.

He is terribly thirsty, he must get up at once and get a drink. But why does he not get up? He tries to move but his limbs refuse to obey him, his body is a stranger to him. Mother will bring him some water at once. He will say to her: "I want to drink." Something stirs beside him. Is it the octopus about to crawl over him again? There it comes, he sees its red eyes. . . .

From afar comes that soft voice:

"Frosya, bring some water!"

"Whose name is that?" But the effort to remember is too much for him and darkness engulfs him once more. Emerging presently from the gloom he recalls: "I am thirsty."

And hears voices saying:

"He seems to be regaining consciousness."

Closer and more distinct now, that gentle voice:

"Do you want to drink, Comrade?"

"Can it be me they are addressing? Am I ill? Oh yes, I've got the typhus, that's it." And for the third time he tries to lift his eyelids. And at last he succeeds. The first thing that reaches his consciousness through the narrowed vision of his slightly opened eyes is a red ball hanging above his head. But the red ball is blotted out by something dark which bends towards him, and his lips feel the hard edge of a glass and moisture, life-giving moisture. The fire within him subsides. Satisfied, he whispers: "That's better."

"Can you see me, Comrade?"

The dark shape standing over him has spoken, and just before drowsiness overpowers him he manages to say: "I can't see, but I can hear. . . ."

"Now, who would have believed he would pull through? Yet see how he has clambered back to life! A remarkably strong constitution. You may be proud of yourself, Nina Vladimirovna. You have literally saved his life."

And the woman's voice, trembling slightly, answers:

"I am so glad!"

After thirteen days of oblivion, consciousness returned to Pavel Korchagin. His young body had not wanted to die, and slowly he recovered his strength. It was like being born again. Everything seemed new and miraculous. Only his head lay motionless and unbearably heavy in its plaster cast, and he had not the strength to move it. But feeling returned to the rest of his body and soon he was able to bend his fingers.

Nina Vladimirovna, junior physician of the military clinical hospital, sat at a small table in her room turning the leaves of a thick lilac-covered notebook filled with brief entries made in a neat slanting handwriting.

August 26, 1920

Some serious cases were brought in today by ambulance train. One of them has a very ugly head wound. We put him in the corner by the window. He is only seventeen. They gave me an envelope with the papers found in his pockets and the case history. His name is Korchagin, Pavel Andreyevich. Among his papers were a well-worn membership card (No. 967) of the Young Communist League of the Ukraine, a torn Red Army identification book and a copy of a regimental order stating that Red Army man Korchagin was commended for exemplary fulfilment of a reconnaissance mission. There was also a note, evidently written by himself, which said: "In the event of my death please write to my relatives: Shepetovka, Railway Depot, Mechanic Artem Korchagin."

He has been unconscious ever since he was hit by a shell fragment on August 19. Tomorrow Anatoli Stepanovich will examine him.

August 27

Today we examined Korchagin's wound. It is very deep, the skull is fractured and the entire right side of the head is paralyzed. A blood vessel burst in the right eye which is badly swollen.

Anatoli Stepanovich wanted to remove the eye to prevent inflammation, but I dissuaded him, since there is still hope that the swelling might go down. In doing this I was prompted solely by esthetic considerations.

The lad may recover; it would be a pity if he were disfigured.

He is delirious all the time and terribly restless. One of us is constantly on duty at his bedside. I spend much of my time with him. He is too young to die and I am determined to tear his young life out of Death's clutches. I must succeed.

Yesterday I spent several hours in his ward after my shift was over. His is the worst case there. I sat listening to his ravings. Sometimes they sound like a story, and I learn quite a lot about his life. But at times he curses horribly. He uses frightful language. Somehow it hurts me to hear such awful cursing from him. Anatoli Stepanovich does not believe that he will recover. "I can't understand what the army wants with such children," the old man growls. "It's a disgrace."

August 30

Korchagin is still unconscious. He has been removed to the ward for hopeless cases. The nurse Frosya is almost constantly at his side. It appears she knows him. They worked together at one time. How gentle she is with him! Now I too am beginning to think that his condition is hopeless.

September 2, 11 p. m.

This has been a wonderful day for me. My patient Korchagin regained consciousness. The crisis is over. I spent the past two days at the hospital without going home.

I cannot describe my joy at the knowledge that one more life has been saved. One death less in our ward. The recovery of a patient is the most wonderful thing about this exhausting work of mine. They become like children. Their affection is simple and sincere, and I too grow fond of them so that when they leave I often weep. I know it is foolish of me, but I cannot help it.

September 10

Today I wrote Korchagin's first letter to his family. He writes his wound is not serious and he'll soon recover and come home. He has lost a great deal of blood and is as pale as a ghost, and still very weak.

September 14

Korchagin smiled today for the first time. He has a very nice smile. Usually he is grave beyond his years. He is making a remarkably rapid recovery. He and Frosya are great friends. I often see her at his bedside. She must have been talking to him about me, and evidently singing my praises, for now the patient greets me with a faint smile. Yesterday he asked.

"What are those black marks on your arms, doctor?"

I did not tell him that those bruises had been made by his fingers clutching my arm convulsively when he was delirious.

297

The wound on Korchagin's forehead is healing nicely. We doctors are amazed at the remarkable fortitude with which this young man endures the painful business of dressing his wound.

Usually in such cases the patient groans a great deal and is generally troublesome. But this one lies quietly and when the open wound is daubed with iodine he draws himself taut like a violin string. Often he loses consciousness, but not once have we heard a groan escape him.

We know now that when Korchagin groans he is unconscious. Where does he get that tremendous endurance, I wonder?

We wheeled Korchagin out onto the big balcony today for the first time. How his face lit up when he saw the garden, how greedily he breathed in the fresh air! His head is swathed in bandages and only one eye is open. And that live, shining eye looked out on the world as if seeing it for the first time.

Today two young women came to the hospital asking to see Korchagin. I went downstairs to the waiting room to speak to them. One of them was very beautiful. They introduced themselves as Tonya Tumanova and Tatiana Buranovskaya. I had heard of

Tonya, Korchagin had mentioned the name when he was delirious. I gave them permission to see him.

October 8

Korchagin now walks alone in the garden. He keeps asking me when he can leave hospital. I tell him—soon. The two girls come to see him every visiting day. I know now why he never groans. I asked him, and he replied: "Read *The Gadfly* and you'll know."

October 14

Korchagin has been discharged. He took leave of me very warmly. The bandage has been removed from his eye and now only his head is bound. The eye is blind, but looks quite normal. It was very sad to part with this fine young comrade. But that's how it is: once they've recovered they leave us and rarely do we ever see them again.

As he left he said: "Pity it wasn't the left eye. How will I be able to shoot now?"

He still thinks of the front.

After his discharge from hospital Pavel lived for a time at the Buranovskys' where Tonya was staying.

Pavel sought at once to draw Tonya into Komsomol activities. He began by inviting her to attend a meeting of the town's Komsomol. Tonya agreed to go, but when she emerged from her room where she had been dressing for the meeting Pavel bit his lips in chagrin. She was very smartly attired, with a studied elegance which Pavel felt would be entirely out of place at a Komsomol gathering.

This was the cause of their first quarrel. When he asked her why she had dressed up like that she took offence.

"I don't see why I must look like everyone else. But if my clothes don't suit you, I can stay at home."

At the club Tonya's fine clothes were so conspicuous among all the faded tunics and shabby blouses that Pavel was deeply embarrassed. The young people treated her as an outsider, and Tonya, conscious of their disapproval, assumed a contemptuous, defiant air.

Pankratov, the secretary of the Komsomol organization at the shipping wharves, a broad-shouldered docker in a coarse linen shirt, called Pavel aside, and indicating Tonya with his eyes, said with a scowl:

"Was it you who brought that doll here?"

"Yes," Pavel replied curtly.

"Mm," observed Pankratov. "She doesn't belong here by the looks of her. Too bourgeois-looking. How did she get in?"

Pavel's temples pounded.

"She is a friend of mine. I brought her here. Understand? She isn't hostile to us at all, even if she does think too much about clothes. You can't always judge people by the way they dress. I know as well as you do whom to bring here so you needn't be so officious, Comrade."

He wanted to say something sharp and insulting but realizing that Pankratov was voicing the general opinion he desisted, and vented all his wrath on Tonya.

"I told her what to expect! Why the devil must she put on such airs?"

That evening marked the beginning of the end of their friendship. With bitterness and dismay Pavel watched the break-up of a relationship that had seemed so enduring.

Several more days passed, and with every meeting, every conversation they drifted farther and farther apart. Tonya's cheap individualism became unbearable to Pavel.

Both realized that a break was inevitable.

Today they had met in the Kupechesky Gardens for the last time. The paths were strewn with decaying leaves. They stood by the balustrade at the top of the cliff and looked down at the grey waters of the Dnieper. From behind the towering hulk of the bridge a tug came crawling wearily down the river with two heavy barges in tow. The setting sun painted the Trukhanov Island with daubs of gold and set the windows of the houses on fire.

Tonya looked at the golden shafts of sunlight and said with deep sadness:

"Is our friendship going to fade like that dying sun?"

Pavel, who had been feasting his eyes on her face, knitted his brows sternly and answered in a low voice:

"Tonya, we have gone over this before. You know, of course, that I loved you, and even now my love might return, but for that you must be with us. I am not the Pavlusha I was before. And I would be a poor husband to you if you expect me to put you before the Party. For I shall always put the Party first, and you and my other loved ones second."

Tonya stared miserably down at the dark-blue water and her eyes filled with tears.

Pavel gazed at the profile he had come to know so well, her thick chestnut hair, and a wave of pity for this girl who had once been so near and dear to him swept over him.

Gently he laid his hand on her shoulder.

"Tonya, cut yourself loose and come to us. Let's work together to finish with the bosses. There are many splendid girls among us who are sharing the burden of this bitter struggle, enduring all the hardships and privation. They may not be so well educated as you are, but why, oh why, don't you want to join us? You say Chuzhanin tried to seduce you, but he is a degenerate, not a fighter. You say the comrades were unfriendly toward you. Then why did you have to dress up as if

302

you were going to a bourgeois ball? It's your silly
pride that's to blame: why should I wear a dirty
old army tunic just because everybody else does?
You had the courage to love a workingman, but
you cannot love an idea. I am sorry to have to
part with you, and I should like to cherish your
memory."

He said no more.

The next day he saw an order posted up in the
street signed by Zhukhrai, chairman of the regional
Cheka. His heart leapt. It was with great difficulty that
he gained admission to the sailor's office. The sentries
would not let him in and he raised such a fuss that
he was very nearly arrested, but in the end he had his
way.

Fyodor gave him a very warm welcome. The sailor
had lost an arm; it had been torn off by a shell.

The conversation turned at once to work. "You can
help me crush the counterrevolution here until you're
fit for the front again. Start tomorrow," said Zhukhrai.

The struggle with the Polish Whites came to an
end. The Red armies pursued the enemy almost to the
very walls of Warsaw, but with their material and phys-
ical strength expended and their supply bases left far
behind, they were unable to take this final stronghold
and so fell back. Thus the "miracle on the Vistula,"
as the Poles called the withdrawal of the Red forces

from Warsaw, came to pass, and the Poland of the gentry received a new lease of life. The dream of the Polish Soviet Socialist Republic was not yet to be fulfilled.

The blood-drenched land demanded a respite.

Pavel was unable to see his people, for Shepetovka was again in Polish hands and had become a temporary frontier outpost. Peace talks were in progress.

Pavel spent days and nights in the Cheka carrying out diverse assignments. He was much upset when he learned that his hometown was occupied by the Poles.

"Does that mean my mother will be on the other side of the border if the armistice is signed now?" he asked Zhukhrai.

But Fyodor calmed his fears.

"Most likely the frontier will pass through Goryn along the river, which means that your town will be on our side," he said. "In any case we'll know soon enough."

Divisions were being transferred from the Polish front to the South. For while the republic had been straining every effort on the Polish front, Wrangel had taken advantage of the respite to crawl out of his Crimean lair and advance northward along the Dnieper with Yekaterinoslav Gubernia as his immediate objective.

Now that the war with the Poles was over, the republic rushed its armies to the Crimea to wipe out the last hotbed of counterrevolution.

Trainloads of troops, carts, field kitchens and guns passed through Kiev en route to the South. The Cheka of the transport services of the area worked at fever pitch these days coping with the bottlenecks caused by the huge flood of traffic. Stations were jammed with trains and frequently traffic would be held up for lack of free tracks. Telegraph operators tapped out countless peremptory messages ordering the line cleared for this or that division. The tickers spilled out endless ribbons of tape covered with dots and dashes and each of them demanding priority: "Precedence above all else ... this is a military order ... free line immediately. ..." And nearly every message included a reminder that failure to carry out the order would entail prosecution by a revolutionary military tribunal.

The local transport Cheka was responsible for keeping traffic moving without interruption.

Commanders of army units would burst into its headquarters brandishing revolvers and demanding that their trains be despatched at once in accordance with telegram number so-and-so signed by the commander of the army. And none of them would accept the explanation that this was impossible. "You'll get that train off if you croak doing it!" And a string of frightful curses would follow. In particularly serious cases Zhukhrai would be urgently sent for, and then the excited men who were ready to shoot each other on the spot would calm down at once. At the sight of this man of iron with his quiet icy voice that brooked no argument revolvers were thrust back into their holsters.

At times Pavel would stagger out of his office onto the platform with a stabbing pain in his head. Work in the Cheka was having a devastating effect on his nerves.

One day he caught sight of Sergei Bruzzhak on a flatcar loaded with ammunition crates. Sergei jumped off the car nearly knocking Pavel off his feet and flung his arms round his friend.

"Pavka, you devil! I knew it was you the minute I laid eyes on you."

The two young men had so much news to exchange that they did not know where to begin. So much had happened to both of them since they had last met. They plied each other with questions, and talked on without waiting for answers. They were so engrossed in conversation that they did not hear the engine whistle and it was only when the train began to move out of the station that they separated.

They still had so much to say to each other, but the train was already gathering speed and Sergei, shouting something to his friend, raced along the platform and caught on to the open door of one of the freight cars. Several hands from within snatched him up and drew him inside. As Pavel stood watching him go he suddenly remembered that Sergei knew nothing about Valya's death. For he had not visited Shepetovka since he left it, and in the unexpectedness of this encounter Pavel had forgotten to tell him.

"It's a good thing he does not know, his mind will be at ease," thought Pavel. He did not know that he was never to see his friend again. Nor did Sergei, standing on the roof of the car, his chest exposed to the autumn wind, know that he was going to his death.

"Get down from there, Seryozha," urged Doroshenko, a Red Army man wearing a coat with a hole burnt in the back.

"That's all right," said Sergei laughing. "The wind and I are good friends."

A week later he was struck by a stray bullet in his first engagement. He staggered forward, his chest rent by a tearing pain, clutched at the air, and pressing his arms tightly against his chest, he swayed and dropped heavily to the ground and his sightless blue eyes stared out over the boundless Ukrainian steppe.

His nerve-wracking work in the Cheka began to tell on Pavel's weakened condition. His violent headaches became more frequent, but it was not until he fainted one day after two sleepless nights that he finally decided to take the matter up with Zhukhrai.

"Don't you think I ought to try some other sort of work, Fyodor? I would like best of all to work at my own trade at the main machine shop. I'm afraid there's something wrong with my head. They told me in the medical commission that I was unfit for army service. But this sort of work is worse than the front. The two days we spent rounding up Sutyr's band have knocked me out completely. I must have a rest from all these skirmishes. You see, Fyodor, I shan't be much good to you if I can barely stand on my feet."

Zhukhrai studied Pavel's face with concern.

"Yes, you don't look so good. It's all my fault. I ought to have let you go long before this. But I've been too busy to notice."

Shortly after the above conversation Pavel presented himself at the Regional Committee of the Komsomol with a paper certifying that he was being placed at the Committee's disposal. An officious youngster with his cap perched jauntily over onto his nose ran his eyes rapidly over the paper and winked to Pavel:

"From the Cheka, eh? A jolly organization that. We'll find work for you here in a jiffy. We need everybody we can get. Where would you like to go? Commissary department? No? All right. What about the agitation section down at the waterfront? No? Too bad. Nice soft job that, special rations too."

Pavel interrupted him.

"I would prefer the main car shops," he said. The lad gaped. "Car shops? Mm.... I don't think we need anybody there. But go to Ustinovich. She'll fit you in somewhere."

After a brief interview with the dark-complexioned Ustinovich it was decided to assign Pavel as secretary of the Komsomol organization in the railway shops where he was to work.

Meanwhile the Whites had been fortifying the gates of the Crimea, and now on this narrow neck of land that once had been the frontier between the Crimean Tatars and the Zaporozhye Cossack settlements stood the modernized fortified line of Perekop.

And behind Perekop in the Crimea, the old world, driven here from all corners of the land, lived in wine-fuddled revelry, blinded by a false sense of security to its approaching doom.

One chill dank autumn night tens of thousands of sons of the toiling people plunged into the icy waters of the Sivash to cross the bay under the cover of darkness and strike from behind at the enemy entrenched in their forts. Among the thousands waded Ivan Zharky, carrying his machine gun on his head to prevent it from getting wet.

And when dawn found Perekop seething in a wild turmoil, its fortifications attacked in a frontal assault, the first columns of men that had crossed the Sivash climbed ashore on Litovsky Peninsula to take the Whites from the rear. And among the first to clamber onto that rocky coast was Ivan Zharky.

A battle of unprecedented ferocity ensued. The White cavalry bore down savagely on the Red Army men as they emerged from the water. Zharky's machine gun spewed death, never ceasing its lethal tattoo. Men and horses fell in heaps under the leaden spray. Zharky fed new magazines into the gun with feverish speed.

Perekop thundered back through the throats of hundreds of guns. The very earth seemed to have dropped into a bottomless abyss, and death carried by thousands of shells pierced the heavens with earsplitting screams and exploded, scattering myriads of minute fragments far and wide. The torn and lacerated earth spouted up in black clouds that blotted out the sun.

The monster's head was crushed, and into the Crimea swept the Red flood of the First Cavalry Army to deliver the final, smashing blow. Frantic with terror, the Whiteguards rushed in a panic to board the ships leaving the ports.

To shabby tunics, over the spot where stout hearts throbbed, the Republic pinned the golden Order of the Red Banner, and one of these tunics was that of the Komsomol machine gunner Ivan Zharky.

Peace was signed with the Poles and, as Zhukhrai had predicted, Shepetovka remained in Soviet Ukraine. A river thirty-five kilometres outside the town now marked the frontier.

One memorable morning in December 1920 Pavel arrived in his native town. He stepped onto the snowy platform, glanced up at the sign *Shepetovka I*, then turned left, and went straight to the depot and asked for Artem. But his brother was not there. Drawing his army coat tighter about him, Pavel strode off through the woods to the town.

Maria Yakovlevna turned when the knock came at the door and said "Come in." A snow-covered figure pushed into the house and she saw the dear face of her son. Her hand flew to her heart and the joy that flooded her being robbed her of speech.

She fell on her son's breast and smothered his face with kisses, and tears of happiness streamed down her cheeks. And Pavel, pressing the spare little body close, gazed silently down at the care-worn face of his mother furrowed with deep lines of pain and anxiety, and waited for her to grow calmer.

Once again the light of happiness shone in the eyes of this woman who had suffered so much. It seemed she would never have her fill of gazing at this son whom she had lost all hope of ever seeing again. Her joy knew no bounds when three days later Artem too barged into the tiny room late at night with his kitbag over his shoulders.

Now the Korchagin family was reunited. Both brothers had escaped death, and after harrowing ordeals and trials they had met again.

"What are you going to do now?" the mother asked her sons.

"It's back to the carshops for me, mother!" replied Artem gaily.

As for Pavel, after two weeks at home he went back to Kiev where his work was awaiting him.

End of Part One

Printed in the Union of Soviet Socialist Republics